Martha
I could never have
written this book w[…]
support of my wife, […]
Martha, are one of her greate[…]
Thank you for all you pour into […]

The DREAM

The DREAM

One man's journey to restore more than a motorcycle

by

Pete Norris

The Dream

Published by Peter R. Norris
7688 Timbers Trail, Traverse City, MI 49685

ISBN 13: 979-8-9891363-0-8

To my amazing wife, Vicki,
whose dauntless venture into her own story
gave me the courage to be curious about my own
and changed our lives forever.

Table of Contents

Acknowledgements

My wife, Vicki, whose perspective, insight and wisdom helped refine chapter after chapter.

Gary Bower, whose countless hours of editing this project were only exceeded by his expertise in guiding each step of the way.

Pat Dolanski, Judy Heine and Annie Solem, whose contributions in this project were invaluable.

Sandy Burdick, who, in response to a Dan Allender Conference introducing his book "The Wounded Heart," started a small group, which became a big group that birthed Open Hearts Ministries (www.ohmin.org). It was here that my journey began.

Amy Anderson, who, early on, helped me identify the "angry, nice boy" who lived inside my heart, and challenged me to tend to him.

Special thanks to Dave Topczewski for the use of the photo of his CA77 Honda Dream for the cover of this book.

Introduction

Doctors ask, "When did you first notice these symptoms?" Mechanics ask, "When did it start doing this?" An appliance repairman may inquire, "How long has it been acting up?" We are quick to respond, and it is helpful to guiding the doctor, mechanic or repairman in identifying the root problem. A similar approach applies to us as well, and we call it story work.

I took my seat, along with five other men and two leaders, in a small living room. It's where I would first share my story – a story I didn't even know I had. My entire life had been forward focused: school, job, house, marriage, kids, starting a business, getting a bigger house, growing the business. Now I was asked to pass a childhood photo around the room while I told them about some of the painful memories that shaped my upbringing.

First of all, I had a perfect childhood. I came from an intact family, and had a healthy balance of farm chores and playtime. We were active in the church. I couldn't remember a single trauma; in fact, my parents created an atmosphere that was pretty much drama free. Some of the neighbors had drama, but somehow, not us. So why was I so reluctant to share that fourth grade picture?

That photo represented everything I had spent countless dollars, hours, and energy trying to distance myself from. The boy in that picture was small and weak, shy and insecure. He wore hand-me-downs and carried a peanut butter and jelly sandwich to school in a bread bag. Why would I ever want to visit those memories, much less share them with a room full of strangers?

As it turns out, being curious about my past has brought more freedom than I ever imagined. When we find ourselves struggling in relationships with people, food, money, possessions, addictions, etc., the backstory is as helpful us as it is to the doctor or mechanic. Story work is a reliable tool for understanding why we show up the way we do. Why the strangest thing can trigger a reaction in us, yet bother no one else. Why we take considerable offense to one thing and remain oblivious to another. Why we struggle to love well.

In First Corinthians 13, the Apostle Paul describes what "loving well" looks like: "patient and kind, not jealous or boastful" (v. 4). The original Greek gives us a clue as to why loving well might be a struggle. "When I was a child (that is, 'immature') I talked like a child, I thought (or 'observed' and 'understood') like a child, I reasoned ('decided' and 'drew conclusions') like a child. When I became a man, I put childish things behind me ('severed' or 'made the things of a child inactive')" (v. 11). Could Paul be suggesting that the understanding and conclusions we acquired as children can keep us from loving well as adults?

I believe so. Many of us have had experiences as children that made such a deep imprint, that the conclusions drawn felt absolute, permanent, and necessary. They likely seemed essential to coping with our environment. Ironically, what once protected us, now encumbers us.

I chose to write this book to introduce the process of story work. A primer, if you will, that allows you to be a fly on the wall of another man's struggle. More than providing answers, I hope it encourages you to explore the questions from your past, possibly with the assistance of a counselor, life coach, or skilled friend.

This book is fictitious, with fictional characters. It is, however, born out of observing patterns in my own life, and over twenty years of sitting across the table from singles and married couples who were trying to restore some aspect of their lives. It is not uncommon for our past to continue to cause pain and devastation decades later. How we responded then shaped how we survived. Unfortunately, it can keep us discreetly loyal to surviving rather than healing. Often, wounds stay carefully hidden in twisted secret memories, until we are tired enough, broken enough, or brave enough to take an honest and compassionate look at our past, in order to bring freedom to our present. Fiction? Yes, but be encouraged if you happen to stumble upon some of your own truth in these pages. Enjoy.

THE DREAM

Chapter One

Interruptions

Thirty-some-odd years of handling lumber kept Jim's six-foot-two frame lean and his hands calloused. Picking up the last cherry board, he bent forward at the waist, as if lining up for a pool shot, and guided it through the table saw. He had gotten an early start on the day and was making good time. The morning had flown by without a hitch — no customers stopping in, no equipment issues, no texts or phone calls to return — just steady forward progress.

He glanced at the wall clock. 2:03. "No wonder my stomach is growling," he said to himself.

Jim switched off the saw and pressed the remote that hung from his apron, shutting off the dust collector. As the sounds of the motors wound down, he snatched his jacket from the coat hook by the door and hung his apron in its place. Few things in life brought him as much satisfaction as the rhythm of uninterrupted production. Little did he realize that sometimes interruptions could be productive, too.

Hustling across the fifty yards between the shop and the house, he heard the crunching sound of tires approaching on the gravel driveway.

"Sheesh, I haven't got time for a sales pitch, and I already know Jesus." He spat the words at a nearby robin as if it actually cared.

He met the car as it stopped. Anchoring his large hands on the roof above the driver's window, he looked over the top of the car to avoid giving the driver the satisfaction of his full attention.

"Help ya?"

Jim's imposing posture seemed to be working on the driver (who remained silent), but not on his female passenger, who was pretty worked up about something. She jabbered on about being Jim's new neighbor, just moved into the place down the road, and that their young son only had a half day of school today, and how after lunch he went out exploring and hadn't come back. She was sniffling non-stop into a tissue, and when she finally paused to blow her nose, Jim seized his chance to break in.

"I'll keep an eye out for your kid," he mumbled without looking down. Then he turned and headed to the house.

A few moments later in the kitchen, Jim dried his hands and swung open the refrigerator door.

"Gail, do we have any leftover chicken from last night? That was amazing."

"In the Tupperware on the second shelf," his wife answered without looking up from the scatter of papers on the dining table. "And there's leftover salad in the crisper."

He put a leg and a thigh on a paper plate and slipped it into the microwave.

"Did you cover that?" Gail asked, glancing over her reading glasses. "I don't want barbecue sauce all over the inside of my microwave."

Jim complied, then rummaged around until he found the salad and ranch dressing.

"Who was in the driveway?" she asked, again without looking up.

"Some new folks. A younger couple, I think. I really didn't get a good look at them. They moved into Danny and Beth's place."

She slipped her readers from her nose and leaned

back in the dining chair. "Just introducing themselves, or did they need something?"

"Something about losing their kid," he replied matter-of-factly as he retrieved the plate from the microwave and scooped a pile of salad onto it. After grabbing a fork from the drawer, he joined her at the table, bowing his head briefly before starting in on the salad.

"What do you mean *missing*?" There was a hint of rebuke in her voice.

"You know," he said nonchalantly. "New place, lots to explore. He's probably a city kid who's never been out in the woods and just lost track of time. I'm sure he'll wander back home eventually."

Before Jim could take another bite, Gail was out of her seat and in the mud room, pulling on her boots.

"Where you goin'?" he asked.

"That mother must be worried sick! Their boy is *missing*, Jim! I'm going out to help them find him!"

By the energy in her voice, Jim knew that he'd better join her if he knew what was good for him.

"Oh, alright. You take the car, and I'll head out to the creek on foot. Kids can't resist a creek."

He grabbed his jacket, phone, and the chicken leg from the plate and headed out the door. As he passed his shop, he felt enough disdain to choke a horse. "I don't have time to wander around the back forty, looking for some stupid little kid who doesn't have the good sense to find his way home," he grumbled.

He made his way through the orchard, due east, towards the woods. At the end of the orchard, barely visible in the tall grass, was a drawn-out tangle of rusty barbed wire and a couple rotted wooden fence posts. They once marked the edge of his property. He always felt a hint of pride when he encountered his property lines. He had purchased the forty acres a few years before he met Gail. He had dreamt of a home, a shop, an orchard, a sprawling yard and, eventually, a wife. Nearly thirty years later, Jim felt pretty good about accomplishing all of those goals (though not necessarily in that order).

He high-stepped over the wire, careful not to catch his pant cuff on a barb, and continued southeast into the woods. It was sunny, but still April, and the jacket felt good. The forest floor was a matt of brown leaves flattened by the winter snow. A few saplings interrupted his path, but not his view. In another month these little trees would be unfurling tender leaves over a carpet of green that would spread out under foot. But not today. Everything still appeared to be asleep, except for a whimpering sound that came from upstream. As Jim got closer, he was dumbfounded.

"What on God's green earth are you doing boy?"

"My boot's stuck," a shivering voice answered.

"Stuck? On what?"

"I don't know. I'm so cold."

"Well," Jim said, shaking his head in disbelief, "of course you're cold! You're in the woods without a coat, standing in the middle of the creek!" He waded into the shin-deep water and took hold of the kid's forearm.

"Come on."

"I can't get my left foot loose!" the boy cried. "And it's really cold."

Jim plunged his hand into the icy water, feeling all around the rubber boot. Sure enough, not only was it tightly wedged between some branches, but the boy's struggle to dislodge it had caused the boot to tear and fill with water. It was stuck, all right. Jim unlaced the top of the boot.

"Can you pull your foot out now?"

"I don't know; maybe?" The little boy sniffled back tears.

"Good enough; the boot stays and we go. I'm gonna lift you up and out of your boot."

Fortunately, the boy was a twig and would be easy to lift. The kicker was, without his boot, he would need to be carried all the way home.

"One…two…three," Jim said, hoisting the child over his shoulder like a sack of potatoes. He stepped out of the creek and gently lowered the shivering boy onto dry ground. Then he took off his jacket and wrapped it around him. "Now, sit down and give me your foot."

The boy did as he was told, timidly extending his leg. Jim released the middle button of his own shirt, took hold of the boy's foot, and placed it against his belly. As he held it there, he texted Gail.

"Hey, honey. I found him. Down at the creek, just like I figured. We'll be heading back soon."

In a few minutes the boy was slung over his rescuer's shoulder again, lost in the large coat, with his bare foot tucked snuggly inside Jim's shirt.

They headed east and picked up the two-track that Danny had used when cutting firewood. He knew it would bring them out into this kid's back yard. As they exited the woods, he figured they had about a half mile or so yet to cover. He found a stump in the sun and set the boy down on it for a bit.

"I'm Jim"

"I'm J.R." the boy answered softly, looking at his foot.

"You mean like, junior?"

"No, just J.R."

Jim took J.R.'s bare foot in his hands and held it for a few minutes until he could see the color coming back.

"Foot warmin' up?"

"It tingles."

"It'll be fine."

Once again, Jim hoisted him up and began walking. It wasn't long before he could see the boy's house. Three or four cars sat in the driveway. *What a hullabaloo over a kid who got lost for a few minutes*, Jim thought to himself. They barely set foot in the yard when J.R.'s mama came running out the door. She snatched him up and buried her face in the boy's neck, blubbering all the way back to the house something about fearing she'd "lost him forever."

Gail was waiting inside the house. Jim made it as far as the porch, but rather than going in, he paused, checked the chains on the porch swing with a tug, and decided to sit a spell. Gail would be out soon enough and he'd catch a ride back home with her. J.R.'s mom was still trying to gather herself, and his dad listened while the boy explained that he wanted to pick some wild flowers for her. And he had found some, too, but they were across the creek, and his boot got caught, and the water was freezing, and that's where that man found him. "He picked me up like nothing, and he put my cold foot and his bare belly to warm it up. Then he carried me all the way home!"

Jim chuckled a bit. *Gee, that kid's makin' me out to be some kind of hero. S'pose it's not a bad first impression on the new neighbors.* Then he remembered the real first impression in his driveway an hour earlier. "Whatever," he sighed.

The porch swing was starting to feel a little too close to all this drama. Jim got up and stepped down to the lawn, back into the sunshine, and made his way across the driveway, He leaned against the trunk of Gail's car. "What's keeping that woman?" he wondered out loud. "I've got work to get back to."

Finally, Gail backed out of the front door, giving J.R.'s mom a hug. Then she bent down, looked the little fellow in the eye, and told him he was welcome to stop over anytime. She gave him a big squeeze, too.

Meanwhile, daylight was burning, and Jim's eyes said so as she approached the car. Gail wasn't fazed. "That was very gallant of you," she said with a grin as she tossed him his jacket. She threw her head back and dramatically proclaimed, "My hero!" Jim just shook his head and got in the car. He may have grinned a little.

In the shop again at last, Jim got back to work. As he ran the cherry boards through the planer, his mind wandered. He recalled being lost in the woods before, probably when he was around J.R.'s age, maybe nine or ten. He remembered the awful feeling when he realized he was lost — everything he loved about the woods became scary. The shadows looked darker. The groaning of the trees in the wind seemed louder. Even the chatter of the squirrels sounded like snickers, as if they were mocking him. How could he be so stupid as to get lost in the woods? When he eventually found his way home, it appeared that nobody had even known he was missing. He remembered feeling small, inept, and grateful no one had noticed he was gone.

At dinner that evening, Gail asked, "Why didn't you come into the house with J.R.? It would've been a good chance to meet our new neighbors."

Jim mumbled between bites that his boots were wet from the river, and they all seemed to have had everything under control. But the reality was that the whole scenario felt a little over the top to him, and he figured J.R. didn't need another spectator at his 'shame fest.'

Gail went on to describe what a nice family they seemed to be, and how grateful they were to Jim for finding J.R. and bringing him home. Hero or not, all Jim knew was that the whole episode made him feel very uncomfortable, but he had no clue how to explain that to her. She went on to share that her brother had called earlier, and something about their niece Steph making the traveling softball team. She kept talking but Jim lost track of the rest of her monologue.

A few days later, Jim was back in the shop assembling some cabinet parts. Suddenly, he sensed someone was behind him. With the air compressor running in the background, he hadn't heard anyone come in, but he'd always had a pretty keen awareness of his surroundings. When the compressor finally cycled off, he set down the glue bottle and turned around. There stood J.R., his hands clasped behind him, silently staring at the floor.

"Well, what can I do for you young man?" Jim asked, wiping the glue from his fingers onto his apron."

"Um…yer…uh…your wife said I could come over anytime."

"Oh. Do you need something?"

"No…well…um…I was just wondering…um…" the boy stammered before finally blurting out, "Do you need any help?"

The mixture of fear and relief in J.R.'s voice made Jim laugh out loud, until he saw the look on the boy's face. His chin had slumped to his chest, and the toe of one shoe had crept over the toe of the other. His knees were tight together as if he had to pee, and he stood stock still.

"Well, let's see here," Jim said, gathering his composure. "You mean you want to earn some spending money?"

"Oh no," J.R. perked up. "I just want to help!"

Jim raised his eyebrows. "Well, I'm afraid there's really not much for a boy to do in a shop." One look at the amount of sawdust on the floor would have exposed his lie, but it was the best he could come up with on the spot. "Besides," he went on, "it's a pretty dangerous environment with all these power tools."

"OK," J.R. replied softly, his chin descending once again. He turned to leave.

Jim stuck his head back into the cabinet and muttered, "I'll think about it." But J.R. had already disappeared.

"I can hear my insurance agent now," Jim said to

himself with a chuckle. "'You let a kid in your shop!?' Yeah, that's prob'ly a pretty bad idea."

Truth be told, he had neither the time nor the patience for a neighbor kid to be hanging around. With each passing year the variables in Jim's life had grown fewer and easier to control, and he had no desire to disrupt a good thing.

Chapter Two

All Work, No Play...

If April showers bring May flowers, they also bring dandelions, and the yard was peppered with them. The grass had really sprung to life, too; and with all the green and yellow, Jim felt like he was traipsing through a John Deere advertisement as he walked from the shop at the end of the day.

Nearing the house, he saw Gail on her hands and knees in her flower garden. Gail loved springtime, when she could finally get her hands into some warm black soil and dream about blooms and bumblebees. The garden was all perennials. Hostas grew in the back; clematis climbed the trellis; spiderwort, hydrangeas, lilies, and hyacinth filled in the remainder.

As he approached her from behind, Jim paused to appreciate the view. With an impish smile, he bent down and snagged a dandelion, intending to sneak up and lightly brush it over her ankle, impersonating a spider. But before he got to her, a bag of mulch with two legs came walking upright from around the garage.

"What the heck?" Jim thought they were alone, but apparently not. Suddenly he was a little embarrassed about where his mind had just been.

As the bag approached, an adolescent voice strained. "Is this where you want it?"

Gail looked over her shoulder. "Yes, honey, you can

drop it anywhere. Those are heavy."

The bag flopped to the ground, and a red-faced little boy was left standing there. "Oh, hi, Mister Jim," he said with a smile.

Gail craned her neck. "Hi, honey. Done for the day?" She noticed the weed in his hand. "Aww, did you pick that for me?"

Not only was Jim's cover blown by this dinky neighbor kid, but somehow he felt reduced to a schoolboy holding a lame flower for his teacher. Not to mention, she had just called them both 'honey.'

"Naw, just picking weeds," he lied. "How long till dinner?"

"Probably twenty minutes or so. I picked up some brats at the store if you want to start the grill." She turned to the boy. "J.R., do you want to join us for dinner?"

"No, but thank you. My mom said I need to be home by six."

Gail glanced at her watch, "Oh my, it's five till. Would you like Jim to run you home?"

"No, but thank you. I've found a shortcut through the woods."

The boy pulled off the gloves that Gail had loaned him and set them on the bag of mulch. "Thank you, Miss Gail," he said. "I liked helping you."

"You're most welcome, J.R., and thank you for your help."

Down the driveway he went, as fast as his skinny legs would take him, and then he disappeared into the woods.

"What a sweet boy," she said.

Jim, on the other hand, was still standing there with that droopy dandelion hanging between his fingers. He loved watching her with kids. She was kind and patient, and had a knack for interacting at their level. She was amazing, yet somehow it bothered him a little, like pricking the longings of his own childhood. Why couldn't he have had a mom like her? It wasn't a conscious thought, just a feeling. He passed it off as not being fond of some neighbor kid's intrusion. *You just never know what kind of upbringing some of those hooligans are getting at home*, he thought.

"Honey, are you ok?" Gail asked.

"Yeah, just wonderin' why he was here."

"Oh, I saw J.R. and his mom at the store when I was picking up the mulch, and he asked if he could come over and help. I told him that I'd like that very much."

The dandelion slipped from Jim's fingers, and he went to start dinner.

Out on the deck, Gail snuck up from behind and slid her arms around Jim's waist. "How was your day, babe?" she asked.

He set the tongs down and turned around to give her a squeeze.

"It was good. The base cabinets are assembled, and the uppers will be by the end of the week. I'm actually a couple days ahead of schedule."

"Oooh, does that mean you could take Friday off? It's supposed to be seventy-four degrees. Could be our first trip to the lake for the year."

"No, babe, it's way too early in the job to be playing hooky. Maybe Saturday after I get the lawn mowed."

"If those brats are ready; I'll grab a plate." Gail spun around to go inside.

"Hey Gail," Jim said, "was A.J. in the garage?"

"Yeah, why?"

"Well, what was he doing in there?"

"He was getting the mulch out of the back of the car. And it's J.R."

"Well, you know I'm not crazy about some neighbor kid rootin' around in my garage." He realized it sounded a little whiny, but it didn't matter; Gail was already inside.

The weekend came. As Jim parked the lawn mower, Gail was backing her car out of the garage.

"Going somewhere?" he said, more as an observation than a question.

"To the beach," she said with a big grin. "And so are you."

"Seriously? In the middle of a Saturday afternoon? You know I've got stuff to do."

"Yes, you do." Gail was still smiling. "And going to the beach is on the list. Wash up and grab your suit. I've got the cooler packed."

Even through her big sunglasses he could see that look in her eyes, and he didn't have the heart to disappoint her.

He returned to the car in a pair of shorts and a tee shirt; it was way too early in the season to be needing a swim suit. He grumbled a little as he buckled his seatbelt, trying to appease the mandate in his head that Saturdays were for working around the property. But he couldn't deny that he secretly loved this playful side of Gail.

He remembered one of his birthdays shortly after they were married. She had showed up on his jobsite in the middle of the day and blindfolded him. She led him away, and when the blindfold came off forty minutes later, he was sitting on the edge of a hot tub in a hotel suite. It had taken Jim a while to comprehend what was actually taking place. That evening they enjoyed a nice dinner. Later, room service delivered a birthday cake, which they nibbled on while soaking in the hot tub. The day had concluded with them feeling exhausted and happy, on a bed that seemed twice the size of theirs at home. It was only one night, but it was a memorable one. She made him feel special. Seen. Enjoyed. It was quite a contrast to the scattered childhood snapshots in his mind, where being seen didn't always mean being enjoyed. When making himself scarce was sometimes a means of survival. Believing he was loved, but sometimes wondering how much he was liked.

Leaving their shoes in the car, they grabbed the camp chairs and cooler from the trunk and followed the path to the shore line. The lake level was down a little this year, and the sand stretched thirty yards between the bluff and the water, but they still parked themselves just a few feet from the shoreline. Jim wiggled his chair, driving the back legs deeper into the sand to create a reclining position. He slouched a little, buried his feet, pulled the bill of his cap down, and closed his eyes. Nothing could carry him away like the rhythm of gentle waves lapping the shore and the smell of the air off the water. It offered a full bouquet of excitement and anticipation with hints of playfulness, followed by a lingering nod to rest. The beach was Jim's idea of aroma therapy and it had soothed him since childhood.

Growing up, the water had always been a place of joy. How many summer days started in the garden, or mowing, or in the orchard, and ended at the beach? Jim's mom always had a list of chores for the day, and when the list was done, he was free to pedal his bike a couple miles down to the lake, where a family from the small church they attended owned some beachfront. Apparently, most of the moms from church had a similar schedule, because around mid-afternoon about a dozen kids would show up. It was bliss diving into the lake after working all morning in the summer heat. They would swim and snorkel and dive for clams to their hearts' content — or until 5:18 p.m., whichever came first. Jim always had to be home when his dad got home at 5:30. Up till then, though, it was paradise — air-drying in the sun on beach towels spread out over the length of the dock, only to dive in to cool down, and air-dry again. The cycle would repeat until the wristwatch Jim left hanging on the handlebars of his bike demanded it was time to return to reality.

Gail interrupted Jim's trek down memory lane with a

gentle hand on his forearm. "Thanks, honey," she whispered. "I really needed this."

Jim knew he needed it, too. But, content to play the martyr, he only whispered back, "You're welcome, babe."

He closed his eyes again, but instead of fond memories, or the washing of the warm breeze anesthetizing his concerns, his mind wandered into next week and the bid that was due on Wednesday. A meeting with his accountant scheduled for Thursday still required him to get some figures together. He also needed to hear back from the tree service so he could have a price for the church board meeting Thursday night.

The sand grew hotter, and the lack of lumbar support from this camp chair was taking its toll. He dug through the cooler and found a chicken salad wrap and a water. Gail was motionless, so he quietly closed the cooler and distracted himself with his lunch. His mind paced over the steps of the previous week and into the month to come. Though he was still sitting right beside her, Gail could tell he was no longer at the beach.

"Ready to go?" she asked.

"If you are," he replied.

Back at the car, they brushed the sand from the chairs and stowed them with the cooler in the trunk. Jim sat down in the driver's seat and brushed his feet off over the parking lot before slipping his shoes on. It was a familiar feeling. He slid his hand around his heal and over the top and bottom of each foot. The clean grit of the sand clung and scrubbed before relenting and falling to the ground. The beach seemed to exfoliate more than just the skin. It could chafe or soothe the soul, too.

Gail's purse buzzed, and she pulled it out from under the seat. Their son Kyle was texting. He wondered if she would have time to talk later that day or tomorrow. Kyle lived downstate, and had for a few years. He found a job after graduating from college and never came back home. That had saddened Jim, but it didn't surprise him. Kyle was a hard worker, no doubt, but a cabinet shop was not his calling. Besides, the pace around here could never compete with the city life.

Gail would be available after seven tonight, or after church tomorrow, whichever worked best for him. As they continued texting back and forth for a while, Jim took a detour towards their favorite drive-thru ice cream shop.

Trying to match their licking to their ice cream's melting, they made short work of their cones. It was good, though. Wiping away any remaining evidence with a napkin, Jim asked, "Who was the text from?"

"Kyle. He wanted to chat and was wondering when would be a good time. He'll call tomorrow."

"Oh."

"Does it bother you that he texts me instead of you?"

Though it did sting a little, Jim minimized it. "He probably knows you're quicker to respond than I am."

"I think he wants to talk about Memorial weekend. I suspect he's not coming home."

"I'm not surprised. We'll probably be busy getting the yard ready for summer anyway," Jim said, dismissing his disappointment.

His mind wandered back to his son sharing his plans for after college. Kyle had hopes and dreams that Jim wouldn't have been able to envision, much less articulate, at that age. Kyle spoke of working in research and traveling, both for work and adventure. He talked about raising support for a two-month trip for his team that far exceeded Jim's annual gross. They wanted to study the economic and social impact of growing tourism on the small coffee plantations in Costa Rica. Kyle talked about grants and being published. He talked about the culture and the energy of the city, the venues he enjoyed, the stadium, and the pubs. When Jim was his age, there was no time or money for romantic notions — just work.

Chapter Three

A Long-Lost Dream

Church was good. The pastor preached about… well, Jim couldn't quiet remember exactly what he preached about, but it was good. He did remember what was said about Martha. She was busy preparing a meal for Jesus and her siblings, while Mary just sat on her butt and listened. Martha was a little miffed that Mary wasn't helping out, and then Jesus got on Martha's case about it. He said that Mary had made a better choice. *Oh sure, that sounds all well and good, until it's dinner time and there's no dinner*, Jim thought to himself.

The pastor suggested that sometimes the busy-ness of our routines and responsibilities can get in the way of really connecting. All the 'doing' sometimes impedes the 'being.' Jim thought about Gail. She could stop what she was doing on a dime and just to listen to somebody, care for somebody, pray for somebody, or just be present. Jim, on the other hand, struggled to see distractions as anything but frustrating.

Kyle did call that afternoon. And sure enough, he wouldn't be home for the holiday weekend. His car was not running, and until he could get it into the shop he was borrowing a truck. A couple from church had helped him nurse his car home. They offered their son's truck, explaining that he was away on active duty and it would be good for it to be driven. Kyle was grateful, but he didn't feel right about presuming on their generosity by making the long trip home in it. Gail commended his considerate perspective, and conveyed her desire to catch up with him as soon as he might be able to make it home. They both agreed that a cup of coffee on a slow morning together was long overdue.

Later that afternoon, J.R. stopped by and found Gail reading on the back deck.

"Why hello J.R.! How nice to see you today!"

"Hi, Miss Gail!"

"What are you up to?"

"It just seemed like a perfect afternoon for a walk, so I thought I'd come over and see you and Mister Jim."

"Well, I'm not sure where Jim is, but I'm tickled you came. How are you?"

"I'm good! I've been helping my mom in the garden. A man came with his tractor with a spinny thing on the back, a roto-something, and made a patch of dirt in the back yard all nice and dark and soft. He said it was good soil for a garden, and maybe someone had planted one there before. Anyway, I got to go with mom and get seeds from the store. We got some small plants, too, and some covers for the plants in case it freezes after we plant them. Mom really likes working in the garden, and so do I."

Gail smiled. "I'm sure your mom appreciates your help," she said. "Say, would you like to give me a hand?"

"Sure!"

"How 'bout we hang the hammock"?

"The what?"

"The hammock."

"What's a hammock?" J.R. replied with a curious look. Hanging something sounded a little scary to him, but he knew Miss Gail would never hurt anything intentionally.

"A hammock is kinda like a net that you secure a few feet above the ground between two posts or trees, and then you lie in it. It sways a little in the breeze, and it's a marvelous place to take a nap."

"Oh! That sounds like fun."

Gail and J.R. went into the garage and found the step ladder. J.R. scurried to the top and pulled the hammock from the shelf. They headed to the back yard where a half dozen mature maples were scattered about, and they found two just the right distance apart. They were perfect, and at this time of day they would offer a little sun and a little shade. While Gail unrolled the hammock, she asked J.R.to go back into the garage and look on the bottom shelf next to the sprinklers to find a couple wide straps for attaching the ends of the hammock to the trees. He returned with a look of triumph, holding the very straps Gail wanted high above his head.

"Splendid!" she cheered from across the yard.

Just then, Jim came around the corner and nearly stepped on J.R. Seeing the straps in the boy's raised hands, he scowled. "Just where do you think you're going with those, young man?" he demanded.

Gail piped up immediately, "Jim, he's helping me hang the hammock."

Jim backed off. "Oh, uh...ok then," he muttered, trying to sound like all was well, but not very convincingly. He kept up the charade, joining them in securing the straps. Minutes later Gail and J.R. were side-by-side in the hammock, looking up through an array of spring leaves into a cloudless blue sky. As Jim tied up the loose ends of the straps, he put his hip into the end of the hammock, causing them to sway gently back and forth.

J.R. savored the moment. Miss Gail was soft and smelled good. She reminded J.R. of his grandmother. He hadn't seen G-ma since they moved. He snuggled in just a tiny bit closer. The sun found crevasses between the leaves and warmed J.R.'s face. He was so delighted he could hardly lie still, while at the same time he didn't dare move a muscle. He was learning to maintain his guard when Mister Jim was around.

Jim returned to the garage and put the ladder away. He paused to glance around, as if he were taking stock. Later, after J.R. left, Jim found Gail on the deck lighting the grill.

"So, why was P.J. in the garage?" Jim asked, still harboring a touch of disapproval.

"Jim, it's J.R. We used the ladder to retrieve the hammock, then I asked him to go back in and get the straps. What's the problem here?"

"Well, I just don't want him thinking he can help himself to my garage any 'ol time he takes a fancy."

"Is this about your motorcycle?"

"No, it's just that…well, maybe a little."

"Jim, there's no reason for him to go near it. Would you like me to talk to him about it?"

"Naw. I just don't want him messin' with it."

"J.R.'s a good boy. He's not gonna hurt it. It's out of the way and under a cover, and he likely doesn't even know it's in there."

"He's a boy and it's a motorcycle. I guarantee you, he knows it's there."

"Oh, whatever."

As Jim settled himself into a chair on the deck, the memories of when his dad first brought the motorcycle home came into focus. Good memories. Exciting memories. It was a white 1965 Honda CA77, 305cc motorcycle marketed as the "Dream." Honda manufactured the Dream in the 1960's for cheap, fun transportation. With its twin cylinders and 16-inch wheels it was more than a scooter; but at roughly 23hp it wasn't quite a performance bike. The sweeping front fender, color-matched side covers, and stamped frame made it unique. Jim remembered hearing that Elvis had purchased a black one for himself and a white one for Priscilla. They were cool. Jim's dad had picked this one up on a whim. It didn't run, and it appeared to have been ridden-hard-and-put-away-wet, but his dad told him they could work on it together. Though Jim was only twelve at the time, he was tall and could touch the ground with both feet when he sat on it. He spent hours perched on its saddle, tipping slightly side-to-side, visualizing going through the corners. He would twist the throttle and squeeze the clutch and imagine the pulse of the engine beneath him. It had its share of dings and scuffs, and even rust was appearing, but Jim kept it clean and polished just the same. Nearly every day after school he would spend time with it. He couldn't wait to help his dad restore it and take it for their first ride. A smile spread across Jim's face as he recalled how he used to imagine sitting on it behind his dad, putting his arms around him, and holding on tight. He could almost smell the Old Spice and feel his dad's tee shirt flapping in his face. It was the closest Jim might ever come to hugging his dad.

As the memory continued, Jim's smile disappeared, as he recalled the day he opened the shed door and the Dream wasn't there. He ran to the garage, but it wasn't there either. He searched everywhere he could think, but to no avail. He hoped his dad had merely taken it to a shop to get the repairs started. When his dad arrived home that evening, Jim met him in the driveway and inquired about the Dream's whereabouts.

"Oh, a buddy of mine wanted it, so I sold it to him. Made fifty bucks on the deal." His dad grinned proudly as he grabbed his lunch pail from the seat of his truck and headed to the house.

Jim stood there speechless. Everything inside him fell like sand to the ground and disappeared into the gravel, yet he was still standing. Invisible, silenced, and without consequence, Jim was familiar with feeling overlooked or misunderstood, but never had he felt so insignificant. Dreaming had never been this painful. His cheeks burned and he could tell his ears were turning red. He felt foolish. He and his dad never spoke of it again. That night as Jim lay in bed, his hurt fostered seeds of anger, his anger slowly budded into mistrust, and in due time, mistrust produced a perpetual harvest of bitterness toward his dad.

Thirty-eight years later, Jim found that motorcycle. A white, Honda Dream caught his eye as he was driving past a swap meet in a neighboring county. He just had to turn his truck around and investigate. When the owner invited him to check it out, Jim opened the tool box cover and removed the pouch. Years ago, the original pliers had been missing from the tool pouch in their Dream, and Jim had replaced them with a small pair of blue-handled pliers. When Jim carefully emptied the pouch onto the seat, the same blue pliers were still there. A flood of memories poured over him.

He put the tools back and secured the cover. Throwing his leg over the seat, Jim grabbed the handlebars and closed his eyes for a moment. He felt reunited with an old friend. Too excited to haggle with the owner, he gladly paid the asking price. With the exhilaration of a twelve-year-old, he loaded up the bike.

Gail was gracious – even excited – when Jim pulled in with it strapped in the back of his truck. She was familiar with the story and had looked at more than a few old Dream motorcycles through the years. She helped Jim unload and push it into the garage. He made space for it in the corner and covered it. There it sat for the last three years.

J.R.'s invasion of the garage must have quietly motivated Jim. Throughout the next week he found himself browsing the internet, looking for a few parts for his Dream. He had a mental list in his head, but hadn't yet even considered starting the restoration. Something had changed though, and he was beginning to imagine what it might be like to take the cover off and enjoy the idea of a project. He found a parts bike online that had the right mirror, both gas tank side emblems, and a good seat, all of which he needed. It also had the taillight lens and a luggage rack. He contacted the seller and made plans to see it over the weekend.

Gail listened quietly as Jim shared his idea with her. It was good to see Jim dreaming again; that wasn't one of his strong suits. He was usually consumed with the day-to-day, saving little energy for imagining the future — unless, of course, it was about work. She remembered early in their marriage having to temper her habit of dreaming out loud. She would fantasize about travel, vacations, camping, or visiting theme parks with Kyle, and it would irritate Jim. He was fairly frugal, and it all seemed frivolous. So, this was a welcome change.

She let him ramble on for a few minutes about how fortunate he felt to find another Dream for parts before she piped up.

"So where is this bike?"

"About four hours from here, just outside Roseville."

"Honey, isn't that near where Kyle lives?"

"Thirty, maybe forty minutes south of Kyle's. Why?"

"What time are you planning to be there?"

"I told the guy I'd text when I got to the Wayland exit. Probably around noon."

"Do you mind if I come along? Maybe we could leave a little early and catch lunch with Kyle."

"Um, sure. Sure, that'll work. You want to call him and see if he's available?"

"Yes!" Gail was delighted. She loved day trips with Jim, and the chance to see Kyle would be the icing on the cake.

Chapter Four

Outside, Looking In

Jim usually slept great, out as soon as his head hit the pillow. But not this Friday night. Earlier in the day he had topped off the gas tank, emptied the back of the truck, put the tie-down straps behind the seat, got the cash (hundreds) for the asking price, plus some twenties and fifties in case he was able to haggle. Still, going through his mental check-list didn't alleviate his restlessness. Something deeper was stirring as he envisioned himself out in the garage, restoring the bike. It unearthed a buried feeling; a longing of spending time with his dad, and the plans they had to restore it nearly four decades earlier. The joy of those memories was quickly swallowed up by disappointment, and the betrayal Jim felt was as fresh as if it had happened yesterday. He finally nodded off, but not until he had soothed the pain with a resolution of "I'll show him" that settled in his gut.

He was up early the next morning, making coffee and scrambling some eggs when Gail came out in her robe.

"Morning, babe. Sleep good?" he asked.

"Like a rock. You?"

"OK, I guess. Had a few things on my mind."

"Like what?"

"Oh, just stuff…about the motorcycle."

"Are you excited?"

"I suppose a little. I mean, it doesn't make sense to have it just sitting out in the garage. It should be restored."

Gail agreed, adding, “It’ll be so good to see Kyle. It’s been since Christmas.”

Jim scooped some eggs onto Gail’s plate in a “let’s keep it moving” fashion. “If we’re gonna get lunch with him, we should probably hit the road pretty soon,” he said.

Gail poured herself a cup of coffee, grabbed her plate and a fork, and slipping her Bible under her arm, made her way out to the deck. She loved this time of year when she could soft-start her morning outdoors. She knew she had time before they needed to leave. Jim was just a little more excited than he was letting on

Jim would have been happy with soup and a sandwich, but Kyle wanted to meet them at one of his favorite cafes. Gail and Kyle quickly found something on the chalkboard menu that they were eager to try. Jim settled for a chicken salad croissant and a pickle. They found a high-top table near the window and settled in, as much as anyone can settle in on an industrial metal stool without a back. These were about as comfortable as the ones Jim remembered from junior high shop class. Gail and Kyle chatted about life, his work, his friends, and a retreat he was planning at his church.

“How’s your car repair coming along?” Jim asked.

“I got a quote,” Kyle said between bites. “Should be able to cover it with next week’s paycheck.”

Jim grunted his approval. His mind wandered out to the sidewalk and the people passing the window. Most were moving quickly, some with lattes in their hands, some in pairs, most chatting or texting on their phones. They all seemed to have someplace to go. And Jim did, too. With their plates clean, Jim waited for a break in their conversation.

“We probably oughta get going, babe. I’m sure Kyle has a full day and so do we.”

Out on the sidewalk, Jim gave Kyle a brief, awkward hug and stepped aside for Gail to say good-bye. She gently pulled her son's face toward her and kissed his cheek, then paused to look him in the eye for a moment. "Your dad and I are so proud of you… we love you very much."

Jim had already unlocked the doors and was climbing into the truck as Kyle crossed the street. "Love you!" Kyle called loud enough for both of them to hear, and then disappeared in the flow of pedestrians.

Jim asked Gail to pull up the address for where they were going on his phone. It showed they were twenty-eight minutes from their destination. They might actually arrive a little ahead of schedule. That was fine with Jim, though Gail would have preferred to spend a few extra minutes with Kyle.

They found the farm and the guy Jim had talked with earlier in the week. He was a pleasant fella. A slight belly filled out his bib-overalls, with one pant leg tucked in his boot and the other one out. His unkempt attire didn't diminish the hearty greeting he offered his two new friends.

"Howdy! Ya found us okay?" he asked, his thick hand leading the way as he almost ran out to welcome them.

"No problem," Jim replied, extending his own hand.

After a quick, firm handshake, the man took Gail's hand in both of his. "Nice to meet you both. Name's Ron."

As the three of them made their way to the barn, Ron said, "I got another guy who's also interested in the bike."

Jim's heart sank, and he felt a little angry. "Wait a minute, we talked. You knew I was driving all the way down here today."

"No, no, it's not like that," Ron said. "I just know that you were looking for a few parts and I wasn't plannin' to part the bike out. But this other fella is needin' wheels and the front fender. I just thought maybe the two of you might work somethin' out."

"Oh," was all Jim replied, feeling a little embarrassed for being harsh. Maybe this could be a good thing. As Jim looked over the bike he began listing the parts he was interested in. He made an offer for just those parts, and the other guy could have the rest of the bike. Ron thought that sounded like a dandy idea, and they shook on it. Together they pushed the bike over to the garage where Ron offered his tools so Jim could remove the parts he wanted.

Ron disappeared into the house and returned with a moving blanket that Jim could have to protect the parts on his trip home. Ron's wife followed him out of the house with a smile just as cheery as her husband's, but she was bearing cookies: fresh, warm, chocolate chip cookies.

Gail engaged her immediately, but Jim seemed oblivious. He focused tenaciously on the wrench in his hand and the parts he was trying to remove.

With the offer of coffee to accompany the cookies, Gail followed the farmer's wife back into the house where a delightful conversation ensued, as if the two were long lost friends.

Eventually, Jim followed Ron through the back door to the kitchen sink. "A little dish soap oughta cut that grease," Ron said as he grabbed a bottle from under the sink and squeezed a puddle into Jim's palm.

Jim scrubbed until he felt confident he could dry his hands on the kitchen towel without leaving a trace. Then he pulled out his wallet and counted out the bills onto the counter top. Once again Ron extended his thick hand.

"Excellent," he exclaimed. "I sure hope your finds today help with your restoration."

Jim shook his hand with a nod. He couldn't shake the awkward feeling that maybe Ron wasn't referring to just his motorcycle. Jim interrupted the women's conversation.

"Gail, I'm ready if you are."

"Oh, come have a cookie," Ron's wife offered Jim as

her husband helped himself to one.

"That's kind of you, but we really should get going," Jim answered. He knew he sounded a little anti-social and Gail's glance confirmed it, but Jim remained in the kitchen.

Ron placed some cookies on a napkin. "Here's a few for the road," he said."

Gail smiled at her new friend. "Thank you for a wonderful visit," she said as she reached across the table and squeezed her hand.

Back on the road, Jim was so pleased with his purchase. As they headed north, he again started anticipating the restoration that had eluded him for so many years. He recalled the hours spent sitting on the Dream, imagining riding behind his dad, or even driving it himself. Maybe, sooner than later, those dreams would come to pass. As for making them come to pass with his dad, well, that ship had sailed. The realization stirred a hint of anger, followed by a trace of sadness.

Gail broke the silence. "You're kind of quiet; everything ok?"

"Yeah, why?"

"Well, you were in a pretty big yank to get on the road. Seems you could've taken a minute join us for a cup of coffee. Carol was so sweet, and funny too. She was telling me about how Ron came into possession of that old motorcycle. They were at a farm auction and he thought he was bidding on a two-bottom plow. He found himself in a bidding war with a lady from the city, and for the life of him, he couldn't imagine what she might possibly need a plow for. He knew his neighbor Ralph was looking for a plow, and he couldn't figure out why Ralph wasn't bidding at all. Imagine his surprise when he realized he was bidding on item sixty-nine instead of ninety-six! She was so comical telling it that I snorted my coffee; was afraid I might pee myself a little. I won't forget her anytime soon."

Jim wasn't amused. "I just didn't see any sense in sitting down with total strangers when we had a couple hundred miles yet to cover."

"You were quiet at lunch too."

Jim was starting to feel a little judged, but with the miles ahead of them he chose his words carefully. "I just don't seem to have much in common with Kyle, I don't really understand his world, and I don't feel like he has much respect for mine."

"Wow, that's interesting," Gail said. "Kyle has a ton of respect for what you do. He loved the desk you made for him in high school. Woodworking may not be his thing, but he's certainly proud of what you do."

"Whatever," Jim replied in a tone that implied he was ready to move on.

Gail's phone rang and she pulled it out of her purse. Jim was relieved; he wasn't fond of her poking around his feelings…asking questions…like there was always something deeper going on. Why couldn't what he said or didn't say be enough for her? Why did she always need to start digging around for clues, like she was Nancy Drew and he was her next case? It made him a little angry. Anger…now that was one emotion Jim was familiar with. He'd watched his grandad pull a 45 out of the glovebox and shoot a hole right through the car door when it left the two of them stranded miles from home on a blistering summer day. He'd seen his dad throw tools and put his fist through more than one door. Growing up, Jim was no stranger to angry outbursts from the men in his world. But he also remembered how he felt when Dad or Grandad would let loose. He didn't like it, and he made a promise to himself to never show up like that. But it didn't mean he wouldn't get angry.

He remembered Kyle's thirteenth birthday. Kyle had begged for a paintball gun; some of his friends had them and he just had to have one too. Against his better judgment,

Jim conceded. After blowing out the candles on his birthday cake, Kyle tore into his gifts. He was ecstatic. Jim handed him the scissors to open the plastic packaging; first the gun, then the helmet and goggles, and finally the canister of paint-balls. Before Kyle even tasted a bite of cake, he was out in the field plinking trees. The following weekend, Kyle had his buddies over and they brought their paintball guns and gear. When it started to rain, Kyle thought, no problem; they could have their paintball fight in Dad's shop. But as much as they tried to clean up the mess, it still looked like a war zone when Jim opened the shop door on Monday morning. Immediately, Jim was standing Kyle's bedroom with the paintball gun in pieces. With his bare hands he had torn and twisted it into scrap while Kyle looked on, speechless. Other than giving explicit instructions on cleaning his shop, Jim never spoke to Kyle about the episode again. There was nothing more to say.

As the miles rolled on, Jim was silent. The memory unsettled him. He felt justified at the time, but looking back, it just felt ugly. Gail, on the other hand was still on her phone. "That's so sweet," she said as she put her phone back in her purse.

"What's so sweet?"

"That was J.R. He wants to stop by later and show us his science project. He got a 100% on it, plus extra credit for having a hand-out for each of his classmates. Sounds like he's very proud of it, and he's excited for us to see it."

"Well, isn't that nice," Jim responded with a hint of insincerity. He knew it was the right thing to say, but seeing the neighbor kid's science project was woefully low on Jim's priority list.

As they continued north, Jim's mind wandered again, this time back to his own early science projects. While the other kids were displaying active volcanoes with vinegar and baking soda, or lighting a bulb with a potato, Jim had made a steam boat. He shaped a piece of balsa wood for the hull.

Then he glued in two tea candles on the top of the hull, one in front of the other. Next, he soldered a cap onto a six-inch long piece of copper pipe and drilled a very tiny hole in the cap. Then, using stiff wire, he mounted the pipe about an inch above the candles, running from bow to stern. He filled the pipe with water and sealed the other end with a stopper. When the candles heated the pipe, the water inside created steam, and with each puff that escaped from the small hole in the pipe the boat would be propelled forward. Finally, he attached a fixed rudder to the bottom of the hull, causing it to turn left. When he put it in a water basin and lit the candles, it would putt-putt-putt around in a lazy circle. He was very proud of it. But his teacher wouldn't let him light the candles in school, so it just sat there in the tub of water while he tried to convince the other kids that it really worked. He got a C.

On the interstate, Jim pushed his speed as much as he dared. Once back on the county roads, he kept it to five over. He didn't need a ticket, but it was becoming a long day and he was ready to get home, unload the parts, and get some dinner in his belly. It felt like he and Gail had caught up on all the small talk and he wasn't interested in "discussions of the heart" as she called them. For the final hour, the miles ticked by in relative silence.

Chapter Five

Mistaken Identity

It was well past dinnertime when they finally pulled in. Jim stopped the truck at the mailbox and grabbed the mail before proceeding up the driveway. He admired the lawn but noted it was almost ready to be cut again. As they neared the house, Jim scowled.

"Oh man, I can't believe I left the garage door up!" He hated the thought of having been gone all day with the contents of his garage exposed.

"Jim," Gail said soberly, "I know you closed the garage door before we left."

Jim stopped the truck short and opened his door. He heard rustling inside. In one fluid motion he released the console between the seats, grabbed his handgun, chambered a round, and was out of the truck. No one was gonna break into his garage without a confrontation. His eyes strained to adjust to the dimness inside the garage. He saw no one. He also didn't see his motorcycle, but he heard noises coming from where the bike was stored. With his gun raised, he made his way in. He was having trouble distinguishing between the muffled ruckus coming from the dark corner and his heart pounding in his chest.

Still in the truck, Gail pressed the overhead door remote to turn the light on. Jim immediately saw the source of the noise. He was dumbfounded, then livid. His Dream was lying on floor with some kid lying there, straddling it.

"I'm stuck" the boy whined. Between the sniffles, Jim could hear him struggling to extricate his leg from beneath the bike, grinding the bike on the concrete with every move.

"DAMMIT!" Stowing the gun in his belt, Jim tipped the bike up a few inches with one hand and slid the delinquent out with the other, with enough force that the kid continued to scoot across the floor after Jim had released his grip.

Stepping forward, Jim snagged the waif by the front of his shirt and lifted him to his feet. "WHAT THE HELL ARE YOU DOING IN HERE?" he bellowed.

Gail hurried out of the truck. She came up behind the boy and put a firm grip on his shoulders. "J.R." she said in a low and steady voice, "are you hurt or bleeding anywhere?" Nervously, he shrugged no. Then, in a tone he had never heard from Miss Gail before, she demanded, "What happened here?"

Now Jim was reeling! This twit was J.R.? Seriously? "FOR CRYIN' OUT LOUD KID! WHAT IN BLUE BLAZES WERE YOU THINKING?"

J.R. couldn't speak. As frightened as he had been stuck under the bike, this was far worse. Jim released his grip and stormed out of the garage.

Gail could see J.R. was shaking, and she slid her hands from atop his shoulders down around his arms. "Let's go inside and have a seat. You can take a minute to gather yourself and tell us what happened."

Under any other circumstance J.R. would have jumped at the invite, but not today. He couldn't even look at Miss Gail. As soon as she released his arm, he tore out of the garage and ran full tilt down the driveway. He stumbled halfway to the road and went spread-eagle in the gravel, but he was up again and running without slowing a bit.

Gail winced as she watched him go down; that had

to hurt, but from the look in his eyes she knew he was in full flight mode and probably wouldn't feel it until he got home. She went inside and dialed J.R.'s mom. Gail filled her in on what had happened, and that J.R. was likely going to need some cleaning up and a few bandages when he got home, along with a safe place to spill his heart.

Jim was nowhere to be found as Gail started dinner. They both needed some space to cool down. She rummaged through the pantry mindlessly before concluding she had just enough energy to empty a couple cans of soup into a pan on the stove. That was going to be good enough. Once it had a chance to warm, she scooped herself a bowl and buttered a piece of bread. Leaving the rest to simmer on low, she collapsed into her recliner and breathed a prayer.

"Lord, thank You…thank You. Thank You for this meal, and would You bless it? Thank You that no one was hurt today. I know J.R. has some scrapes on his hands and knees, but I can't help but believe the wounds to his heart went a little deeper. Give his mama wisdom as she comforts and tends to him over the next couple days. Lord, give me wisdom. I know Jim is a twisted mess inside right now. I want to support him without minimizing his responsibility in this situation, and I certainly don't want to come across like his dad. Thank You for being more intimately aware of what's really going on here, than I can imagine. Give me Your perspective, Lord. In Jesus name I ask, amen."

She picked up the TV remote and then set it back down. The disruption going on inside was all the noise she could handle right now.

A half hour later, Gail was sitting motionless in her chair. Her soup had gone cold, and the slice of bread was only half eaten. She was trying desperately to sort out her anger from her fear before she confronted Jim. She knew he had been robbed before, in his early twenties, in the city at knife point. He has also caught some teenagers trying to break into his shop a few years ago. He chased them off, but it never went any further with the police. That's when Jim purchased a handgun. But today…well, today was way over the top. It needed to be addressed.

Her internal debate was interrupted by voices out in the driveway. She listened without moving. It sounded like two men. One of the voices was Jim's, but she didn't recognize the other.

"There was an intruder — in my garage! I had every right!" Jim was still hot.

"Yes, Jim, but there was no confrontation, no threat. You pulled a weapon on a 10-year-old boy."

"How was I supposed to know who it was? Besides, if there was one in the garage, there may have been two more in the house!"

Gail made her way to the window. There was a patrol car in the driveway, and Jim was talking with an officer. Her heart sank. She had wondered if the other voice might have been J.R.'s dad. She hadn't even considered the police would be involved.

"Listen Jim, I don't think they're gonna press charges, but I just wanted to stop by and check things out, for your sake as well as theirs.

Jim was incredulous. "Press charges!?"

"Jim," the officer said calmly but firmly, "the kid's upper arm is black and blue with a huge hand print all the way around it. If push came to shove, I'll bet it would match yours."

Jim remembered snatching the boy from under the bike. He had grabbed him by the right arm all right, but certainly not hard enough to leave a mark, he thought.

The overhead door was still up, and the officer asked if he could take a look around. Jim nodded and followed him inside, turning on the lights. The bike was still lying on its side. Everything else looked untouched. Then Jim noticed the bike's cover was folded neatly and placed on the workbench. Next to it was a piece of cardboard with a large "A+" drawn in red marker. Sitting on the cardboard was a deflated balloon mounted atop a small paper plate, and a caption that read, "How a Hovercraft Works." Jim's head started to spin as he remembered J.R.'s call to Gail earlier in the day, wanting to show them his science project. They had arrived home later than they planned, and J.R. must have gotten bored waiting for them.

Jim followed the officer out of the garage and offered an obligatory, "Thanks for stoppin' by" as the officer climbed back into his cruiser. Jim pressed the code into the keypad and watched the overhead door slowly descend, sealing in the evidence and leaving him standing alone in the driveway.

He felt the night air on his neck. The sun hung low in the west, and the shadows stretched across the yard. The moon peered over the trees and began its night shift as Jim started toward the front door. But he couldn't go in; not yet anyway.

He brushed off a couple landscape bricks on the perimeter of Gail's flower garden and sat down. Elbows on his knees, he planted his face into his hands. Everything in him wanted to rewind or erase the scenes that had unfolded since pulling into the driveway. The more he tried to push them from his mind, the more vivid each scene replayed. Jim was shaken with how quickly he had escalated from curiosity to caution, to fear, to anger, to rage…and then shame.

He wasn't sure how long he sat there, but his nether regions were falling asleep and the stars had come out. A coldness crept through his body that he was unable to shake, and he knew it was time to go inside.

What a day, was all he could think — and he knew it wasn't over.

Sitting down on the bench just inside the door, he leaned forward to untie his work boots, tugging the laces loose from their worn positions. One at a time, he kicked them off and slid them underneath the bench. For a moment he just sat there, arms straight, grasping the front edge of the bench with each hand. He loved the feel of furniture, and he remembered coming across the rare, curly oak he used to make this bench. He really enjoyed the process of making custom furniture. He appreciated the parameters that each piece provided; size, purpose, aesthetics, species. They created the boundaries wherein his imagination could flourish. His role as a craftsman was well defined, and he knew where he belonged when he was in the shop.

Not so much in the world of people, though, where the parameters of what was expected often conflicted with what was modeled for him growing up. He remembered as a kid the searing pain of a dislocated shoulder. His mom had called him in for dinner, but it was such a perfect summer evening that he had ignored her and continued to ride his bicycle round and round the driveway. He had mastered riding with no hands. The breeze felt good as he kept a steady, easy pace. With his arms outstretched, he imagined he was flying. His eyes were all but closed as he made the sweeping curve past the front porch, when suddenly he felt his dad's iron grip lock securely around his forearm. His dad was angry and anchored, and Jim was instantly flat on his back in the gravel. He could hear the words as clearly as if they were spoken yesterday: "Boy, your mother said dinner was ready."

Jim released his grip on the front of the bench and rubbed his shoulder, recalling how it seemed to take forever for his aunt to get there and pop it back into place. He took a deep breath; he knew that pausing in the familiarity of memories and work was his lame attempt at stalling the inevitable. He got up and walked into the living room.

"Hi, hon," Jim said nonchalantly.

"There's soup on the stove," Gail replied.

"I'm not really hungry."

"I saw the police here."

Jim downplayed it. "Yeah, Dean stopped by. Just wanted to fill in the blanks."

"Fill in the blanks?"

"Well, yeah, the kid's folks musta called the cops and Dean was on patrol tonight."

"What did they tell the police?"

"That the kid was here, just waiting for us, and that when we got home, I went all ballistic. Pulled a gun on him and bruised him up. Dean didn't think they were gonna press charges, but he wanted to get my side of the story."

"What did he want you to do?"

"Nothin' that I know of."

"What are you going to do?" Gail pressed.

"What do you mean?"

"Just what I said. What are you going to do?"

Jim fidgeted. He didn't like where this was going. "The kid broke into my garage!" he snapped, feeling backed into a corner. "Listen here, woman! If you think I'm gonna apologize to that stupid kid, you got another think comin'!"

"I didn't say anything about apologizing," Gail said firmly, "but if that's what you think you should do, it sounds like a good place to start…man!" She had no problem going toe-to-toe with Jim.

"I'm going to bed"

"I don't think so Jim."

"Why in tarnation am I the bad guy here?" his voice escalated.

"Jim! You are not a bad guy. You are a wonderful man. But your response to what happened in the garage was way out of proportion. It's almost like it touched off a fuse connected to some stored-up explosives from who-knows-where. And you need to look at that!"

Her tone had a resolve that Jim couldn't dodge. It was as if she saw something in his soul that he had no concept of.

"I'll sleep on the couch," he grumbled.

"Maybe later, but we're doing this now! You are not walking away, Jim. You grabbed that boy like a rag doll and nearly threw him out from under that bike. What was going on with you?"

"I DON'T KNOW!" His anger created more distance than he anticipated. Immediately, he felt very alone. "I don't know. I was angry. I was just…so…angry…" His voice trailed off as he walked to the dining room and slumped into a chair.

Gail took a minute before going into the kitchen. She pulled a bowl from the cabinet and ladled some soup into it. She buttered a piece of bread, grabbed a spoon and napkin, and brought it out to Jim. Quietly, taking a seat across the table from him, they sat in silence. Jim picked up the spoon and ate slowly, deep in thought. Finally, Gail spoke up.

"Jim, besides angry, how did you feel?"

Jim stared into his soup for a bit. Then, slowly and brokenly, he replied, "Like someone...was taking something…something that I really valued…and there was not one…single…thing that I could do about it."

Gail honored his vulnerability with a long pause, allowing the weight of his words to settle before she continued. "When else have you felt that, Jim?"

He pushed his bowl away and buried his face in his hands. He said nothing for a while, but then she saw his bottom lip quiver as he whispered:

"When Dad got rid of the motorcycle…like I was losing it all over again…like my dreams still didn't matter."

Gail got up slowly and quietly gathered his bowl and napkin. She brushed the few bread crumbs left on the table into the bowl and took it to the sink. She returned with a box of tissue and sat down, beside him this time, and put her hand on his leg. For the next ten minutes they just sat in silence. Silence on the outside; Jim's thoughts ping-ponged between the past and the present. Gail was praying. Jim reached over and pulled two tissues from the box and blew his nose, then wiped his eyes indiscriminately on his sleeve as he got up from the chair. Gail got up too and quietly said, "I'll be there in a minute. See you in bed."

By the time she had tidied the kitchen, locked the doors, switched off the lights, and finished brushing her teeth, Jim, true to form, was asleep.

Chapter Six
Thwarted

Jim tossed most of the night, and around four in the morning he woke up in a sweat. He had been dreaming. He rolled to his back and looked at the dark ceiling. Closing his eyes again, he replayed the dream in his mind.

A boy was making his way across a sandy field or a dune with occasional clumps of knee-high grass and thistles. He avoided both as best he could as he headed toward a stand of trees in the distance. He wiped his brow with the back of his hand, and his new jeans chafed in the heat. The clean, white tee-shirt he was wearing seemed much more appropriate for these temperatures. He saw a makeshift structure near the trees and adjusted his course toward it. He also noticed people in the distance, who also seemed to be heading toward the structure, but they were much farther off.

As he neared, he realized that it was an old hand-dug well. It had a brick perimeter that rose a few feet above the ground, and had a dilapidated metal roof overhead. The boy paused to catch his breath and spotted a wooden bucket in the dirt next to the well. His excitement grew as he anticipated a cool, wet reprieve. When he finally reached the well, he picked up the bucket only to find there was no rope. He peered into the pit, hoping the water wasn't too deep. But it was. Very deep. The boy thought for a moment, then slipped his belt from his jeans and attached it to the handle. Leaning over the dusty brick ledge, he lowered the bucket as far as he could, but it wasn't even close.

By this time, one of the strangers who was traveling alone arrived. It was a little girl, wearing a pale yellow dress with a white bow, shiny white shoes, and ankle socks with frills on the top.

"What are you doing?" the little girl asked. Her curls bounced around her face, and deep dimples punctuated her cheeks.

"I'm thirsty," the boy replied. "Tryin' to get some water from this old well."

"I'm thirsty too," said the girl. "Can I help?"

He eyed the bow on her dress. "Do you think we could use your ribbon?"

"Sure," she said, untying the bow and handing it to him, looking quite pleased that she could contribute.

The boy tied the ribbon to his belt and lowered the bucket again. Still too short. He considered his tee-shirt. He knew his momma wouldn't be pleased if he came home with his shirt messed up, but their thirst overruled. He pulled it off, tied it to the bow, and once again leaned over the brick edge and lowered the bucket as far as he could. Still too short.

Her shoes had a buckle, but his had laces. Removing them from his shoes, he knotted them together and then tied them to his shirt. He added his socks to the length as well. Still not long enough. Discouraged, he pushed himself from the brick ledge and sat on the ground, his back leaning against it.

"Does your tummy hurt?" the girl asked.

"I'm a little hungry I guess."

"No, you're bleeding."

The boy looked at his stomach. Leaning over the brick had left his skin scraped and bloody. The blood caked quickly with the dust and sweat that now covered his torso.

"I'm fine." He said with his most grown-up voice.

Two adults approached — a man and woman — and

the little girl went to greet them. It was apparent they didn't know her, and at first they were cautious of her advance. But her cheery disposition quickly won them over as she chatted freely. The woman even picked her up and carried her as they continued toward the well where the boy rested. Upon arrival, the adult travelers looked him over and frowned their disapproval. He was small, disheveled, barefoot, and dirty.

The little girl squirmed to get down, but the woman held her tight. The boy jumped to his feet. "Put her down! She wants down!" he demanded as the wiggling little girl began to panic. But the woman only sneered.

"Oh, no you don't. You're coming with us, you pretty little darling!"

At this, the man grabbed the boy's arm and threw him to the ground. He tied the boy's hands with the shoe laces, and with the rest of the makeshift rope he tied the boy's body to the well. Then the man stepped back and glared.

"Too bad you're so filthy. And that nasty attitude of yours…nope, that just wouldn't work for us."

The boy twisted and turned, trying desperately to free himself. But he could only watch as the strangers disappeared with the helpless little girl.

Jim got out of bed and went into the bathroom to splash some water on his face. *What was that all about?* he wondered. The entire episode seemed so bizarre, yet somehow familiar.

He quietly made his way out to the living room. Finding a pen and paper, he began jotting down the dream as best as he could remember. He had seen Gail do this countless times, and it usually made for entertaining discussion the next day. He eventually put down the pen and finished out the night on the couch.

Gail rose with the sun. She slipped passed Jim and picked up her Bible on her way to the kitchen. With a fresh cup of coffee, she made her way out to the deck. Before opening her Bible, she paused to watch the stars fade as the sun crept over the tree line. Between sips of coffee, she quietly hummed a new worship tune they had learned in church. The words escaped her memory, but the tune had stuck with her. She hoped they would sing it again today. She glanced at her watch. Jim could sleep for another fifteen minutes before they would need to get ready for church.

Church was really good. Jim even remembered the text. It was Luke chapter fifteen, the parable of the lost sheep. It took Jim back to his week-long summer visits to his uncle's farm as a boy. He loved being in the pasture when the sheep were out of their pens. He'd read that sheep can recognize faces, and he believed it, for after only a few days with them, they would race toward the fence when they saw him coming. He wondered why they seemed so eager to see him, almost like puppies. Good memories.

Anyway, Jim was familiar with the passage, but the pastor's take on it was different. When this sheep went missing, the shepherd risked leaving the other ninety-nine in the open country to search for it. Almost like it was seen as an individual rather than part of a flock. Jim couldn't remember ever risking the security of ninety-nine of anything for the sake of one. He imagined being at a park and pulling a hundred dollars out of his wallet and dropping a dollar bill. A big wind catches it and it's gone. Then he puts the ninety-nine back in his wallet, leaves the wallet on the park bench to chase after the one-dollar bill. *Ain't never gonna happen*, he chuckled to himself.

Yet, as the pastor pointed out, knowing the risk, the shepherd searched. And not just around the area. Not just for a few minutes. Not just for an hour. Not only until he assumed it had been attacked by a predator, or until a predetermined search area was covered, or timeframe met. Not until he felt justified that he had done enough. No, he searched until he found it. By the time he found it, the shepherd himself may have been exhausted, hungry, thirsty, and nearly lost. Maybe he had to venture into a thicket to retrieve the little lamb and get stuck by a few thorns himself. Jim could imagine himself tromping through briars with a shepherd's staff, hooking the sheep and dragging him free, then venting a little frustration by prodding him all the way back to the flock with the blunt end.

But that's not how the story went. The sheep was hoisted onto the shepherd's shoulders and carried all the way back, while the shepherd rejoiced. Now, in Jim's mind that little sheep had been bad. It had wandered away, risked the wellbeing of the rest of the flock, and caused the shepherd a lot of anxiety. The little rascal deserved a punishment, a lesson, a reminder that it better not happen again. There needed to be some sort of restitution before it could be all right. But no. All that was required of the sheep was to submit to being rescued, carried, and celebrated.

While Jim was certainly intrigued by the premise, he had little context for processing it. Every relationship he'd ever experienced was affected by, if not based upon, his performance. If Jim showed up well, if he didn't disappoint, and if he met or exceeded expectations, then people liked him. They were favorable toward him, and they even treated him with respect. In the work world this meant recommendations, promotions, and raises. Jim understood that he was saved by grace and that his sins had been forgiven; but he was also taught that, once saved, he'd better "straighten up and fly right." This pastor was making a very different point: the shepherd loved the sheep even when it screwed up, to the point of hunting him down and rescuing him. The bottom line? It was Jesus' job to save us. Our job is to believe that He can. And that happens to look very much like resting on His shoulders. Jim remembered snatching J.R. from the river and hoisting him to his own shoulder.

He had to admit that he liked the way it sounded. But

Jim was still pretty committed to making sure he was good enough, too. In light of the incident in the garage with J.R., he knew he wasn't. He had been bad, and he knew he had to make it right. He just wasn't totally clear on what that was going to look like.

After shaking the pastor's hand, Jim slipped through the crowd and out the double doors. He pulled the keys from his pocket and fidgeted with them on his way to the truck. When he was within range, he pushed the unlock tab. It chirped in response and he climbed in. He didn't know if J.R.'s family attended here yet, or anywhere for that matter, But if by chance they were here, he wasn't ready to face them just yet. Not in the church parking lot anyway.

He pulled his phone out and checked the weather for the week. Gail was nowhere in sight. She was always the last one out; it didn't matter if they were in their home church or visiting one three states away. She would eventually climb into the car and start going on about meeting so-n-so, and how they were related to so-n-so, who used to be neighbors with so-n-so. All very interesting, mind you, but Jim preferred to wait in the car. Checking his phone, the forecast looked good, warming, with rain on Tuesday.

Gail finally made it to the truck and, true to form, filled Jim in on all the latest community information. "Jeanie's mom is doing better and, Lord willing, hopes to be out of the hospital tomorrow. Lois said Bill got a new job; started a week ago and he seems to like it. Donna and Bud are grandparents again; Dena had a little girl and everyone is doing just fine. They hope to go down to see her next week. That's four for them, you know. Oh, and by the way, I asked pastor Jackson if he was doing any counseling."

Jim raised his eyebrows. "Why? Are you looking to get some more counseling?"

Gail hesitated, choosing her words carefully. "I just wondered if you might want to talk to someone about what happened yesterday, that's all."

The rest of the drive home was silent.

After lunch was cleaned up, Gail took a book and settled into her hammock. She forgot her reading glasses but figured she wouldn't last more than a page or two before falling asleep anyway. It had been a restless night for her, too. She was worried about Jim. She had seen his temper before.

It was Jim's temper that had driven a wedge between Kyle and him years ago. Jim was calculated; Kyle was carefree. Jim was resourceful with things; Kyle was more relational. Jim got stuff done; Kyle researched, planned, saved, and then got things done. Jim was a stickler for maintenance; Kyle, not so much. That had been an ongoing sore spot since Kyle was little.

She recalled one particular day when Jim came home from the hardware store. Kyle had left his remote-control car in the driveway. Jim claimed he never saw it, but it was bright yellow and would have been hard to miss. It was a birthday gift from Gail's parents, and Kyle was so excited when he unwrapped it just three weeks prior. He played with it every chance he could...until that day. Jim showed no remorse, and suggested that maybe now Kyle would remember to take better care of his things. Kyle had gathered the pieces into a box and put it in his closet. Something happened that day. Ever since, Kyle and Jim didn't talk much; at least not about things that mattered.

Gail had tried to encourage Jim to soften up towards Kyle back then, and even a few times since, but Jim could be so hard and unrelenting if he felt justified in his position. The episode with J.R. yesterday smacked of the same rage that she had seen toward Kyle all those years ago. Gail had learned through her own counseling a few years back that when the response is out of proportion to the offense, the problem is usually not the problem.

Jim spent the afternoon tinkering in the garage. He

tipped the motorcycle up and inspected it for further damage. The front fender was bent and scratched, and there was a dent in the gas tank and the exhaust pipe. He was also going to need the left mirror.

"I should have bought the whole bike yesterday," he thought out loud. "Who knows how long it'll take to find more parts?"

He knew he was just licking his wounds, and his justification for his behavior with J.R. was wearing thin. In fact, as he replayed the scenario in his mind, he was starting to feel a little embarrassed. After all, he had seen a couple other parts bikes online that were only a few hours away. So why did he get so angry?

Maybe I ought to talk to somebody, he thought.

By the time evening rolled around, Jim knew he needed to say something to J.R. or his folks. He didn't want to start the week with this knot in his gut.

"Gail, do you have J.R.'s number?"

"I have his mom's number. He uses her phone when he calls. Why?"

"I just want to apologize for yesterday."

Gail knew better than to say anything, but was pleased to see the shift in Jim's attitude. She found her phone and gave Jim the number.

Jim dialed and waited. Four rings and then, "Hi, sorry I missed you. Leave a number and I'll get back to you when I can." Jim hated leaving messages.

"Hi…uh…this is Jim. Your neighbor. I…uh…just want to…uh…listen, there was a big misunderstanding here yesterday with J.R. See, I thought we were being robbed. Anyway, I want to apologize if I hurt J.R. or scared him or anything. Anyway, sorry. Bye."

When Jim hung up, he knew it sounded lame. He was glad Gail was in the bathroom and didn't hear it. But it was off his plate now, and he could get on with his week.

Gail returned to the kitchen. “How’d that go?”

“Great.”

The next morning, Jim was feeling pleased with himself for apologizing to J.R. the night before. He sat at the kitchen counter with his coffee and bagel, planning out the day. The forecast called for upper 70s and plenty of sunshine, which put a spring in his step on his way down to the shop.

But as the temperatures rose throughout the morning, so did Jim’s apprehension. As much as he tried to put the weekend behind him, the scene from the garage continued to play in his mind like a TV in the background. It was hard to focus on his work; the nagging images of holding his gun on the unidentified intruder fueled something. An intense desire to get even. To protect what was his, whether from a felon or a ten-year-old kid. To make sure what came and went in his life was by his choosing.

He could feel his blood pressure rising, and the next thing he knew, he had miscut two boards in a row. Jim wasn’t fond of making mistakes or wasting material. It was a clue. He needed help.

At lunchtime, Jim scrolled through his contacts and found Pastor Jackson’s number. The pastor answered.

“Well, hello, Jim. How are you?”

“Hello, Pastor. Pretty good, I guess.”

“Great to hear it. What can I do for you today?”

“I was wondering if you might have a few minutes some evening this week to chat for a bit.”

“Let’s see,” said the pastor said, pausing to dig out his calendar from under some reports stacked on his desk. “Tuesday evening I’ll be here at the church for a few hours after dinner. Want to stop by then, maybe around seven?”

“Hey, that’d be great. Thanks a lot.”

“My pleasure Jim.”

“Okay, see you then.” Jim hung up the phone and drew a deep breath.

Chapter Seven

NAME _______

Tuesday morning came and the sunny forecast held true. But two-o'clock brought a good spring soaker that hung around the rest of the day. After dinner, Jim excused himself.

"Pastor Jackson wants me to stop by the church and go over a couple things," he told his wife.

Gail smiled as she cleared the table. "Say hi to him for me."

Jim's wipers were doing double-time as he pulled into the church parking lot. He parked as close to the front doors as he could. Since nothing was scheduled on Tuesday evenings, he opted for the handicap space.

He shook off the rain once he got inside but kept his jacket with him. Only a few sconces lit the lobby, and he could see the office light under the door. He knocked lightly.

"It's open."

Jim let himself in, and Pastor Jackson scooted his chair back from behind his desk and stood to greet him.

"Burnin' the midnight oil?" Jim quipped, trying to hide his apprehension.

"If I finish this tonight, I can sneak in a couple hours of fishing tomorrow morning before the day gets into full swing. Have a seat, Jim. So, what can I do for you?"

Jim lowered himself into a chair. He didn't have a clue where to start. "Well, I...uh...I kinda get angry sometimes. My wife thought I should…well, maybe I might want to talk to somebody about it."

"Do you want to talk to somebody about it, Jim?"

"Not particularly."

"But you're here."

"Yeah, well, maybe I do. I don't know. There's a strong likelihood that I'm not very good at it."

"Oh, I don't know, Jim; I've always considered you to be a pretty good communicator. Your presentations at the board meetings are always thorough and precise."

"That's different, Pastor Jackson."

"I know." He shot Jim a quick grin. "And, please, just Deon. How 'bout you give me a little presentation about what's going on for starters, and we'll take it from there?"

"Fair enough." Jim replied.

He spent the next fifteen minutes describing the scene in the garage with the neighbor kid, then with the cop, and then with Gail. When Jim was finished, Deon took a second to process all he had just heard, and then responded.

"Jim, you've given me a great description of the physical evidence, timeline, and characters. Even to the point of self-incrimination. If I were a detective, you might be my star witness, if not my star suspect. Are you hoping I might find you innocent or guilty?"

"Maybe? I don't know."

"Sorry, Jim. Not my role in this story. Plus, I get the sense that you've already got that covered."

"Yeah, to be honest, I've felt like crap ever since I pulled my gun on that kid. I just hate that I get so angry. What's that about anyway?"

"Do you really want to know?"

"Well, yeah, I think so."

"Jim, I could give you some Scriptures about anger and self-control, and even recommend a couple of books. But I imagine you want to get to the root of it."

"Yeah. I can fix somethin' a whole lot better if I know

why the hel…" Jim caught himself, "…why it broke."

"Fair enough. If you really want to know, I think you'd benefit from meeting with a counselor."

"Seriously? I thought that's what you were gonna do."

"I could take you a little ways, Jim, but I'd like to recommend a counselor who recently moved into the area. I've known him for quite a while and he's worked with me in the past. I trust him. I think you would benefit from his expertise."

"Hmmm."

"Jim, I imagine this may feel like I'm trying to pass you off, but if you're willing to do the work, Joel is really skilled at taking you to the root of an issue."

"I'm not afraid of work!"

Deon smiled. "I know you're not, Jim. If you're looking to address the wound rather than just finding a better Band-Aid, I think Joel can help. Albeit, this won't be anything like the work you're used to."

They both chuckled. Pastor Jackson jotted Joel's name and number down on a sticky note and passed it to Jim.

"Thanks for coming in and having the courage to look at the deeper issues, Jim. I'll be praying for you."

With that, Jim slipped on his jacket and extended his hand. Their eyes met as they shook. The pastor's eyes were damp. Jim wanted to look away, but the chance that Deon understood more than he let on was so encouraging.

I think he gets me, Jim thought.

"Stay dry out there tonight," said Deon.

"Thanks, and good luck with your fishing tomorrow," Jim replied.

Jim spent what was left of the evening mindlessly flipping through a trade magazine while Gail painted her nails at the dining table. As they got ready for bed, Gail's curiosity got the best of her.

"How'd your visit with Pastor Jackson go?" she called from the bathroom.

"Fine." Jim replied as he climbed into bed.

"What'd you talk about?"

"Just some stuff."

"Oh, you just seemed pretty quiet after you got home."

"I just wanted to get some help dealing with what happened over the weekend."

"What'd he say?"

"He thinks I'd benefit from talking to a counselor friend of his. Apparently, he's supposed to be pretty good at helping guys deal with where I'm at."

"Do you think you'll see him?"

"Yeah, probably. I've got his number."

Gail paused from washing her face and raised an eyebrow of approval in the mirror. She hung the towel up, flipped the bathroom light off, and had to feel her way into the bedroom. Jim hadn't left the lamp on. Lying down, she pulled the covers up to her chin, grinning as she pondered what she had just heard.

The rest of the week was sunny and warm, giving Gail a chance to be in her flower gardens again. It was therapeutic in so many ways, like yoga for her body, twisting and reaching and pulling and bending. It calmed her mind too. The plants were simply beautiful, grateful for any attention they received without making any demands on her. They always seemed to give more than they took.

She pulled the few weeds that didn't belong and then strung out fifteen feet of hose from the reel. Searching the garage to find the sprinkler, she noticed a piece of cardboard on the workbench. It had a big "A+" written on one corner in red marker. It was J.R.'s science project, a model hovercraft.

"Clever boy," she whispered to herself. She gently bit her lip. She hated everything about that horrific Saturday evening. The intrusion. The speed that Jim went from disappointment to rage. The gun. The anger. The terror that gripped J.R. harder than Jim's large hand. The bruises that were surely left on J.R.'s heart, not to mention his arm.

Gail stood barefoot on the cold garage floor. It was nothing compared to the coldness that swept through her body as she remembered her own childhood. She had been in J.R.'s shoes. Her dad had a temper. Her two brothers took the brunt of it, and being daddy's girl helped. But he was a man who could turn on a dime. She had never been so confused as the first time his big hand came across the side of her face. They were home alone, and she had tried to make him lunch. As she brought a bowl of hot soup to the table, she spilled some on his leg. Immediately his chair shot backwards and he exploded out of it, unleashing on her six-year-old body a hand that only that morning had held her in a warm embrace. It felt like her head came unhinged, and suddenly she was in a heap on the floor. He disappeared and left her to clean up the mess. Obviously, her clumsiness must have deserved such a reaction, she thought. She must be more careful from now on. She never spoke of it. But now, hot tears escaped her eyes, and her cheeks burned, much like they did that day, and many others, so long ago.

Gail missed J.R. Would he ever stop by again? Would his parents even let him? Picking up his science project, her mind raced, trying to imagine scenarios where she could return it to him. But as quickly as they were conceived, they were also dismissed. It wasn't her place, and she knew it. No, Jim would have to return it, or J.R. would have to ask for it back. Everything in her wanted to fix this, but her own journey had taught her well that you can't fix someone else. She wasn't willing to shortchange Jim the opportunity to take full ownership of what had happened.

She set the project down on the workbench and found the sprinkler.

She positioned it near the center of the garden and turned the water on about half-way. She moved it a couple more times, adjusting the water pressure until it reached all the plants. As she stood and watched it gently shower the garden from left to right and back again, she began to pray.

"Lord, wash me with your gentle grace. Wash the tension and worry away. Help me trust that today, right now, that You are working on my behalf, on J.R.'s behalf, on his parents' behalf... on Jim's behalf. I know You can make good come from this. Show me how to help facilitate Your good and not merely seek out the comfortable place in all this."

The sprinkler needed one more adjustment. As she watched the water bead on the tender petals, these words whispered in her mind: "Consider the lilies of the field." Gail smiled and went inside to get dinner going.

After dinner was cleaned up, Jim asked Gail if she wanted to go for a walk. Gail rarely passed up a chance to go for a walk, especially with Jim.

With the heat of the day behind them, and a gentle breeze to keep the bugs away, they made their way down the driveway and across the road. A sandy two-track led them through a meadow that seamed golden in the evening light. Blue jays could be heard calling back and forth from the trees up ahead, and a robin hopped along thirty feet in front of them.

As they entered the woods, the trail descended gradually and stopped in a small clearing next to a large pond. Years ago, someone had partially dammed the creek and formed this pond for watering their livestock. Now it made a splendid place for a picnic or an evening stroll. Gail kicked off her sandals and waded in just past her ankles. Their conversation was light and they both were in good spirits.

Returning home, Jim took Gail's hand as they headed back uphill through the woods. By this time the wind had died, and shadows blanketed the field. Night was falling, and the mosquitoes would find them soon enough.

Crossing back over the road, Jim stopped at the mailbox. There were only a few pieces of junk mail, a bill from the gas company, and a fat envelope addressed to Jim. The chill of the evening followed them up the driveway. Gail paused to rinse off her feet before coming inside. As Jim passed through the kitchen, he dropped the mail on the counter, except for the envelope addressed to him, which he kept as he continued on to his office. He returned to the kitchen, where Gail was sorting through the rest of the mail.

"I'm gonna make some decaf; want any?" Jim asked as he deposited a pod into the coffee maker.

"No thanks, I'm good." Gail replied.

"Oh, I know you're good, I just wondered if you wanted coffee," Jim teased. She rolled her eyes as Jim searched the fridge for the creamer.

Back in his office, Jim set his coffee down and eased into his leather chair. Opening the envelope confirmed his suspicion; it was from that counselor. He had made the call and was told to expect an intake questionnaire in the mail. He felt the tension build in his shoulders. Was he really going to do this? It's one thing to chat with his pastor, but a counselor? In an office? It was starting to feel a little too formal. Maybe he could just find a good book. Gail had read two or three when she was in counseling.

He emptied the envelope of its contents. It stated "Client Intake Form" across the top, but it looked more like federal tax forms. Six pages of questions and places to sign.

"For cryin' out loud!" he fussed. "I just thought it would be a good idea to talk to somebody. No, Gail thought it would be a good idea. She oughta be fillin' this stuff out."

Jim rolled his chair back and, leaving the forms on his desk, found Gail on the living room couch, where she was just starting to enjoy a fresh batch of popcorn.

"Want some?" she offered as he passed by.

"Absolutely."

She poured some onto a napkin and handed it to him.

"Whatcha watchin'?" Jim asked.

"Thought I'd find a movie. Want to join me?" She pulled back the blanket to make a place next to her.

"Sure," Jim said. Anything sounded better than the paperwork he had just walked away from.

The next morning, Jim started his work day in the office as usual. He went through his emails and checked his schedule for the day. Although his calendar cleared him to head out to the shop, the Intake Form still lay there, silently beckoning him to take a few minutes and fill it out. It kept doing so each morning for the next week and a half, but Jim always had a reason to push it to the side.

At last, on a rainy Saturday morning, he got tired of looking at it and ran out of excuses. He unfolded the papers and pulled a pencil from the cup on his desk.

Should probably use a pen, he thought. He put the pencil back and found a decent ballpoint.

Page one. **Name_________.**

Jim jumped up. *I should have some coffee.*

He returned with a warm mug in his hand, settled into his seat, and again stared at the first line of that first page.

Name_________.

I'm hungry. I wonder if Gail picked up a Danish for the weekend?

There was no Danish, but this time Jim returned with a piece of toast with strawberry jelly.

Name_________.

By now it seemed like the word was staring at him. Grudgingly, he began making his way through the form.

Contact information___________________________.

Insurance____________________________________.

General health________________________________.

"For cryin' out loud, how often do I exercise?" he asked himself out loud. "I'm on my feet in the shop eight hours a day. If that ain't daily exercise, I don't know what is."

Past or present psychiatric medications? Jim recalled his college days with a chuckle. *Well, not prescribed per se.*

Alcohol use? Tobacco use? He chuckled again. "Don't drink, don't chew, or hang out with girls who do," he quipped. He was starting to have fun with this.

Daily supplements? There's no way he was listing all of those. He simply jotted down, "Vitamins."

Areas of concern: Anxiety? *Nope.* **Anger?** *Nope, unless they've got it comin'.*

Eating issues? *Nope, appetite is excellent.* **Issues with children?** *Nope, unless they hang around uninvited.* He grinned.

Issues with co-workers? *Nope, I work alone*, he thought with a smile. **Suicidal thoughts? Suicide attempts? Schizophrenia?** *Nope, nope, and nope.*

Gail had heard him chuckling in the office and poked her head in. "What are you working on?"

"A questionnaire for that counselor Pastor Jackson wants me to see. Look at this question: **'Sexual Abuse?** They're asking if I've ever sexually abused anybody! This is crazy!" he said, chuckling again.

"Or, if *you've* ever been sexually abused Jim."

His smirk disappeared. He picked up his pen again. "NOPE." He spoke the word as he wrote it, but his demeanor perplexed Gail. She thought better of pressing him on it, so she retreated to the kitchen.

Jim continued with the form, but there was no more giggling. When he was finished, he folded it up, tucked it into an envelope and shoved it into a drawer.

Maybe I can just find a good book to fix me, he thought again.

Two weeks passed before Jim came to terms with the fact that he was fooling himself. He addressed the envelope, stuck two stamps to the corner, and laid it on the kitchen counter with the rest of the mail that needed to go out.

Chapter Eight

What Brings You Here?

He couldn't remember exactly what the pastor had said during his sermon, but something made Jim want to start the week with a clean slate.

After lunch, Jim gathered up J.R.'s science project and took it over to his place. It was time to put it all behind them. But J.R. wasn't home; in fact, no one was home. He carefully set the project on the porch swing. He thought about leaving a note, but told himself it probably wasn't necessary.

That evening he took Gail out for ice cream. She really enjoyed Jim when he was playful, and lately he had been. He struck up a friendly conversation with a couple old friends in the ice cream parlor, and even left a hefty tip for the waitress.

On Tuesday he received a down payment on a nice project, and was really looking forward to working with this new client.

On Wednesday morning he got a call from Danny inviting him and Gail out for dinner. Danny and Beth were going to be driving up to empty the storage unit they rented after the sale of their house. They planned to spend the night and head south with the load the next morning. Jim accepted the invitation. He was pretty sure Gail was free, and he knew she'd be thrilled to catch up with Beth.

Though they had only been neighbors for a few years,

Jim really enjoyed Danny. He was an electrician, a heck of a welder, and thought like an engineer. Danny always had a project going on. Jim could stop by just about any night of the week and find him in the barn, up to his elbows in an engine, or replacing the rigging on a sailboat, or welding pans for boiling maple syrup. Beth took night classes and Danny filled the evenings with projects of his own, or helping out a neighbor. For being a younger guy, Danny could say a lot without saying much. He had a rough go of it in high school, and in his early twenties he spent two years in prison. He became a Christian before he got out and it stuck. Then he married Beth, who was a real sweetheart and perfect for him. Then he hired on with an electrical firm. Danny had made some updates to their house, and Jim helped him with the new windows and siding. Danny was someone who was easy to be with, and they got a lot done when they worked together. It was a big disappointment for Jim when Danny's work transferred him to Ollarsville. When the time came to put the house on the market, it went quick. They stayed until Beth wrapped up her classes, and then they were gone.

At dinner, Beth was curious about the new owners. She had done more work on the inside than Danny had on the outside: patching drywall, painting, tearing up carpets, and refinishing the maple flooring. She also remodeled the bathroom. Beth's dad was a contractor, and she knew her way around a job site. She was thrilled to hear that the new couple and their young boy had settled in nicely. She even feigned jealousy when she heard how helpful J.R. was with Gail. "Man, could I have used the energy of a ten-year-old when I was stripping those floors," she said.

The fellas finished their meals and waited patiently, while the gals spent more time talking than eating. It was a fun night, and Danny had slipped his card to the waitress before she laid down the bill, denying Jim the opportunity to pay for dinner. They parted ways on the sidewalk with hugs and goodbyes.

Jim took Gail's hand as thy walked back to the car. It was a perfect evening. The sun was setting later, and just a breath of warm breeze kept the bugs away. They probably could have walked all the way home if they hadn't needed the car in the morning.

Jim remembered evenings like this when Kyle was a baby. They would bundle him up for an evening stroll, and he would be out for the night by the time they got back home. Then the challenge was to get him unbundled and into his crib without waking him. They had about a fifty-fifty success rate. They had so much fun as a young couple. Dating varied from dinner and a movie, to fishing. Jim didn't mind shopping with Gail, and she enjoyed following him to car shows and swap meets. They hiked and swam and loved watching stars. A few dates even included bailing hay. Even into marriage their dating continued, usually more spontaneous than planned — a bike ride, a walk, or a swim in the pond on those warm summer evenings. A road trip to pick up a new tool for the shop would often include dinner and a nice hotel. There was a refreshing playfulness in their relationship all those years ago…then something changed. Kyle was born.

They had struggled to get pregnant, and Gail miscarried twice before delivering Kyle just a week shy of full term. He was healthy and happy, and Jim and Gail were over the moon. It wasn't long, though, before Jim began to pull away. He helped with the baby, but seemed to take a step back so the infant could have Gail's full attention. Jim supported Gail however he could to ensure that she was the best mom she could be. Somewhere though, the unspoken connectedness they once delighted in started to wane. They were a great team, but when it came to parenting, Gail was the captain and Jim was the water boy. His awareness as a parent was excellent, but he was tentative to fully engage in that role. A provider? Yes. Protector? Yes. Teacher? Yes. Someone who embraced the nuances of a father son relationship? Not so much. Jim was as responsible as they come, but when it came to parenting, his approach seemed more obligatory than desired. He loved Kyle, no doubt, but just wasn't very good at connecting with him.

When Jim and Gail got to the car, he opted to take a detour west of town, where a winding road climbed to the highest elevation in the county. Jim turned right and followed the familiar gravel road under a canopy of hardwoods. The gravel turned to sod and ended in a clearing, where Jim put the car in park and turned off the key. To the west, the terrain dropped away abruptly, and the tree tops spread out before them, followed by fields, farms, and more forests. It was a plethora of springtime greens geometrically divided by occasional ribbons of narrow county roads, two-tracks and fence rows. Further still was the haze of the horizon and what was left of the setting sun, casting a warm glow on everything it touched, including Jim and Gail. As they watched it disappear, they felt the same sense of awe as the teenagers who sat in the other parked cars in the clearing.

When they arrived home, a message was waiting for them on the answering machine. It was the counselor confirming Jim's first appointment: four o'clock on Thursday. Jim was glad he had listed this number on the intake form; he wouldn't have wanted to take that call on his cell phone in front of Danny and Beth. But four o'clock? He hated the idea of cutting his workday short, but it was probably as good a time as he could hope for. He pulled out his phone and put it on his calendar before connecting it to the charger for the night.

The next day, Jim worked until 3:40 when he dusted himself off with the air hose and made his way up to the house. He took off his work shirt and slipped into a clean one, washed up, and headed out to the truck.

On the way to his appointment, Jim marveled at how well the last few weeks had gone. Work was good, he and Gail were enjoying each other, and he had even had a decent conversation with Kyle the other day. Jim wondered if maybe he didn't need counseling after all.

His thoughts were interrupted with the blare of an air horn up ahead. A truck was approaching in the oncoming lane. Jim checked his mirror. Sure enough, some idiot was passing him. Jim hit his brakes to let him in as the oncoming semi blew by, air horn still blasting. Then the idiot had the nerve to flip him off as he sped away.

Jim could feel his blood pressure rising as he buried his foot in the accelerator. After a few seconds he thought better of it and backed off. His truck would never catch the jerk anyway. It was an unexpected confirmation that he might still have something to talk about with the counselor.

Pulling into the parking lot, Jim drove past the front door and around to the back of the office, where he parked in one of the two spots available. He moved the lever into PARK and tapped the steering wheel for a few moments.

It was a cute little office, with brick up to the window line and gray vinyl siding the rest of the way to the roof. The lawn was manicured with flowers bordering the sidewalk. A slightly faded sign in the yard identified the business as an insurance agency. Apparently, this counselor was subleasing part of the building. Jim finally turned off the key, took a deep breath, and stepped out of the truck.

With a measured amount of bravado, Jim pulled open the front door and was immediately met with two more doors. On his right, the insurance company; on his left, what felt like an accident waiting to happen. A temporary sign that simply said 'Counseling' was taped to the left door. He pushed it open and found himself in a sparsely furnished lobby that felt more like a tiny living room. There were a couple chairs, a couch, a coffee table, and a small nook with a coffee maker. Next to the coffee were cups, and two toy dump trucks, one with a variety of sweetener packets in the dump box, the other with the little single servings of creamers. Jim smiled at the cleverness. Under the counter was a dorm size mini fridge with cans of soda, bottles of iced tea, and water. Jim grabbed a water and was looking for a place to pay when he noticed a sign on the counter: "Let him who thirsts, take freely." He chuckled. At least I'll get something for my money.

He barely sat down before a nice-looking man opened another door across the waiting room. He looked to be in his mid-thirties. He had dark hair with a little wave, a trim build (probably a runner, he thought), slacks and a striped, button-down shirt with rolled-up sleeves and no tie. Jim suddenly realized it must have appeared that he was trying desperately to size this guy up, but he couldn't help himself.

"Jim?" the man asked.

"Yeah, that's me."

The man extended his hand. "Hello, I'm Joel. Come on in."

The office was also sparse. Joel settled in at his desk, and an empty chair waited for Jim on the other side. A slew of books were stacked haphazardly on the floor and along one wall. On the wall opposite where he had entered was a second door, with a sign reading 'EXIT'.

Jim pulled the chair away from the desk and sat down. He was glad he had grabbed a water. Between sips, the bottle was something to keep his hands busy.

"So, tell me Jim, what brings you here today?"

"My truck." Jim was desperate to relax, and his reluctance to being there was already showing. Joel smiled graciously. Then Jim took the next ten minutes beating around the bush, explaining his wife's concern about his occasional angry outbursts, and how she thought he might benefit from some counseling.

"So Jim, what brings you here today?" Joel tried again.

A little flustered, Jim replied, "I kinda just told ya, didn't I?"

"Yes, sort of. How about you tell me straight up, why you believe you're here today?"

"Because you had an appointment available today?" Jim knew he was being resistant, but he couldn't help it. He wasn't about to spill his guts to this guy yet.

Joel opened the file in front of him. "What do you say we take a few minutes and go over your intake forms?"

Jim relaxed a little. Joel was backing off, and it felt satisfying to have some control. But at the same time, it felt like he was copping out. Maybe in their next session he would open up a little more.

Jim spent the rest of the session expounding on some of the answers he had hastily written on the intake. Eventually, Joel put his pen down and slipped Jim's forms back into the file. Jim knew his fifty-minute session was drawing to a close, so he reached into his shirt pocket and pulled out his checkbook.

Joel noticed and smiled, "Still using checks?"

"Old school" Jim replied, reaching for a pen from the cup on the desk.

"How about you don't pay me today?"

That caught Jim off guard. "Whadaya mean, not pay you?"

"I mean, not pay me today." Joel replied. "I'd like to meet with you once more to see if this is a good fit for you, Jim. If it is, we can discuss a payment schedule. But if not, I'd rather not charge you for the two sessions."

"Are ya sure?"

"I'm sure. I'll see you next Thursday at four." Joel

rose and glanced toward the door with the EXIT sign on it.

Jim put his checkbook away as he stood. He pushed his chair in and turned to Joel, searching for a clue as to whether or not they were supposed to shake hands again. But Joel was already gathering the file, and when their eyes didn't meet, Jim made for the door. It took him into a short, empty hallway that led to another door with another EXIT sign over it. This one opened into the parking lot, only a few feet from his truck.

Ha, he thought, taking a deep breath as if he'd just been let out of the principal's office. *Two reasons to park back here: close to the exit, and no one will see my truck.*

After dinner, Jim tried to read an article touting the benefits of waterborne spray finishes for furniture, but he was really struggling to concentrate. His meeting with Joel had unnerved him, and he wasn't quite sure what he was feeling or what to do with it. Thankfully, Gail brought work home and was too busy to notice.

Closing the magazine, he got up and went out to the garage to change the oil in his truck. Then he figured, while he was at it, he'd change Gail's, too. Both vehicles were nearly due, and Jim always kept extra filters and a case of oil in the garage. He turned on the old radio that was perched on a shelf and pulled on a pair of disposable black rubber gloves.

While waiting for the oil to drain, Jim checked the other fluid levels and all the lights. The left turn signal was out on the back of the truck. He scrounged through a drawer in his tool chest that was a catch-all for electrical stuff, but there was no bulb. He'd have to pick one up at the store.

His mind wandered back to his appointment, and he found himself contemplating whether or not he liked Joel.

He's professional. Pleasant enough. A little disorganized, maybe. And hard to read. He makes me uncomfortable. I half expect him to start hunting for clues like Gail when she's concerned about me. 'Are you ok?'How does that make you feel? Do you want to talk about it?' Not really!

From the radio on the shelf, a tune with these lyrics was playing on the country station:

"Come watch your broken dreams,
dance in and out of the beams,
of a neon moon.
Oh, watch your broken dreams,
dance in and out of the beams,
of a neon moon."[1]

The song faded out but the words hung heavy somewhere between Jim's head and his heart. He knew he had dreams that far exceeded this farm, or his business, or the motorcycle in the corner. Dreams to be more like Gail in a way — maybe Joel, too. Dreams to feel like he belonged. Dreams to quiet down on the inside, and pretend a little less on the outside. He was tired of feeling like he was usually on the outside looking in when it came to people.

He opened the box with the new oil filter, then lowered himself onto the creeper and rolled back under the car. Working on something was always a good antidote for feeling too much.

Bobbi swayed on her porch swing, lost in a book. If Joel knew he'd be working late, he'd plan to bring dinner home. It was too frustrating for Bobbi to make something and try to keep it warm if she wasn't sure when he would get there, and this was a compromise they both enjoyed. On those evenings, she afforded herself time to read from 5:00 until whenever he came up the driveway, and now that the nights were growing warmer, the porch swing had become her favorite spot. She had sewn cushions for it from a print that reminded her of their honeymoon in Hawaii, and it was

---

[1]Brooks & Dunn, "Neon Moon", June 1991, from the album *Brand New Man.*

as comfortable as any seat in the house. She slipped a bookmark into the page and lowered her book. The unmistakable rumble of a Harley-Davidson motorcycle downshifting could be heard from the road.

A single headlight swept across the porch as Joel rolled up the driveway. He smiled seeing Bobbi waiting for him. The last golden rays of daylight wove between the trees in the yard, illuminating the root-beer-colored metal flake of the Harley's paint. Joel squeezed the clutch and braked to a stop in front of the porch steps. Unstrapping his helmet, he hung it on the mirror, swept the kickstand down and stepped off.

Bobbi came down the steps and kissed his cheek as he opened the tour-pak behind the seat and retrieved a pizza. He paused, and slipped his free hand around her waist and returned the kiss, but on the lips.

"Good day?" she asked. "Ooh, this smells so good!" She took the pizza to the porch swing while he gathered his satchel from the saddlebag.

"Long, but yes, good. Where's J.R. tonight?"

"He's spending the night at a friend's house, so it's just you and me, baby." She gave him a wink and patted the cushion on the swing for him to have a seat. "Take a load off, babe. I'll grab some paper plates. What do you want to drink?" she called over her shoulder as the screen door slammed behind her.

"I'll have whatever you're having." Joel's satchel dropped to the porch as he slouched into the swing, stretching his legs out in front of him as far as he could. He closed his eyes and let his chin rest on his chest. The tree frogs and crickets had started their evening serenade. A blue jay was taking turns with a pair of cardinals at the feeder that hung at the end of the porch. The warmth of the day surrendered to a pleasant evening breeze. Joel took a deep breath. As much as he enjoyed his work, he loved coming home to this.

Chapter Nine

A Broken Chair

"Let's see…I can be there next Tuesday, say, around 3:00 if that works for you? Very good. I'll see you then."

Jim hung up the phone. It was 10:45 a.m. and he was still in the office. He had been chasing his tail all morning, and a call from a former customer just added a few more laps. Her cabinet doors needed adjusting. Of course they do, Jim thought. After all, he installed her new cabinets in December when the furnace was running and the humidity in the house was 35%. Now it was summer, and the last week had been in the 80's with 80% humidity. Wood was bound to swell a little, and doors were gonna move.

Pressing on, he looked at the calendar and grabbed a job file from the front of the rack on his desk.

I need to order hardware yet today if I want it here by the first of next week.

Noticing the tax forms sitting next to the files, he clenched his jaw, closed his eyes, and let his chin dip forward, as if swallowing a curse word. Quarterly taxes had to be in the mail by tomorrow.

By 1:30 he finally made it to the shop and began sanding the legs of a fireplace mantle. Once he was in the shop, he could feel his blood pressure return to normal. No interruptions; just him and his tools and a project. Jim smiled. Predictable. Controllable. Enjoyable. If only all life could be this gratifying.

With the sanding completed, he set the legs aside and started on the brackets that would receive them. Every piece was a separate task, each with its own setup and procedure. Each step was built on the previous one until eventually a mantle would take form, which in this case would become a part of a complete fireplace surround. Jim loved the planning as much as the process. He also valued being able to see marked progress every day. He didn't have to wonder what he had accomplished; he could feel it, smell it, and show it to Gail if she poked her head in the shop. There was decisiveness about his impact in the shop – even if it was only with wood – and it felt good.

It was Thursday afternoon again, and Jim continued to glance at the clock on the shop wall. 3:40 stretched to 3:45, then 3:50. Finally, he shut down the edge sander and dust collector, dropped his shop apron on the bench, and double-timed it to his truck. With no time for a clean shirt today, he brushed the sawdust from his sleeves while he ran.

It hadn't rained in over a week, so the dust curled up behind the truck as he raced down the gravel driveway. He finally slowed as he pulled into the parking lot for his counseling session. Like before, he drove past the front of the building and around the end, tires chirping on the hot asphalt as he swung into "his" parking spot, hidden from the road. He looked in the rearview mirror and hastily combed his hair with his fingers. Good enough.

As he entered the lobby, Jim noticed Joel's door was open. He grabbed a bottled water at the mini fridge before edging toward the office. Joel appeared in the doorway.

"Come on in Jim."

They both took their places, and Joel opened Jim's file. As Jim sat down, he noticed the wall clock – 4:12. He fussed with a loose corner of the wrapper on his water.

"So Jim," Joel began, looking up from the file. "How would you like to describe a perfect day to me?"

Jim grinned slightly, thinking he had dodged the tardy bullet. He took a few seconds to reorient. "Ahh, the perfect day." He enunciated slowly, as his imagination engaged. "The perfect day would begin at six a.m. I'd enjoy a cup of coffee while frying up two pieces of bacon. Then, in the bacon grease, I'd fry two eggs over easy, and toast a slice of whole wheat bread. I'd read my devotional while eating, and then head out to the shop by seven."

"What would you do in the shop?"

"I'd start with running rough lumber through the planer."

"What kind of lumber?"

"Oh, hmm. Maple…curly maple." Jim took his time answering, as though he was speaking of a favorite childhood vacation, or his first bike. "When curly maple is rough cut from the mill it doesn't look much different from regular maple, ya know. It's coarse and full of slivers. But, as you run it through the planer, the grain appears, and it's almost magical. Suddenly, it's smooth and consistent in that beautiful maple blond. Then the daylight from the window lays across it, and the way the light is refracted – it's called chatoyance – when the waves in the grain look like they're turning from wood into rippling water."

Jim noticed Joel trying to stifle a grin, and realized he must sound like a schoolboy after his first kiss. Dialing back his passion, he went on. "After that, I might glue them into a larger slab, like for a table top. Then I'd sand it smooth and flat, trim it to size, sand it some more, and apply a finish. That's when it really comes to life." Jim's eyes danced with passion for his work. "At the end of a long, productive, uninterrupted day, I can see and feel exactly what I've accomplished, and it is usually very satisfying."

Joel looked up from his notepad, smiling. "Thank you, Jim. That was very descriptive. How does thinking about that day make you feel?"

"Good?"

"Okay, any other feelings?"

"Hmm…happy?"

"Excellent, Jim! Now, I'm curious. Is there any one element that could singlehandedly ruin the day that you just described?"

"INTERRUPTIONS!" Jim blurted out without even thinking. "I HATE interruptions!"

"I gathered." Joel chuckled, enough so, that Jim had to chuckle at himself too.

"Now," Joel continued, "how about describing a bad day. But this time I'd like you to use a real-life event."

Jim's mind immediately went back to the images of J.R. trapped under his motorcycle. He wasn't ready to be that real yet, so he chose another memory. "I remember running out of gas on a sloppy fall day. It was half raining, half snowing, temperature in the upper thirties. Gail had borrowed my truck the day before and returned it with the tank on empty. I only made it two miles and had to walk back home in that slop to get a gas can, and then two miles back on a bicycle, trying to balance a five gallon can on the handle bars. I threw the bike and the emptied gas can in the back of the truck and raced straight for the gas station. I was forty-five minutes late to my meeting with an architect, mud all over my pant legs and smelling like gasoline. I don't think she asked to borrow my truck for a year after that, and it's probably a good thing."

"Very good, Jim. Excellent. I noticed the energy in your voice built as you shared that story. How did recounting it make you feel?"

"Angry!"

"Okay, good. Anything else?"

"You mean, besides angry? I don't know. I suppose disrespected?"

"Are you asking?"

"No. Disrespected. I felt disrespected!"

"Good, Jim. Would you say then that interruptions make you feel disrespected?"

"Hmm, maybe? Sometimes. I often plan out my day and when stuff messes with those plans it can really bug me."

"Did that ever happen to you as a boy?"

"Huh?"

"As a boy, were your plans messed with?

"Oh, well yeah. Mom would have a list of chores she needed done before I could play. But sometimes when Dad was leaving for work, he'd 'remind' me of some big project he wanted done, and we had never even talked about it. It didn't matter if I'd made plans with my friends or had other stuff to do." Jim's voice went soft. "And there'd be heck to pay if I didn't have it finished when he got home."

Joel continued, "So, someone imposing their desires on you, without regard for your time, feels disrespectful?"

"Exactly! Interruptions make me feel like what I'm doing isn't important."

"Does meeting with me feel like an interruption?"

"Wait. What? No…I mean, no, I don't think so."

"Sounds pretty convincing," Joel replied with a smile.

"What do you mean?"

"Does meeting with me — counseling, looking at your stuff — feel like it's interrupting your life? Like maybe the world you've worked hard to create is being put upon, or not important?"

Jim thought for a moment, and then asked solemnly, "Is this about me being late?"

"Only if it's the reason you were late." Joel let that sink in before continuing. "Jim, I get that this probably isn't comfortable for you. Much like the first day of class. You don't know what you don't know, and you're not crazy about having 'what you don't know' exposed."

Jim imagined the look on his face fluctuated between shame and confusion. Joel continued:

"Maybe this will help. When I was growing up, I had an uncle who restored furniture. Occasionally, someone would bring in a very old piece, an antique. Sometimes the piece may have been built in England or Germany or Japan. He wouldn't be able to start the repair work without doing some research first. What species of wood was used? Was it solid or a veneer? What was the origin of the stain? What type of glue or finish was used? And also, he needed to know what type of joinery held it together so he could disassemble it without causing further damage. He had to answer a lot of questions before he could consider addressing the needed repair. Rarely was the customer much help in his quest for information. They simply knew it was passed down from their grandmother, and it was broken and they wanted it fixed. Does that make sense Jim?"

"Absolutely. I've done a fair amount of restoration work myself."

"Okay. Now, in light of that scenario, what would you think if the piece being restored – let's say it was a chair – was embarrassed and tried to hide that it was broken?"

Jim's brow furrowed. "That's just goofy. The chair didn't break itself. Somebody probably misused it or didn't care for it properly."

"Excellent point, Jim. Now, what if the chair viewed being subjected to a craftsman for some repair as an inconvenience or interruption?"

"Well then, I'd have to say that the chair didn't have a very good perspective of its purpose. It's missing the whole point of being a chair."

"Jim, I couldn't have said it better myself." With a broad smile, Joel leaned in. "If there's something amiss or not working right – something broken in your life – I'd be honored to help you with some research to find out why or how it broke, and chart a good path for restoration."

Jim processed this silently. He connected with the

chair. Something inside *him* was broken too, and he knew it. He imagined himself as a chair, wanting to be roped off, with signs posted saying, "Don't touch." *Children are too busy. I don't want them climbing on and off of me. I don't want to bear the weight of some personalities. If you expect me to support you...* His eyes looked to the floor as he let the internal dialogue continue. *I am broken...I won't be able to... I'll only disappoint.*

"Jim, what's going on for you right now?"

"I think I get what you're saying. I may be a little messed up myself. Probably oughta get some help if I don't want to miss the purpose of being me."

Joel pulled a box of tissues from a case on the floor behind him, opened it, and set it on his desk.

"Buying 'em in bulk now, huh?" Jim tried to lighten the mood as he helped himself to a tissue and blew his nose.

"I like your perspective, Jim."

"Okay, what now?"

"Well, if you'd like to continue, over the next week I would like you to spend some time listing bullet points from your childhood. A chair is rarely damaged when it is being cared for properly, so, I'd like you to pay special attention to events that may have left you feeling bruised or injured."

"Are you talking physically or emotionally?"

"Yes."

"Yes?"

"Yes, both. Both can be equally damaging Jim."

"All right. And you want me to bring that with me next week?"

Joel stood. "I would. Next Thursday then? Four o'clock?"

"Sounds like a plan."

Jim rose and dropped his empty bottled water in the waste basket at the end of the desk and waited to make eye contact with Joel. Joel reached out his hand.

“You might find some childhood pictures helpful in jogging your memory as you begin to put your story on paper.”

“Thanks.” Jim gave Joel a firm handshake and made his way to the exit door, down the hall and out into the warm summer afternoon.

Chapter Ten

Making a List

Jim cleared the dishes from the table as Gail hung up her phone. "Bummer!"

"What's up?"

"My meeting has been canceled tonight. Not that I was that excited about the meeting, but I was really looking forward to hearing how Donna was enjoying her new granddaughter." She rinsed a few dishes before putting them in the dishwasher. "Well Jim, it looks like my evening just opened up. What are your plans for the rest of the night?"

"I was gonna work on some stuff for Joel."

"What stuff?"

"He wants me to list out my childhood in bullet points."

"Your whole childhood?"

"Yeah, well, not everything. More like a framework and then things that were bad. He suggested I look through some childhood pictures too."

"Oh, that sounds like fun! Do you need any help?"

"Gail, it's not supposed to be fun, remember? The bad stuff."

"Oh yeah, I'm sorry. I just meant the photo album stuff. I remember outlining my story when I was in counseling too. It was very helpful. Anyway, I'd be happy to help if you'd like."

With dinner cleaned up, Gail went into the guest bedroom and returned with the photo album that Jim's mom had given him, along with a shoebox of loose snapshots and Polaroids. She set them on the coffee table, then returned to the kitchen to pour each of them a glass of wine before joining Jim on the couch. Page by page, Jim's life unfolded before them, as Jim recalled and Gail recorded the highlights on a yellow legal pad:

1. Born on a small farm, only child.
2. Dad worked 8 to 5, Monday-Friday, factory work.
3. Dog, chickens, stray cats. Scraggly fruit trees left on the property from the previous owner.
4. The new bike I got for my birthday.
5. Sunday afternoons at my uncle's farm.
6. The sheep "Sammy" that my uncle gave me.
7. The school play where my part was the rear half of "Clifford, the Big Red Dog."
8. The pumpkin I grew that weighed 32 pounds.

The list continued to grow throughout the evening. When they finished going through the box of photos, Jim remembered Joel's words: "bruised or injured." He asked Gail to start another list:

1. The orchard
2. The bike
3. The Dream
4. Sammy.

"I don't ever remember hearing about Sammy. It was a sheep?" Gail said.

"Yeah, a lamb actually. My uncle gave him to me, kinda."

"What do you mean, 'gave him to you, kinda'?"

"It was nothing. Just a misunderstanding."

"But honey, you listed it in the 'hurtful' list."

Jim didn't respond, and Gail decided to let it go. She remembered a few years back, when she was in counseling and had to list out the elements of her story. It was a major accomplishment just to label some of the events on paper. There was a level of shame that shrouded a season in her childhood, and she had never discussed it prior to counseling, much less written about it. She was proud of Jim for having the courage to look at his story.

"Can I pour you another glass?" she asked, placing the pen and pad on the coffee table and rising from the couch.

"I'm good." Jim got up, too, and gathered the pen and pad and took them to his office. Laying them on his desk, he looked out the window. The sun was low, and blanketed the field across the road in bronze. The grass was tall and waved ever so slightly, changing its sheen in the breeze like someone drawing their hand over a velvet dress. His thoughts took him back to his uncle's farm and running through such a field with Sammy. The memory made him smile. Then he remembered Caroline. Closing the office door behind him, he made his way back to the living room.

"Maybe I'll have a half a glass if the wine is still out."

Gail obliged and poured him another while Jim found the TV remote and started channel surfing. When he couldn't settle on any channel for more than a few seconds, Gail decided to press a little.

"Are you all right?"

"Yeah. Why?"

"You seem a little agitated."

"There's just nothing on tonight."

Gail knew what numbing out looked like, but if Jim didn't want to talk, it was better to let it go. His restlessness was a pretty good indicator that he was disrupted. That was always her cue to pray.

The weekend came and Saturday was filled with

maintenance. They both worked in the orchard in the morning, and later Jim mowed the yard while Gail tended her flower beds. Finally, Jim scraped the brick molding around the garage door and applied some primer, while Gail prepped a rack of ribs for the grill. It wasn't long after dinner when they both fell into bed exhausted.

Jim could hardly pull himself from bed the next morning for church. Three hours later he wondered why he had. Church was awful. Three of the four worship songs were new. Who can worship when you're trying to learn a new song? There should be a limit of one new song per month and no more. Then they had a guest speaker, and he was terrible. He preached the whole sermon from the twenty-third Psalm; how we were like sheep, not always too bright, no natural defense like claws or venom, and prone to follow the crowd. For whatever reason, Jim was in no mood to be dwelling on sheep and this guy went on for thirty-five minutes. Jim was never so ready to exit the front doors.

He bee-lined to his truck, hopped in and cracked the windows, enough to let in some fresh air, but not enough to encourage conversation if someone walked by. To appear busy (as opposed to anti-social), Jim foraged around in the glove compartment for a turn signal bulb. It was a long shot, but he had been known to toss a spare bulb in there on occasion, and he still hadn't picked one up from the store. No bulb and still no Gail. *That woman could talk the hind leg off a mule.* Jim thought.

He pulled out his phone and checked the weather for the week. Then he read a couple news stories and even played a Sudoku before Gail finally appeared in the parking lot. He started the truck, turned on the air, and rolled the windows up. Gail hugged three more people and had one more quick conversation before she finally hopped in. Kicking off her heels while buckling her seat belt, she adjusted her skirt and then the dash vent.

“Thanks for cooling the truck down Jim. I had the nicest visit with…”

Jim pulled out of the parking lot, not really hearing a word she was saying. He must have grunted or ‘mmm’d’ a couple times because she prattled on for about ten minutes. Finally she asked, “How did you like the guest speaker today?”

“Fine.”

“I really liked when he described how even without the physical attributes that some creatures have, like claws, teeth, or stingers, our words can unleash venom, or cut, or bruise. Then did you hear him say the blood of a sheep has natural anti-venom in it? I loved the imagery of the Blood of the Lamb protecting us from the venomous things we sometimes experience. We can respond with empathy and forgiveness rather than anger and fear. Isn’t God just so good?”

Jim didn’t respond. Actually, he hadn’t heard much after the preacher compared him to a simple-minded sheep. He was both familiar and disgusted with the label. He remembered as a boy, being scolded by his father for taking so long to do a job, without appreciating that Jim only took extra time because he liked to do a good job. His dad seemed to value shortcuts. Whether mowing the lawn or cleaning the garage, Jim wanted to do it right, which often brought his father’s reproach. “You’re so slow,” he would chide. “You’re destined to be a dumb laborer if you don’t start figuring a faster, better way to get your work done.” Scheming to get someone else to do it; that’s what he really meant. Even his uncle goaded him about how detailed he was when tending to the livestock or mucking out the stalls. “They’re just gonna crap again as soon as you’re done.” He’d laugh as Jim would pitchfork every last trace of manure into the wheelbarrow.

But Jim couldn’t help himself. He figured if he was gonna do something, he wanted to do it right, and it was this quality that made him a good cabinet maker. But his dad would never relent with his sideways comments about Jim's career choice, as opposed to getting a job in the factory. "Yer out there sweating and hustling lumber around, breathin' sawdust all day, when ya coulda been sittin' in an office, overseein' a dozen guys crankin' out parts. Good bennies, paid vacations, gettin' somebody to punch the clock for ya so you can really take a lunch break, if ya know what I mean." Jim didn't even want to know what his dad meant. He enjoyed his work, and that meant something to him even if his dad couldn't appreciate it.

No, that morning he really hadn't heard much of the sermon at all.

Chapter Eleven

My Truck Is Fine

Jim tucked in a clean shirt with one hand while shuffling through the papers on his desk with the other. A piece of deli meat hung from between his lips as he tried to make up for working through lunch. He desperately searched to find the legal pad Gail had used to write down his life events, and if he didn't find it soon, he was going to be late for his appointment with Joel again.

Finally, he saw a corner of pale-yellow peeking out from under a hardware catalogue. He snatched it up and gave it a glance. It was the list alright, although it seemed far less pertinent right now than it did when he and Joel talked about it last week. He grabbed another piece of ham from the fridge as he passed by, jumped into his truck and headed east.

Approaching an intersection, Jim hit his left turn signal and slowed to a stop at the four-way stop-sign. He proceeded when it was his turn, glancing in the mirror. A patrol car was behind him.

"Aw, shoot!" Jim grumbled out loud. "I hope he didn't notice my signal is out."

When his turn came, the officer also turned left and followed (or at least went the same direction as) Jim. The car between them turned off within a few blocks, leaving the officer directly behind him again. Jim didn't want to be late as much as he didn't want to be pulled over. He was careful not to do anything to draw attention to himself, but knew if the officer didn't turn soon, Jim would have to make another left directly in front of him. Approaching Joel's office, he slowed well in advance, then slipped into the turn lane. Dang it! The patrol car filed in right behind him. Jim pulled into the parking lot with the cop in tow, but as quickly as it entered, the patrol car spun around, hit its lights and siren, and sped off in the direction it had come from.

Jim took a deep breath as he watched it disappear from his mirror. He could feel his heart thumping. With a micro dose of adrenalin surging through his veins, he rounded the back side of the office. Swinging wide into his parking space, he noticed, too late, a motorcycle was parked in the spot next to his. He cranked the wheel hard but still felt the slightest thump as his bumper passed by it. As if in slow motion, the motorcycle started to topple. It was almost graceful as its weight transferred from the tires and kickstand to the highway bars, then the fairing, and saddlebag guards.

Jim slammed the lever into PARK and raced around the truck. He hoisted the bike upright, secured the kickstand, and looked around. No one in sight. Hmm. He stepped back to survey the damage. It was a beautiful, root-beer and tan-colored Harley-Davidson. Newer, and fully decked out for touring. Upon closer inspection, he saw some scuffs on the fairing and the saddle bag, but nothing broken. He straightened the mirror, then spit on his finger and rubbed the scratches on the fairing.

I'll bet that'll buff right out, he tried to convince himself. Satisfied with his appraisal, he grabbed his legal pad from the truck and headed inside.

The clock on the coffeemaker read 3:56. *Breathe, Jim. Grab a water and relax.* Joel's door was closed, so Jim took a seat on the couch and tried to settle down. Soon enough, Joel poked his head out the door.

"Hi, Jim! Come on in."

Jim fumbled with the water bottle cap and nearly

dropped his legal pad as he pulled the door closed behind them. Fortunately, Joel's back was to him. He felt like such a fraud. As they sat down, Jim placed the pad and the water on the desk in front of him.

Joel began. "You OK? You seem a little undone."

"Oh, yeah, maybe a little. A cop followed me into the parking lot. I was sure he was gonna write me a ticket for having a blinker out."

"Did he?"

"No, he left as soon as he pulled in."

"I heard the siren."

Jim breathed a little easier. *Good cover*, he thought. *No need to say anything about the motorcycle. It likely belongs to someone from the insurance company next door. Probably well-insured. Besides, they should've parked more in the center of the parking space.*

"Is that all?" Joel said, glancing through Jim's file.

The silence seemed deafening, and Jim realized he wasn't breathing.

"Well, I kinda bumped into someone's motorcycle parked out back."

"Oh?" Joel's interest was piqued. "Any damage?

"Oh, no; my truck is fine."

"And the motorcycle?"

"Well, it went over a little bit. I think the kickstand must have already settled into the asphalt because it went over so easy. There might be a little scuff on the fairing… and maybe a saddle bag. But I'm sure it will buff out, no problem. It might have already been there, I don't know."

Jim paused, a little embarrassed by the dismissiveness of his own words. With a little more consideration, he continued. "Why? Do you know who owns it?"

"Oh, I wouldn't worry about it, Jim. Sounds like no real harm was done."

"Yeah, um…okay, yeah." Jim was at a loss for words.

It wasn't the response he had anticipated, but he was relieved. He took a deep breath and exhaled a load of anxiety. He knew the owner would see it eventually, but he felt justified he had done his part to acknowledge it.

"I see you brought your list," Joel said. "Shall we take a look?"

For the next 40 minutes Jim described the scenarios on the pad in greater detail. He actually enjoyed reminiscing about most of the topics listed: life on the farm, critters to care for, fresh eggs, the occasional apples or pears from the orchard. But his voice quieted and details became scarce when they came to his uncle's farm and Sammy.

Joel scribbled something in Jim's file and encouraged him to continue. "I see your list has two parts."

"Yeah, the first is general information, like you asked for. The second is the hurtful stuff."

"Are you ready to talk about the painful events?"

"Sure, why not," Jim said with a grimace. "Let's see…the orchard. When Dad bought the farm, there were a couple dozen fruit trees behind the barn. They hadn't been cared for in a while and he tasked me with the chore. My dad told me, 'There should be a saw hanging somewhere in the barn. Just cut any sagging branches and any in the middle if it seems too crowded.' So that's what I did. I had no idea where to cut, or how to cut, or how much to cut. That old saw was so dull it did more tearing than cutting. But I stuck with it and accumulated a pretty impressive pile of limbs. It was kinda fun playing tree trimmer, and I looked forward to wintertime when we would make a huge bonfire out of the branches. I'm not sure if Dad ever checked on my work, but he was expecting the next year to produce all the apples and pears we could possibly want. When the next fall came and there was even less fruit than before, Dad was furious. He said I must've screwed up, and he wondered why I hadn't talked to the farmer down the road to figure out how to trim them proper. He said now he knew why the farmer asked if he needed a hand with trimming. Said he was embarrassed; that I was an embarrassment. He was so mad he made me spend the rest of the month cutting down every tree in the orchard with an ax. He told the neighbor that we wanted to clear out the orchard and put it to seed. But he never did pull out the stumps, and it was at least three or four years before we gathered up the trees and burned them."

"What did you think about that, Jim?"

"It made me mad, really mad. I felt stupid. I thought I was doing a great job, and I was enjoying it, only to find out I did it all wrong for the whole community to see." Jim's voice softened. "He always made me feel dumb. No matter how I tried, I could never do anything right, or good enough, or fast enough."

Joel stepped in. "Did he ever teach you how to do it right, or good, or fast?"

Jim hesitated. "No."

"Jim," Joel continued, "I'm sorry that, as a boy, you were burdened with responsibilities without ever being prepared to carry them out, and then ridiculed or punished as a result." He paused. "You deserved to be trained and taught and given responsibility accordingly. And then celebrated when you did well, and corrected and encouraged if you made a mistake.

Jim had never heard such words before. Now his face was in his hands, and his breathing was staggered. He allowed himself to begin to imagine the environment that Joel described. It connected with something deep inside him, something he hadn't felt since he was a kid. It was a longing. He wanted so badly to believe Joel's words, but had abandoned the possibility long, long ago. As he looked up, his cheeks were wet. He grabbed a tissue from the box on the desk.

"May I ask what your tears are for?" Joel said.

After a pause, Jim replied. "I had a friend whose dad treated him the way you just described. I always thought he was soft, a sissy. But secretly, I envied him."

Joel quietly gave Jim a moment to linger in what he was feeling. He jotted in Jim's file: "*This is foreign territory for Jim, but territory that needs to be traveled if he is serious about this journey.*" Joel finally broke the silence.

"Our time is over for today, Jim. If you're not opposed, I encourage you to keep a journal."

"A journal? Like Gail does?" Jim wrinkled his face in disapproval.

"Ok, maybe we call it a log. A record, or notes, like you might jot down at the end of the day while on vacation. It may serve as a narrative as to where you're coming from and where you've yet to go.

"Are you gonna read it?"

Joel smiled as he stood up from his chair. "No, Jim; it'll be for your eyes only."

Jim tossed his wadded tissue in the waste basket and made for the door.

The motorcycle was still standing beside his truck as Jim carefully backed out from his parking spot. He gingerly shifted from REVERSE to DRIVE, and slowly exited the lot. He was feeling a little undone and didn't want to make another bonehead move like that again.

Jim closed his laptop and turned to his clients. They liked his design, especially incorporating a Murphy bed into the study. Since meeting with this couple two weeks ago, he had been working on drawings to convert and extra bedroom into an office/study. They wanted one wall of floor-to-ceiling bookshelves and a desk, but they weren't ready to give up the sleeping space; it would still be needed when their adult kids returned home with their families. Jim had reworked their ideas a little, moving the bookshelves to the south wall with the window and creating a window seat for reading. This made room for a desk on the east wall and allowed space for a Murphy bed to fold out from the closet. Jim had quoted it in oak as they requested, but also offered the option of cherry. The kitchen was cherry, and she loved the soft, unassuming charm it added to the room. Jim thought she might appreciate the choice.

Leaving the proposal on the table, Jim rose and shook hands with each of them. They wanted to think about it over the weekend, but they seemed really excited about the prospect of finally getting an office in the house.

On his way out to his truck, Jim noticed the time. *That meeting went well, and quicker than I anticipated. It doesn't make sense to go home and then come back for my appointment with Joel. I could burn up a few minutes at the auto parts store and pick up a blinker bulb.*

He pulled into the parking lot and strolled into the store. Flipping through the bulb application catalogue, he identified the bulb he needed. *Probably oughta change them both while I'm at it.* He grabbed two from the display. Then he picked up the catalogue again, wondering if they might have bulbs for his Dream. He flipped the pages until he came to 'Motorcycles/Scooters.' He followed his finger down the list. Make, Honda. Year, 1965. Model…hmm. It didn't even list his bike. This was gonna be a bigger challenge than he thought. He'd have to try to find them online.

It felt good to think about the restoration again. It had been a while since he had even considered it. The scene with J.R. had been so ugly, and the police, and Gail. Remembering his bike lying on the floor, he could feel the anger rise up again as he stood there in the store. Suddenly, his mind turned to Joel's parking lot and the Harley lying on the ground. For a moment, he allowed himself to consider the contrast between the two incidences. On the one hand, an irate man waving a gun around, violently dragging a kid out from under the bike, who then scurries home with his tail tucked. On the other hand, nothing besides a couple questions. No escalating anger or energy. No threats. No pause to even go take a look at the damage. No accusations or hint of shaming.

Jim was tempted to simply assume it was his good fortune and dismiss it. He really wanted to forget that it even happened, but he couldn't deny the reality that he really had screwed up, and even though the offense was similar, the response was significantly different. Watching that Harley topple in slow motion made him feel so small, like a little boy. Shame had immediately flooded over him, and he had braced himself for someone to come flying out of the insurance company screaming bloody murder at him. That's what his dad would have done. But no one came; no one saw. And when he mentioned it to Joel, it was met with nonchalant indifference.

Jim knew what a Harley cost. He also knew the scuffs wouldn't just buff out, and the mirror should really be replaced, and maybe the saddlebag guard too. Jim fought the inclination to not care, to dismiss it with "that's what insurance is for." When his dad came down hard, it seemed easier to not care, to distance himself from the offense and the offended. He learned at a young age to isolate his feelings. He was tempted to chalk up Joel's apathy to ignorance. It could be that Joel had no idea of the potential cost of the damage Jim had caused. Maybe Joel didn't even know what a Harley-Davidson was. He may have just assumed it was some kid's dirt bike parked out back. What would another scratch or ding matter?

But what if Joel *did* know what a Harley was? What if he could accurately ascertain the damage caused by being struck and toppled onto the pavement? Could he so easily have minimized it then? Or was he just unconcerned because it wasn't his? There were too many variables in this internal monologue. All Jim could conclude was that he was grateful no one came charging out of the office waving a gun and manhandling him until he went scurrying home with his tail tucked.

Jim paid for the two bulbs and headed back out to his truck. He would be early, but there wasn't enough time to do anything else, so he headed to Joel's. He parked in his usual spot and had the back lot all to himself. He grabbed his laptop, thinking he might work on some billing while he waited in the lobby.

The fridge was freshly stocked and he grabbed a soft drink; a little caffeine sounded pretty good. Taking a seat, he noticed a boy sitting on the couch, reading. Something about that kid seemed familiar. The boy looked up.

"J.R.?" Jim exclaimed.

"Hello, Mister Jim," J.R. responded politely, barely above a whisper.

"J.R., What are you doing here?"

"Waiting for my dad. He's in there." He pointed to Joel's office.

Popular guy, this Joel must be, Jim thought. He tried to remember if he had actually ever met J.R.'s dad. He had spoken to his parents — or listened to them, rather — in his driveway the day J.R. was lost. But he was pretty sure he never looked into the car and saw who was talking to him. He had hoped no eye contact would help convey his displeasure in having his day interrupted. Now he was grateful for the office's rear exit, and hoped Joel would call him in before J.R.'s dad could come around to retrieve him from the lobby. When 4:00 rolled around, Joel poked his head out, smiled at the boy, and invited Jim in.

"How are you today?" Joel asked as they sat down.

"I'm fine." Jim wondered if the brevity of his answer

betrayed him. "Yeah, I'm doing pretty good."

"Good, I'm glad to hear it, Jim. I see you brought your list again this week. Would you like to continue with it?"

"Yeah, I figured we would."

"Before we start, I'm wondering if there was anything from our last meeting that you wanted to talk about?"

"No, I'm good."

"Alright, what's next on your list?"

Jim shared about how much he loved riding his bike as a boy. He enjoyed riding to the beach or the store, or discovering where roads he'd never been on would take him.

"What did you love most about riding your bike?"

Joel's question felt like more than fact-finding. As if he really wanted to know what Jim felt as he pedaled down an unfamiliar road or through sweeping curves! This kind of question felt foreign, but welcome just the same.

"I think it was the freedom. I could go wherever I wanted. There was no wrong way to do it, no wrong way to go. I could just enjoy myself with no boundaries…well, except for the endurance of my legs, I guess."

"Sounds wonderful Jim. So why is your bicycle on the painful list?"

"Oh, my dad knocked me off of it one day. I was pedaling around our circle driveway with no hands, my arms outstretched and my eyes closed. One minute I felt like I was flying; the next, I was flat on my back in the gravel. My shoulder was dislocated and hurt like nobody's business, and my dad just looked down and said, "Boy, your mother said dinner was ready."

Jim subconsciously rubbed his shoulder; the words were as fresh as if it had just happened. He went on:

"That evening I went out to put my bike away and found that after my dismount, it had continued on and slammed into a tree. The front wheel was bent and the tire was flat. When I told my dad the next day and asked if he could get the wheel fixed, he said he'd see, and reminded me if I had obeyed my mother, I wouldn't be without a bike right now. He never did get it fixed. I finally found a junk bike with a good front wheel and swapped it out. It wasn't the right size but it worked ok."

"Jim, I understand the pain of a dislocated shoulder. I'm sorry that happened to you. I wonder, though, was there any other pain you felt that day?"

"You mean like emotional pain don't you."

"Was there emotional pain?"

Jim thought hard. "I felt small, really small, like I didn't matter," he answered.

"That sounds more painful than the shoulder."

"Took longer to heal, too." Jim replied.

"Do you want to tell me about that?"

"I was pretty pissed at him for prob'ly a month or so."

"Then what happened?"

"I got over it."

"Can I ask what that looked like?"

"Well, I realized it was pretty rude to ignore mom the way I did. I guess I could see how selfish I was."

"So, it was all right for your dad to jerk you off your bike like that?"

"Well…yeah, I guess. I mean, I was misbehavin' right?

"Yes, you were."

"So, I guess I got what I deserved, right?"

Joel remained silent, allowing Jim's declaration to linger in the room.

Two days later the statement was still rattling around in Jim's head. *I did deserve it, right?*

Jim spent the whole day sanding parts with a palm sander, which gave him plenty of uninterrupted time to ponder. He remembered running over Kyle's radio control car years ago. He wasn't exactly proud of it, but he could still justify it in his head. He also remembered the disappointment on Gail's face when it happened. It made him mad at the time. It was one thing to be a disappointment to his dad; but his wife? She was supposed to agree with him, be on the same page. He was a man, a dad himself. Hadn't he outgrown the moniker of disappointment? Yet that was the very label he embraced with his entire being as he watched the Harley tumble to the ground in Joel's parking lot. Everything in his life had been acquired to combat that label. His farm, his family, his business, his skillset. But one stupid little mistake and he felt so small again. Sometimes it seemed like 'insignificant' could be his middle name. The other day, though, when Joel asked about his story (kinda like Gail did), he did it without drawing conclusions. *It felt like my story was important to him, like maybe I didn't deserve some stuff, or maybe deserved something else.* That felt good.

But if he didn't deserve his dad's harshness, what about Kyle? Or J.R.? Or everybody else, for that matter, who was on the receiving end of Jim's righteous wrath?

Not liking where this line of thinking was going, Jim popped his earbuds in, turned up the music, and focused his attention back on the sanding.

Chapter Twelve

Caroline

A newer pick-up truck rumbled past the shop and stopped at the house. Jim watched to see who got out. If it was a couple of young people in white shirts, they could just leave their brochure. Nope. A middle-aged gal hopped out and made for the front door. He didn't recognize her as one of Gail's friends; he should probably go see who it was. He hung up his apron and pulled the door closed behind him. As he walked toward the house, the woman came down off the front porch.

"Jim? Jimmy, is that you?"

"Aw, shoot," Jim mumbled in a panic, without a clue of who was calling his name like a long-lost friend. As he neared, she approached him at twice his speed with her arms open wide. She must have seen the confusion on Jim's face as she paused abruptly only a few feet away.

"It's Caroline, your cousin, you silly boy!"

Jim's confusion turned to relief as she threw her arms around him. Jim gave her a squeeze and stepped back. Now he recognized her.

"Dang girl, it's good to see you! It's been so long. What brings you out this way?"

"Daddy. But it's so good to see you, too. I knew I was taking a chance, but I found your address and thought I'd at least stop in and say hi."

"Can you come in for coffee?" Jim led her back up on

the porch and through the front door.

"I'd love that, and maybe I could use your bathroom too?"

"Absolutely. First door on your left."

Jim pulled a couple mugs from the cabinet and made them each a cup. "Anything in your coffee?" he asked as she came into the dining room.

"Maybe a splash of creamer, if ya got it?"

Soon, Jim and Caroline were sitting across from each other at the dining table. He'd always thought she was pretty, though the years were starting to show. Her infectious smile and big curls hadn't changed a bit. They were the only two cousins, and as kids they had been best friends. Sunday afternoons were usually spent at her farm. It had been thirty-five years, give or take, since they'd seen each other, and there was a lot of catching up to do.

"Remember fishing in the creek? Jim asked. "Your mama would pack us sandwiches, and we'd spend the better part of the day there."

Caroline remembered. "Yes, and I also remember the time we got so hot, we went swimming to cool off. But we didn't have our swimming suits, so we just swam in our clothes."

Jim broke into a grin. "We both got a lickin' for that. And I had to wear a pair of your shorts and a blouse while my clothes dried on the line."

"Ah, and remember the fort we made from Daddy's scrap lumber?"

"Yeah, and I remember being bummed they wouldn't let us sleep out in it. Remember sledding on the hill behind the barn and your momma making hot chocolate for us?"

The thought brought a warm smile to both of them.

"And swinging from the ropes in the barn after the hay was in," Jim went on. "That was the best."

Caroline winced. "Yeah, until I broke my wrist. But

then you stayed at the farm for a few weeks to help out with my chores. I really appreciated that, Jimmy."

"Remember that older boy you met when you were fourteen. Dan, or Don was it?"

Caroline didn't respond, so Jim continued. "That next summer you two were together all the time. I hardly saw you at all, and then suddenly you were gone. Nobody talked about you after that. When I asked my mom, she just told me you had to go away. Your momma said you probably wouldn't be coming back anytime soon. I didn't have the nerve to ask your daddy."

Caroline stared past Jim and out the window as the conversation was becoming more inquisitive than reminiscent. Taking a deep breath, she proceeded matter-of-factly:

"Delbert. I called him Del. They vacationed up here in the summer. He was nineteen and I got pregnant. I went back with him to Georgia, where they were from."

She hesitated, holding the warm cup in both hands. "I lost the baby."

Her voice drifted, as if she had forgotten to brace herself to hear the words she had just spoken. She took another deep breath and continued.

"Two months later we broke up. Momma was pretty hurt about me leaving, and Daddy was madder than a wet hornet. Said he never wanted to see my sorry a…well, he didn't want to see me again. To tell the truth, I didn't want to see him anymore, either. I bounced around for a while after that. It was a pretty dark season. Got married a couple times. Both losers, I found out later. Finally settled in Florida. The warm agrees with me." She smiled and took a sip of coffee, as if to say, "That's enough information for now."

Jim chose his words carefully. "You said you were here for your Daddy. I thought he moved years ago. Is everything alright?"

"Daddy passed."

"Oh, I'm so sorry, Caroline."

"That's kind, Jimmy, but don't be. I hated that son-of-a…that man."

"I hated what he did to you."

"Well, Jimmy, I hated what he did to you too."

They both sat in silence staring into their coffee for the longest minute before Caroline reached across the table and took Jim's hand. Smiling, she looked him squarely in the eye. "Jim, you were a good friend to me; far better than I realized at the time." And with that, she slid her chair back and stood abruptly.

"I've got to get going. I need to stop at the bank in Berrington before they close, and empty his safe deposit box, then a meeting with his attorney."

"Would you like me to come along?"

"Oh no, Jim. I'm a big girl." She threw her purse over her shoulder and gave him a kiss on the cheek on her way past.

Jim followed her out to the driveway. "Are you sure you can't stay a bit longer? Gail will be home soon, and I'd love you to meet her."

"Maybe another time Jimmy. It was really good to see you."

Her eyes met his and lingered curiously for a moment, like she was savoring a memory from an innocent era. Then, she jumped up into her truck and was gone.

When Gail pulled in thirty minutes later, Jim was still sitting on the front porch steps. He barely noticed her.

"Jim, are you ok?"

"Hi, hon. I'm fine."

"Sitting on the front steps at four-thirty in the afternoon isn't fine for the Jim I know. What's up?"

"Caroline stopped in."

"Caroline? Like your cousin Caroline?"

"Yeah, my cousin Caroline." He had a distant look on

his face, as well as a touch of red lipstick. He followed Gail inside. She put down her purse, got a damp paper towel, and handed it to him.

"Here, honey. Clean off your cheek and tell me about it."

Jim explained that his uncle had passed, and that Caroline was in the area tying up loose ends. He shared how good it felt to reconnect after so long.

"If you two were so close, why didn't you keep in touch?" Gail asked.

"She left."

"I don't understand. She left?"

"When she was fifteen, she met a boy and she left. Nobody heard from her for years. I think she was married a couple times. I'm pretty sure she's alone now."

"Any kids?"

"There was a pregnancy, but no kids."

"Were things bad at home?"

"Her dad…he did things."

Gail sat down beside Jim and put her hand on his back. "Things?"

Jim looked away from her as his eyes grew damp.

"He did stuff to her."

"I'm so sorry Jim. Do you want to talk about it?"

"Naw. Maybe. I don't know."

Gail sat patiently, offering Jim space to share if he wanted. He tried to put words to images that had been buried for decades.

"It was after church, and we drove out to their farm for Sunday dinner like we usually did. It was fall, and I had on brand new school jeans with the cuffs rolled up. Mom warned me not to get them dirty. I took off my new shirt and left it in the car; it was warm enough to be in a tee shirt, anyway. I ran into the house and asked my aunt if she knew where Caroline was. She thought maybe in the barn. So I ran across the yard and pushed open the barn door and hollered for her. Nothing. I was about to leave when I saw my uncle up in the loft. I asked if he knew where Caroline was, and he said she was busy, but he had something to show me. Their ewes had produced eleven lambs that spring. We walked to the back of the barn, and he swung open a window that looked out over the pasture. He said I could pick one of the lambs and name it, if I wanted to. He said he'd care for it, but I could call it mine, if I'd like. I was excited and knew immediately which one I wanted. I had already been giving him treats when no one was looking. He'd always come to the fence when he saw me, hoping I'd have something for him."

"How old were you?"

"Oh, nine maybe. Caroline would've been ten. Anyway, when we went back through the barn, Caroline was coming down from the loft. She was still in her Sunday dress but it was all messy and she had hay in her hair. I asked her if she wanted to play, but she said she had to go change, and we never did play that day.

"About a month later on a Sunday afternoon, I ran down to the pasture to see Sammy — that's what I named the lamb. For some reason, a few of the sheep were inside the barn, so I went in and found Sammy in a stall with a few others. I pulled a carrot from my pocket and sat down in the straw and let him nibble it. It was almost like he smiled when he saw me, and I loved how soft he was. Then I heard something around the corner where the bales of straw where stacked. When I went to look, I saw my uncle. He was kinda kneeling on his hands and knees, and his trousers were down. Then I saw Caroline…under him. Without thinking, I charged at him with all my might and tried to knock him off her. He was strong, like my dad. He grabbed the front of my shirt, and before I knew what hit me, he pinned me down with his hand across my chest and throat. 'Not a peep from you, boy, or else.' He tightened his grip and twisted my face into the straw."

Jim choked up. "He wouldn't let go. I remember feeling like I was in a tunnel. I could faintly hear him say, 'This is what men do, and if you ever became a man, you'll do it too.' When he was done, he climbed off her and glared at me as he pulled his trousers up. Then he leaned over, stuck his finger in my face and said, 'I'll butcher that puny lamb of yours in a second, if there's ever a peep outa you about any of this! Ya hear?'"

Gail's cheeks were wet as Jim went silent. Shame filled his eyes. She grabbed the tissue box from the counter and set it on the table.

"I couldn't do anything…" Jim could barely speak the words. "I just laid there."

He took a moment to dry his eyes and continued. "After my uncle was gone, Caroline got up, pulled up her panties, straightened her dress, and walked past me like she didn't even know I was there."

Gail honored his words reverently before responding softly. "Jim, I am so sorry that happened to you, and to Caroline. You were so brave to attack a full-grown man who was hurting your friend."

Jim couldn't help but deflect her words. "I felt so small…so weak…so invisible."

Gail continued, "Your actions called him out. You were very strong on the inside." But she could tell that Jim was struggling to make a place in his mind for her words to land.

He finally jumped up. "I think I need some air." He went out the patio door onto the back deck, and across the yard toward the orchard. Gail knew better than to follow. She whispered a prayer before going into the kitchen to start dinner.

Chapter Thirteen

Who Made You Pay?

"Jim, would you mind going with me in the morning to the farmers market? I'd like to get some cherries."

"Can we go first thing? I want to mow the orchard tomorrow."

"Sure, but you might have to take me out for breakfast." Gail loved starting the day with a cup of coffee across the table from Jim, especially if someone else was waiting on them.

"Sounds like a plan to me," Jim said.

The next morning, they rolled into the park at seven sharp. The grass was still wet with dew, but the vendors were set up and ready for customers. Gail wanted at least a lug of tart cherries, and maybe some sweets if they were ready. An hour later, Jim was carrying a lug of cherries, topped with two quarts of blackberries, and a bag of fresh snap peas. Gail carried a bag of green beans.

With everything loaded into the back of the truck, Jim considered his work complete and was ready for some eggs and sausage at the diner. Gail was ready for breakfast too, but was also excited at the prospect of pitting and freezing cherries the rest of the day.

Jim rolled down his window and steered past the rows of cars toward the park entrance. He was visualizing the breakfast menu in his mind when Gail started waving at someone pulling into the park.

"Who you waving at?" he asked.

"J.R. and his dad."

"Where are they?"

"Right there."

"Where?"

"On that motorcycle," she replied as it rumbled slowly toward them.

Sure enough, there was J.R. with his head floating inside his helmet, grinning from ear to ear on the back of a Harley. As the motorcycle approached, the sun reflected off its fairing, changing it from a shaded silhouette to a brilliant root-beer metal flake.

Jim felt his chest tighten. He wanted to sink down behind the steering wheel, but he held firm. J.R kept waving, and the driver nodded and smiled at them as they rolled past.

"THAT WAS JOEL!"

"Who?"

"Joel, my counselor!"

"Oh, I didn't know J.R.'s daddy was a counselor."

"He's MY counselor! And it's HIS brown Harley!"

Jim was so flustered he turned left from the park and headed for home.

Gail was bewildered. "Aren't we doing breakfast this morning?" she asked.

"No, let's just get home."

"Okay, I suppose we can just have some blackberries on cereal." She popped one in her mouth.

"Yup," Jim replied without even hearing her. They drove in silence the rest of the way home, but a monologue raged in Jim's mind the whole way.

After they brought the produce in, Jim hardly touched his coffee before heading outside to hook the brush hog to the tractor. Once he got to the orchard, he engaged the brush hog and started to mow. Now his mind was free to wander.

He replayed the events of the recent months with his new-found information in mind, and he became more enraged with each episode. J.R. tipping over his motorcycle. Jim chasing J.R. out of the garage with a handgun. The visit from the sheriff. Joel knowing who Jim was, but Jim not having a clue who Joel was. And knocking over Joel's motorcycle! What were the chances? And to top it all off, Joel showing no concern at all about the Harley — not even claiming it was his! He had gone on with their session as if nothing had happened. Jim was fuming. He felt played, and was so furious he could hardly mow straight.

By Thursday afternoon, Jim was more than ready to give Joel a piece of his mind, and at 4:00 he burst into his office without waiting to be invited. "Who the hell do you think you are? Making a fool outa me when I hit your Harley in the parking lot!"

"Hello Jim, would you like to sit down?"

"No, I don't want to sit down. You've basically been lying to me ever since we've been meeting. Operating under false pretense or something like that!"

"Jim, why don't you tell me what's bothering you."

"I'll tell you what's bothering me all right. You knew all along that I was the jackass who scared the crap outa your kid because he tipped over my old piece of junk motorcycle. And you didn't even flinch when I hit your $15,000 Harley with my truck! How do you think that makes me feel, huh? How do you think that makes me feel!?"

"How does it make you feel Jim?"

"Like CRAP! It makes me feel like crap!"

"Why does it make you feel like crap Jim?"

"You should've told me you were J.R.'s dad! You should've told me it was your Harley! You should've gone out and looked at the damage, got an estimate, made me pay to get it fixed…or at least cover your deductible. You should've made me pay. After what I did to J.R. you should've made me pay!"

Jim was pretty undone. Eventually, he settled into the chair.

"Where else did you pay, Jim?"

"What?"

"In your story, in your childhood, where else did you have to pay?"

"What are you talking about?"

"Who made you pay?"

"My Daddy made me pay!" Jim blurted out.

"How did your daddy make you pay?"

"If I broke something, even a worn-out old tool, he made me replace it with a new one. The axe I used in the orchard, he said I lost it. I know I put it away, but he was sure I lost it. So I had to wear the previous year's winter coat that I had outgrown until I saved enough to buy him a new axe. And I dropped one of Mama's china dishes one time. It broke in a million pieces. Mama said not to worry, but Daddy kept my lunch money for a month. That's just the way it is. When somebody screws up, they've gotta pay!"

When it seemed like Jim was finished, Joel leaned back in his chair and simply asked, "What if somebody else pays instead?"

Jim was silent. Joel proceeded. "In simplified terms, 'mercy' is not getting what you deserve. 'Grace' is getting what you don't deserve. Are you familiar with these terms?"

"Well, yeah, of course. I've heard them in church."

"Have you ever experienced them?"

"What are you talking about?"

"Has anyone offered you grace or mercy?"

"Well, Jesus did, right? That's how we get saved. We believe that he paid so we wouldn't have to."

"Okay. Have you ever received grace or mercy from someone besides Jesus?"

"You mean like a friend or family member? Gail cuts me a lot of slack, I suppose."

"How does that feel?"

"Feels pretty good, but she's my wife. She's supposed to be on my side, right?"

"Okay, anyone besides your wife?"

Jim had to think about it. "I borrowed my neighbor's trailer once to get some gravel for the driveway. Loaded it a little too heavy and bent the tongue. Danny, a friend of mine — in fact, he's the fella you bought your house from — he straightened and reinforced the trailer. Made it even better than before, and didn't charge me a dime. Danny was like that."

"Did you and Danny spend much time together?"

"Some, yeah; I suppose we did. I really liked him. I was bummed when he got transferred."

"Why do you think you liked him?"

The question caught Jim off guard. He'd never considered why he liked somebody. He either just did or didn't. Joel gave him time to ponder, and eventually Jim replied. "The first time I saw Danny was at the grocery store, he was in line ahead of Gail and me. The woman in front of him didn't have enough money, like twelve or thirteen dollars short. Before the gal could begin sorting out what to exclude, Danny slipped a fifty into her hand and told her to keep the change. He was so subtle about it that only the gal and me, ever knew it happened. I was pretty impressed. A couple weeks later I found out he was my neighbor."

"What did you think about the woman that accepted the fifty dollars?"

"Well, I guess I thought it was cool that she didn't make a big fuss about it; you know, make it all about her. It's like she honored his stealth generosity. It was really cool."

"So, now I'm curious Jim. Why was it cool for her to receive grace from Danny, but not cool for you to receive mercy from me?"

Jim was stumped. Each rationalization he came up

with fell short before he could articulate it. Jim was many things, but stupid wasn't one of them. He was starting to see that his reasoning was faulty, but he couldn't understand why. "I guess I don't know," he finally conceded. "Do you?"

Joel smiled empathetically. "Not necessarily, but I wonder if you've just experienced a conflict between your longings and your beliefs."

"My what and what?"

"Your longings, your desires, versus what you think you deserve. In the scene in the store, who would you rather have been? Danny or the gal who was short on cash?"

"I thought it was cool how Danny addressed the problem before it even became a problem."

"So you'd want to be Danny then?"

"Hmm, maybe. But the gal was pretty cool too. I mean, he slipped the fifty into her hand, she looked at him, he nodded and said keep the change, and she just smiled and paid for her groceries. She didn't even make a stink about the change, just slipped it into her purse and gathered her kid and took her groceries. It was all pretty classy."

"So, you'd want to be the gal?"

"I don't know. What are you getting at?"

"Jim, I wonder if you long to deal in the currency of grace, but you've been taught that it's only for other people. You're limited to dealing in the currency of justice."

"I'm sorry…I'm lost."

Joel was opening a door that Jim had walked past a thousand times, but never seen. "Jim, did your dad love you?"

"Of course he did!" Jim was quick to respond.

"Okay, do you mind if we take a minute and look at a passage in the Bible?"

"Sure."

"Remember First Corinthians 13? It describes love as 'patient and kind, not jealous or boastful or proud or rude. It does not demand its own way. It is not irritable, and it keeps no record of being wronged.' Jim, I'm not suggesting your dad didn't love you; in fact, I'm pretty sure he did. But does this verse better describe how your dad loved, or how Danny loved?"

Jim couldn't answer fast enough, "Danny!"

"And you admired him for it?"

"Absolutely!"

"Jim, I don't know your dad's story, but it's possible that grace and mercy were never modeled for him."

"Heck no! Grandad was a jerk. He'd whoop ya just as soon as smile at ya."

"Okay," Joel continued, "it sounds like, from what you've shared so far, your dad was just passing on what he learned. Do good, that's expected. Do bad and you'll pay."

"Pretty much. And never let you forget it either!"

"So, your truth is what was modeled for you, what you experienced as 'normal'," Joel said, making air quotes around the word 'normal'. "In your case, would it be out of line to say that your 'normal' included a warped sense of constant judgment?"

"It sounds awful when you put it that way."

"I'm sorry, Jim. How would you describe it?"

"I didn't say it was inaccurate; it just sounds awful."

"Fair enough. On the flipside, your longing is to experience the very environment that God designed for us to operate in: grace and mercy."

Jim was starting to come out of his chair. "So how do I do that!?"

"Easy there, cowboy," Joel chuckled. "For lack of a better term, we call it 'story work'. Together we'll look at your story, the incidences that shaped and confirmed your belief system that defined the currency that you're limited to, i.e. justice. We may approach your story from a different perspective; maybe challenge some of the conclusions your 'little boy' devised to make sense of his sometimes-confusing world. We'll likely pause on occasion and offer a little care for a difficult memory. It will take time and energy, but you've already made some pretty good headway. For now, why don't you bring your list with you next week, and we'll continue with that?"

Jim's head hurt. He had been so wound up when he came in, and now he was weirdly looking forward to coming back. "Sounds good if you say so, Doc." He rose and stuck out his hand.

Joel met it with a firm shake. "Next week then."

Chapter Fourteen

Label Maker

"Hi Mom." It was Kyle, and Gail was always tickled when he called.

"How are you? It's so good to hear your voice."

"I'm good. Really busy, but doing good."

"I'm so glad."

"Work has been taking up a lot of my time. We're implementing new software, and I've been putting in ten to fifteen hours of overtime per week during the last month. It cuts into my social life, but sure helps the paycheck. How are you and Dad doing?"

"Oh, we're good, honey, but I want to know what's new in your world? Any progress with your desire to go on a mission trip yet this year?"

"Well, that's what I wanted to talk to you about. Our church has sponsored an orphanage in Mexico for a few years now. Last year we started a school there and it's going pretty well."

"That's exciting. Are you going down there to help?"

"Yes, actually I am. There's a team heading down this winter, which I'll be a part of, but the church board has asked if I'd consider staying and helping out with the school after the team returns."

"Wow. How long would you stay?"

"At least through the end of their academic year, maybe longer. They're struggling with some administration and software issues the board wants me to address. Anyway, I'm starting to raise support for the trip and wanted not only to let you know what's going on, but also give you a heads-up that I've talked with your pastor. He's invited me to share with your congregation for a few minutes on a Sunday morning. You know, my plans and how the congregation can help, that sort of thing."

"Kyle, that's wonderful. When will you be coming home for that?"

"There's no date yet, but sometime this fall. I just knew you'd want to be kept in the loop."

"Absolutely. I can't wait to tell your dad. Is there anything we can do?"

"Well, since you asked, while I'm gone I really can't justify paying rent here just to keep my spot in the apartment. I'm wondering if I can move my stuff home while I'm away. My bed is just a blow-up mattress, so we're talking a dresser, a TV, a bookshelf, and a desk. Oh, and my winter clothes."

"I'm sure we can make room for your stuff, honey. I'll let your dad know. It would probably be easiest just to come down with the truck and trailer when you're ready to leave. Then you won't have to mess with it at all."

"Oh, Dad will love that!" Kyle said sarcastically.

"We'll figure it out when the time is closer."

"Sounds good Mom. Hey, I gotta scoot. Love you."

"Love you too, Kyle. Bye."

Gail couldn't help but feel pleased. This was right up Kyle's alley. He loved travel, adventure, serving, and problem solving. She could hardly wait to tell Jim.

When Jim came through the door, he was carrying a box under his arm.

"What's that?" Gail asked.

"A box; what's it look like?" Jim replied with a grin.

Gail rolled her eyes. "Duh. What's in the box?"

"It was sittin' on the front porch. I imagine it's parts I

ordered for the motorcycle."

Gail could tell Jim's playfulness was directly related to his excitement about making progress on the Dream. A couple weeks ago, he'd started disassembling and organizing parts, determining what could be repaired and what needed to be replaced. Before tearing it apart, he was actually able to get it to start. It only ran for a few seconds, but Jim was ecstatic. A tune-up was going to be far less expensive than a rebuild.

"Don't be long," she hollered as Jim disappeared through the laundry room and into the garage. "Dinner will be ready in five."

When Jim returned, he washed his hands and dried them at the kitchen sink. "The parts for the carburetor came," he said. "What's for dinner?"

"Salmon and salad, and don't get my towel dirty!"

"Mmm…smells wonderful." He grabbed a couple glasses and filled them with water while Gail took the fish out of the oven.

"Are you gonna drizzle that glaze over it?"

"Already done, babe." She gave him a wink.

At the table, Jim bowed his head. "Thank You, Lord, for a great day, for meaningful work, and the health and strength to accomplish it. Thanks for Your provision in every area of our lives and for this meal. We ask that You'd bless it, in Jesus' name, amen."

Before releasing Gail's hand, he raised it to his lips and gently kissed it, then slipped his napkin into his lap and piled some salad onto his plate.

"How was your day?" he asked as he drowned his salad in ranch dressing.

"It was good. I talked to Kyle."

"How's Kyle?"

"He sounded great. He's excited about a trip he'll be taking this winter."

"Oh? Where's he going?"

"A group from their church are going to Mexico to work with a school they started there. They've asked Kyle if he'd consider an extended stay to help out with some of the startup struggles."

"Is he gonna, stay? Babe, this salmon is amazing!"

"Thank you, hon. Yes, I think he will."

"Good for him. He loves that kind of thing."

Gail was pleasantly surprised at his supportive attitude. Jim had been unexpectedly upbeat over the last few weeks. She figured this was as good a time as any.

"He can't really justify keeping his apartment while he's gone, and wondered if we could store a few things for him."

"How much has he got?"

"Not much, it would easily fit in his old room."

"Will it fit in his car or do we have to go get it with the trailer?"

"The trailer would make the most sense."

Jim continued to enjoy his dinner without any more mention of Kyle's plans.

Later in the evening, Gail came across a note pad with Jim's writing on it. It was among a pile of accumulated papers she was going through on the kitchen counter. She called to him in the office.

"Jim, what's this?"

"Not sure, babe. Whatcha lookin' at?"

"Something you wrote down on a scratch pad. A story maybe? About a boy, and a well?"

She had Jim's curiosity stirred, and he came into the kitchen to see.

"Oh, that's a dream I had a few months ago. It was pretty vivid, and I couldn't get back to sleep, so I jotted it down."

"Do you mind if I read it?" Gail asked.

"Go ahead, if you can make any sense of my handwriting."

Gail set it aside, and when she finished sorting the rest of the pile, she brought it into the living room with a cup of decaf. Smelling the coffee, Jim got a cup of his own and joined her on the couch while she read quietly.

"Jim, some of the imagery in your dream sounds familiar," she said.

"What do ya mean?"

"You talk about new blue jeans and a white tee shirt."

"Yeah?"

"Do you remember sharing with me about Caroline, in the barn. You had new blue jeans and a white tee shirt on."

"Huh. I guess I hadn't made that connection."

"And here it talks about the girl being taken. That's terrible." Gail kept reading. "You were tied up? Jim, this is too weird. You weren't able to help her, just like with Caroline. Oh, honey, this must've been an awful dream!"

"Well, I couldn't get back to sleep after it."

"There just seems to be a lot of parallels here. When did you have this dream?"

"Not sure. Is there a date on it?" Jim checked the upper corner of the page. "Hmm…this was right after the incident with J.R. in the garage."

"I wonder if you might want to share this with Joel. See if he can make any sense of it."

"Oh great; bring up that whole fiasco with Joel? I don't know...maybe I'll think about it, anyway."

Jim didn't have to think about it too hard; by the time Thursday rolled around he was ready. Armed with his scribbled recollection of the dream, he waited for Joel to invite him into his office. Jim had previously shared with Joel what happened in the barn when he and Caroline were children. Now Joel listened as Jim shared the dream.

"Jim, what are your thoughts about dreams?"

"Well, Gail thinks that sometimes they can be a window into our emotional state. I don't know."

"What are your thoughts concerning this dream?"

"When Gail read it, she was surprised at the similarities between this and the story I'd shared with her about my uncle and Caroline in the barn."

"Would you like to tell me about the similarities?"

"Yeah, I guess." Jim took a deep breath. "Even though Caroline was a year older than me, I looked out for her, ya know? I'd bait her hook and take the fish off if she caught one. I'd be the first to go into the fort to clear out the spider webs. I'd always make sure there was enough hay where we were gonna land before swinging from the ropes in the barn. Stuff like that. I looked up to her, but I looked out for her, too."

"How about the girl in the dream?"

"I suppose I wanted to protect her, too. Especially when those people wouldn't let her go."

"So, you're the boy in the dream?"

"What do you mean?"

"Well, you just said 'I wanted to protect her too."

"Oh wow, I guess I did, didn't I? Anyway, when he – or I – tried to help the girl, I got tied up." He paused. "When I tried to help Caroline, I was pinned down. I was completely thwarted both times. I felt so useless."

"Jim, can you identify the victim in both scenarios?"

"That's easy."

"Is it?"

"Yeah, Caroline in the barn, and the girl in the dream."

"Any other victims?"

Jim was confused. "Whadaya mean, another victim?"

"In both scenarios you tried to protect someone whom you perceived was a victim, right?"

"Yeah."

"In both situations, weren't you also a victim?"

"Huh? How so?"

"In each circumstance, who was physically subdued? Who was minimized, dismissed, and abandoned?"

Jim's brow wrinkled. "Wow, I'd never thought of it like that before."

"I wonder how it would have felt if somebody had shown up to help protect both you and your friend?"

Jim stared blankly across the room. He had no idea what that might have felt like. There was no reference point in his memory to draw from, no recollection of someone standing up for him. He found himself feeling as alone as he had in the dream watching the strangers disappear with the little girl.

"Jim, was there a coach or teacher, some adult who seemed to notice you?" The question echoed the hundred miles across the desk, and Jim barely heard Joel ask it.

"What?"

"When you were a boy, who had your back? Who was always happy to see you?"

Jim rummaged through his memories. Then the slightest of smiles lifted the corners of his mouth.

"Mister Elhurt."

"Who was Mister Elhurt?"

"He was the shop teacher. I think he liked me. I liked his class and I always got an A." The interest in Joel's eyes encouraged him to continue. "I was good with the tools. He let me use the band saw by myself, and even the table saw if he was nearby."

"Anything else?"

"One day during class, he found a nice piece of walnut that had been cut in two in the waste barrel. If we miscut our material, we weren't allowed to just throw it out. We had to show it to Mister Elhurt, and he would make a note of it in his gradebook before issuing another piece. Only two of us were working with walnut at the time, and the other boy accused me right away. Mister Elhurt looked directly across the room at me, and I looked at him. Then he walked over, put his hand on the other boy's shoulder and walked him out of class. And the boy never came back for the rest of the year."

"How did that feel?"

"I remember thinking that he trusted me, and it felt really good, but then I thought maybe I had just gotten lucky or something."

"Why lucky?"

"Because I wasn't used to someone actually looking out for me."

"Did you deserve to have someone looking out for you?"

"I don't know. I always thought it makes you more self-reliant if you're on your own."

"Yes," Joel said, "I suppose it does." He jotted something down in Jim's file. "I have some homework for you, Jim. Remember making a vow to your wife when you were married? It was an agreement, a position or posture that became an absolute in your mind. I wonder if you've made less-public declarations in your life that seem just as binding. They may have started out with 'I will never' or 'they will never' or 'I'll always.' Over the next few weeks, I'd like you to be curious about your story, and vows you might have made in the pain of the moment."

Jim was intrigued. "You mean like 'I'll never trust my dad again'?"

Joel was surprised by Jim's quick response. "Is that something you said?"

"I carved the letters NTD on my headboard." Jim could see Joel didn't get it. "Never Trust Dad."

"Wow. How old were you?"

"It was when I came home and found out he had sold the Dream. He had disappointed me before, but I always saw where I might have played a part in it. But not that time." Jim was feeling angry just thinking about it. “One minute he brings home a project for us to work on together, and the next minute he sells it to a friend who wants a project to work on with his kid. I decided then and there it wasn’t about me. Dad was a piece of crap when it came to caring about what I wanted. I swore I’d never trust him again.”

“I’m sensing a lot of energy as you’re sharing that with me. Are you still angry at your dad?”

“A couple years later, I remember pulling into school with Grandpa’s old pick-up. As I walked across the parking lot, I saw a bunch of girls huddled around something on the sidewalk. When I got close enough, I could see a guy in the middle, sitting on my Honda Dream. He and his dad got it running, and while I was driving Grandpa’s tired old farm truck, this kid was riding a chick magnet. In that moment, I hated my dad.

“Do you still hate your dad?”

“Dad’s dead, he’s been gone almost ten years.”

“Do you still hate him?”

“How can you hate something that is no more?”

“Do you still hear his voice when you’re late, or make a mistake, or lose a tool?”

“Yeah, I suppose I still do.”

Joel waited a moment before continuing. “Jim, your dad and mom created a few labels for you.”

“I have no clue what you are talking about.”

“Imagine your dad painting the word ‘Irresponsible’ on a scrap of wood, and drilling a hole in each end to attach a chord, and then hanging it around your neck. Then imagine he made another that said ‘Lazy,’ and another read ‘Dreamer’. Now imagine that your mom made a couple and painted ‘Not worth protecting’ and ‘Too sensitive.”

“When would I have to wear them?”

“All the time.”

“That would be embarrassing.”

"What do you think you would do?"

"I'd probably try to cover them with a jacket or something."

"Why would you want to cover them?"

"Because it would be hurtful."

"What would be hurtful?"

"If people saw them."

"Why would that be hurtful Jim?"

"Because they might believe them."

"I suppose they might, and it might be a good warning as to your character… if it were true." Joel paused again. "Is it true?"

"I don't know. I mean, Daddy called me all of those things on more than one occasion, and I suppose Momma did too, at least by her actions, or lack of. Yeah, I suppose they're true."

Joel leaned back in his chair and slowly swiveled until his back was to Jim. "Irresponsible. Lazy. Dreamer. Worthless. Sissy." Joel spoke each word slowly, deliberately. "I wonder if Gail would choose these words to describe you. Or Caroline? Or J.R., or Pastor Jackson, or Danny?"

Joel continued to rotate his chair until he was facing Jim again. Jim felt the conflict within. As he considered the perspective of the people Joel named, he sensed it was different from what he believed about himself.

"So," Jim asked, "you're saying those labels aren't true?"

"What matters isn't what I believe. What matters is what you believe."

"C'mon, Joel, what are you saying?" Jim was starting to feel played and frustrated.

"OK, let's say at eight-years-old you did something irresponsible, and your dad hung that label around your neck. It seemed appropriate at the time; after all, you did just do something irresponsible. But if he never removed that label — like, by telling you at some point how proud he was about how responsible you are — then you'd probably continue to wear it, believing you deserved it. Maybe you decided it was appropriate. In fact, you may even have worn it proudly. More likely, though, you'd become hyper responsible just to dissuade people from agreeing with the label. When a customer or a friend would comment on how attentively and responsibly you handled a situation, it would feel good…for a moment. But then the label would reappear and you'd have to try harder."

"So being responsible is a bad thing?"

"No Jim. But the reason you are responsible determines whether it brings freedom or condemnation. If I'm trying to distance myself from the label 'irresponsible,' I'll never be able to relax. If the label is 'lazy,' I'll never be able to play. If the label is 'dreamer,' I'll never enjoy taking a risk. Until I see those labels as nothing more than someone's opinion about my behavior, rather than a judgment on my character, I'll likely be in a constant battle somewhere in my soul."

"I remember hearing Gail say I'm a human 'being', not a human 'doing'," Jim said. "When I asked her what that meant, she said, 'Our worth is based simply on the fact that we are, not on what we do.' I kinda struggle with that. With Dad, it sure felt like it was all about what you could do."

"I wonder what your heavenly Dad thinks?"

"Yeah, that's probably more important." Jim smiled an exhausted smile. "Are we done yet? My brain hurts."

"We can be if you'd like."

"Great. See ya next week."

Joel smiled and rose with Jim. "I'll walk you out."

In the parking lot, Jim stopped in front of his truck. Noticing Joel's Harley, he just had to ask, "Joel, why didn't you make me pay for the damage I caused to your bike?"

Joel had already turned to go back inside when he

said over his shoulder, “Why didn’t you charge me for the damage J.R. did to your bike?”

Chapter Fifteen

Where There's Smoke...

Jim rolled over in bed. The clock glowed 4:45. For some reason he was wide awake. He loved early mornings this time of year, and before he knew it his feet hit the floor. Donning his slippers and robe, he quietly pulled the bedroom door closed behind him. He stopped in the kitchen just long enough to make a cup of coffee, and then he was out on the deck.

The warm morning air meant there was no dew on the furniture so he settled into a chair. He let his head tilt back and his eyes adjust. A million specks of light vied for his attention, strewn across the darkness above him. The silence almost felt sacred at first, but gradually he realized it wasn't silent at all. The tree frogs laid down an unending chorus. The crickets chimed in here and there. A pair of ducks made their way across the morning sky, a gentle whistle pulsing over their wings. Jim sipped his coffee as though he were taking communion. It was Saturday, and by an unusual turn of events his day was without an agenda. He had planned to help some guys from church replace the roof for an elderly couple. Somehow, somebody forgot to order the dumpster for the tear-off, so Jim got a call just before going to bed informing him that it had been rescheduled for the following weekend.

The sun pushed against the night sky with a slow, steady resolve. The trees stood as dark silhouettes in the yard, patiently sipping hues of green. A blue jay swooped in and laid claim to the feeder. Gathering his fill, he ascended to the roof and unabashedly announced the day had arrived. A hummingbird lit on its feeder for a quick drink, and he was on his way. Three haunting notes of a loon echoed from the pond nearly a mile away. The air barely stirred, but when it did it carried a fragrant blend of summer: fresh grass, the orchard, smoke...

SMOKE! Jim jumped up and stepped off the deck. The further from the house he walked, the more he could feel a breeze. It was coming from the east.

Jim climbed into his truck and headed down the driveway. He rolled down the windows and made a right turn into the wind. Slowly he drove, sniffing like a hound dog as he went. Just before coming to Joel's place, the smell stopped. He turned around in Joel's driveway and paused to make sure the smoke wasn't coming from any of the buildings before heading back to the west.

About halfway between his place and Joel's he pulled over and parked. There was no reason for there to be a fire in the woods, but it sure seemed like that's where the smoke was coming from. To avoid getting his robe snagged, Jim left it in the truck. In his PJs and slippers he shuffled across the road into the forest. As he pressed through the lower branches, he realized that he hadn't been in these woods since rescuing J.R. from the creek. The foliage was thicker now and the forest floor was lush. It had rained hard earlier in the week, so the ground wasn't dry, but Jim still didn't like the idea of his property being downwind from a wildfire. The smell was getting stronger now, but there was still no sign of open flames.

Jim squinted trying to make out details of the forest in the early dawn. He knew he must be nearing the creek, and could hear it splashing as the current made its way past rocks and limbs. Or was that sizzling? He stopped to let his senses acclimate. It was sizzling, all right; he could smell bacon. Then, with a couple stealthy steps to the right, he saw the source.

There was a tent. A few more steps revealed a campfire, and a couple guys reclining in camp chairs drinking coffee and frying up breakfast. Jim wanted to get a better idea of who he'd be dealing with before confronting them in his PJs. He could hear low conversation.

Jim crouched as he advanced slowly, seeking the cover of a towering beech tree. Hidden behind it, he could hear them plainly. He quieted himself by leaning against its smooth trunk, and focusing his attention on listening. It was definitely two people, men, maybe a man and a boy. The younger of the two spoke up.

"Dad, do you know why leaves turn color in the fall?"

Aha! Jim thought, a father and son.

"Why do you think they turn color?" the father asked.

"It's because as the days get shorter and there's less sunshine, the trees produce less chlorophyll. The chlorophyll is what makes the leaves green."

"That's fascinating son. Is that what makes the leaves fall off the trees, too?"

"Naw, they're just tired after hanging on all summer."

The dad chuckled and reached in to flip the bacon. "I suppose I'd get tired after hanging on all summer too. Are you excited about school starting this fall?"

"I suppose."

"That wasn't very convincing. Are you concerned about something?"

"Dad, we didn't get to see Grandma all summer."

By now Jim was convinced the situation was benign and decided against a confrontation, especially considering his attire. He planned to exit undetected while it was still dark, but the boy said something that stopped him in his tracks.

"I really missed spending time with Miss Gail too."

"I'm sorry you didn't get to see her much this summer. Was that because of what happened with Mister Jim?"

"Yeah, he doesn't like me."

"Why do say that?"

Jim knew he was privy to a conversation he had no business hearing, but he couldn't move as the boy continued.

"Dad, he was really mad at me."

"Yes, I remember. We talked about that."

"I asked him why he bought a motorcycle that didn't run, but he said I wouldn't understand. Then he said there's nothing quite like riding a motorcycle on a warm summer day. That day that I was waiting for them to come home, I just wanted to sit on it and see if I could imagine what it might be like."

"Then it tipped over and pinned you?"

"I was so happy to see them come home. Then… Dad, I was so scared."

"I know you were, son. I would have been, too."

"Why was he like that, Dad?"

Jim braced himself for Joel's assassination of his character. Joel wasn't quick to answer, but he finally asked, "Do you think Mister Jim might have been scared too?"

"Of me?" J.R. seemed incredulous at the thought.

"I'm not sure Mister Jim knew it was you. You said it was kind of dark in the garage. Maybe he thought he was being robbed."

"By me?"

"J.R., maybe he didn't know it was you, at least not at first."

J.R. though about it. "He did let go of me when Miss Gail came in and called my name." J.R. thought some more. "I just can't imagine Mister Jim being afraid of anything!"

Jim knew he had to get out of there. As quickly and quietly as possible he made his way back to his truck.

Gail was up and in the kitchen. She laughed out loud when Jim came through the door in his PJs. "Well, where have you been?"

Jim explained and her laughter subsided. "That's nice that Joel would take J.R. camping," she said. "Making some good memories, I'm sure." She carried two plates to the table, each with an over-easy egg and toast. Jim grabbed some silverware and sat down.

"Thanks, honey. This looks great. And thanks, Lord, for this day, and for this food. We ask that You'd bless it, and bless Joel and J.R., too. In Jesus' name, amen."

Jim pretended to enjoy his breakfast, but was still undone by what he heard in the woods. It almost felt like an impromptu intervention. He was subjected to J.R.'s perspective, which he had never considered, as well as Joel's thoughts on his whole gun-raising fiasco. Both felt so foreign; they were actually considerate of what he might have been feeling. There was no judgment. Not one mention of his shameful behavior. When he heard Joel say, "Maybe Mister Jim was scared too," it rocked Jim to his core. His gut response was defensive, followed by an immediate feeling of being defended. The way Joel had said it made it seem like it was okay, even normal, for a man to be afraid. That was a far cry from what Jim's dad and grand-dad had taught him. Somehow, Joel's words felt far more inclusive than the words he'd grown up with. Being tough, having the answers, being independent, always left him feeling somewhat alone.

Gail interrupted his thoughts. "Do you remember taking Kyle camping?"

It took Jim a moment to conjure up the memories of camping with Kyle.

"Jim, are you okay?

"Yeah, why?"

"You seem a little quiet. Is your egg too done?"

"No, breakfast is great. I was just thinking."

"About?"

Jim couldn't help but notice the contrasts between his recollections with Kyle, and what he witnessed just this morning. "It really looked like Joel and J.R. were having a good time," he said.

"I'm sure they were. Didn't you and Kyle have a good time camping?"

"You'd have to ask Kyle."

"Oh, come on, honey. I think he probably had fun."

"I'm not sure. When I was with Kyle, I always felt like I had to teach him stuff; you know, like how things worked, or why this had to happen before that could happen, or the best way to do something."

"Why do you suppose you did that?"

"I guess I never thought about it. Maybe because I felt like I was left to figure a lot of things out for myself, and I didn't want him to have to?"

Gail stacked their empty plates and pushed them aside, inviting him to continue.

"It was interesting observing Joel with J.R. He treated him more like a friend, like he was enjoying J.R. instead of fulfilling a role."

"Did you feel like fulfilling a role was more important when Kyle was growing up?"

"Maybe…I think so. I mean, it was so strange to hear J.R. explain to his dad why the leaves turn color, and when he said they fall off because they get tired, Joel just went right along with it. It was almost like, making sure J.R. got it right wasn't really important at all. Like, just enjoying each other was more important."

"Were they?"

"Yeah, it seemed like they really were."

"Do you remembering enjoying Kyle?"

"When he was a baby, but less as he got older."

"Why, do you suppose?"

"I'm not sure. I think I always felt like I should be teaching, or shaping, or influencing him. I never put much thought into just enjoying him."

"Do you ever remember your dad enjoying you?"

Jim was silent for a long time before shaking his head. "No."

Jim spent the rest of the day in the garage. He had about thirty minutes of sanding to finish up before he could start priming some of the parts for the Dream. But sanding and painting didn't fully occupy his mind. He remembered Joel encouraging him to be curious about his childhood, his story, and so he was. All sorts of questions wandered in and out of his thoughts.

Why would Dad pass up the opportunity to restore this bike with me? Wasn't I enjoyable enough for Dad to want to spend time with me? Why wouldn't Dad take time to teach me stuff, like how things worked and how to fix stuff? I always felt like he just expected me to know it. I think that's why I was always teaching Kyle. I never wanted him to feel as stupid as I did when Dad would tell me to do something but not show me how.

Jim had enjoyed hearing J.R. that morning, but he really hadn't missed him over the last couple months — not like Gail had. She didn't say much, but Jim could tell it still hurt a little that J.R. didn't feel free to stop by like he used to. Jim wondered what it was about kids that he shied away from.

He thought about Caroline. She was more like a sister than a cousin. His memories with her were almost all happy ones. Her folks weren't as harsh about chores as his parents were, so when they were at her farm it was pretty much all about play. Her momma was nice too. If they were going fishing or hiking, or whatever, she'd pack a lunch for them with sandwiches wrapped in wax paper, and some fruit, and then some cake or pie or fresh cookies, and always, two of bottles of Orange Crush. She even bought Caroline her own little cooler for the two of them to use.

But that all seemed to stop when he was around ten, around the time he got Sammy…when he saw what her daddy did to her. Jim remembered asking his dad if it was normal for daddies to "do stuff" to their girls. When his dad asked what he meant, Jim told him that he thought he might have seen his uncle do something to Caroline in the barn. "Was Caroline hurt?" his dad demanded. "Well, no, not that he could tell," was Jim's answer. "Sometimes daddies play a little rough," his dad said. "If she wasn't bleeding or something broke, I'm sure they were just playin'. No need for you to go stickin' your nose where it don't belong, ya hear boy?" Jim understood.

He remembered going out to Caroline's a few weeks later for Sunday dinner. He went straight to the barn like he usually did, but this time he couldn't find Sammy. When he asked his uncle where Sammy was, he just replied, "Gone." They had lamb chops for lunch that day. It wasn't unusual to have lamb when they were there; they would occasionally butcher some of their stock for meat or to sell. But on that day, after finishing the prayer, his uncle glared at him from across the table and nodded at the plate of chops. It was the same look he got that day in the barn when he tried to protect Caroline. He wondered if his daddy had said something, and now his uncle was sending a message. Jimmy limited his plate to mashed potatoes and corn that day.

When Jim stopped for lunch, he asked Gail if she remembered his uncle.

"Caroline's dad? Oh, yeah. That man gave me the heebie-jeebies."

"What? What do you mean?"

"Remember at our wedding? In the reception line? He gave me a big kiss right on the lips! Then he smiled a creepy smile and said, 'Welcome to the family, sweetie!' You don't remember that?"

"What did I do?"

"Nothing. You were busy with somebody else, and I didn't want to make a scene. And when I told you about it later, you just got a really strange look on your face, so I dropped it."

"What kind of look?"

"It was weird…like…helpless. Like a little boy. What's this about Jim?"

"I'm sorry, Gail. I'm sorry I didn't protect you."

"Oh, I protected myself after that incident. I wouldn't let him get near me. But what's bringing all this up?"

"I think seeing Joel with J.R. this morning made me realize how the men in my childhood weren't as normal as I thought they were. I don't remember any man ever enjoying me, or listening to me, or asking me questions. In fact, I probably would have been suspicious if they had."

Gail smiled to herself. She remembered when she started to realize the "normal" in her story wasn't healthy. She could see Jim's world starting to rock.

"I'm sorry you never got to meet my dad," she said. "He would have loved picking your brain and finding out what makes you tick. He restored a few cars when he was younger. One was a nice Mustang he fixed up for me when I was in high school. I think it was a '68."

"It was a '67, hon. I've seen the pictures."

"Anyway, I'll bet he'd have loved to come over and help you with your Dream."

"That would've been a strange turn of events. My own dad wouldn't, but my father-in-law would've."

Gail thought for a moment. "Is that why you liked Danny so well?"

"I'm not sure what you mean."

"Danny was a man who was 'for' you. He'd help you out with anything you asked. He respected your thoughts, and he didn't need anything in return. It seemed like you just enjoyed each other."

"Yeah, Danny was one in a million."

"I don't think so."

"Huh?"

"I think if you could believe that men in general were 'for' you...wanted good for you... you might find a lot more 'Dannys' in your life. But you're right; growing up, you just saw men using people to get what they wanted. Not all men are that way, you know. You're not."

Chapter Sixteen

Expensive Vows

Jim and Gail filed out of the sanctuary into the lobby. Gail was quickly swept into conversation with some of her girlfriends, while Jim made for the door. One of the guys from the work team caught up with him in the parking lot and asked if he had an extension ladder for next weekend's roof project. Jim responded that he did, and would bring it. Then he retreated to his truck.

The sermon was okay, but something the preacher said troubled him. Gail climbed into the passenger side and fastened her seatbelt.

"Donna's little granddaughter is teething already,' she said. "Can you believe that?"

As Jim pulled out of the church parking lot, he started in. "So, who's this disciple that Jesus loved?"

"What?"

"In the sermon, when the pastor was reading, he read it a couple times. 'The disciple that Jesus loved.' Who was this disciple? Why didn't they just say his name?"

"Wow, hon, this has you really bothered doesn't it?"

"I'm not bothered. I'm just wondering why didn't they just say which disciple they were talking about? I mean, Jesus loved all the disciples, right? It's not like it was a secret that he loved them, right?"

"It was John."

"How do you know that?"

"You'll only find it in the book of John. The writer was referring to himself."

"That seems a little arrogant."

"Or endearing. You're right, Jesus did love all the disciples, but John got it."

"What do you mean, he 'got it'?"

"To some, Jesus was just a teacher. To others, a prophet; and to a few, the Son of God. To John, he was the very Son of God who loved a simple fisherman. I think it took Peter and a few others a little longer to grasp the depth of Jesus' love for them."

Jim chuckled. "Yeah, Peter wasn't the sharpest tool in the shed. So, you're saying that John wasn't bragging, but that he was just relishing the thought that the Son of God — sitting next to him with skin and bones, eating bread and soup — loved him?"

"Yup."

"Hmm. Never thought of it that way."

Jim spent the afternoon tinkering on the Honda. Uninterrupted in the garage, he considered what Gail had said earlier. So, John understood what it was to be loved by God. Jim tried to imagine introducing himself as 'the cabinetmaker loved by…' Gail maybe? She was his wife, so that's a given, right? His dad? His uncle? This was weird, and he couldn't help chuckling to himself. Yet, he still struggled with the concept of identifying himself by who loved him. Then a question gently settled into his mind that caught him off guard: Might John have simply acquiesced to being loved by Jesus, enough so that it actually became his identity?

He stood there for a moment, thinking. Gail. Gail's love had changed him. Not overnight, and not a lot, but he was a better man for being married to her. She usually thought better of him than he did of himself. She had confidence in his goodness, and even when he disappointed her, she trusted his heart. He thought about being introduced as "the one Gail loves." Probably not at the lumber yard, but where people knew and respected Gail, he could see how it might feel good. That was kind of why they wore wedding rings, right?

He looked at his. It was a simple gold band, the shine long worn off. His hands had grown thicker and weathered, and he wondered if he could remove it even if he wanted to. He couldn't imagine ever wanting to. She was one of the few people in his world who made him feel really safe, and he valued that.

He remembered feeling like he had done something right when they became engaged, and she would show off her ring. It wasn't big or fancy, but she seemed so happy to show it whenever someone asked. Was it less about the ring and more about belonging? He hoped so. Maybe that's how people were supposed to feel in their relationship with Jesus, like they belong. Was that what John meant?

Jim knew God loved him; he'd heard it his whole life. A few months after getting married, he had knelt in the front of a church, accepting Jesus' offer of forgiveness of his sin. In that moment he felt valued. It seemed strange that Jesus, or anyone, had thought of, much less made provision for, his future. He was so accustomed to making his own way that the freeness of salvation felt very foreign. But the pastor had made it clear it was for anyone who wanted to be saved. He had never received anything nearly as wonderful, and Jesus picked up the tab. It was a little mindboggling.

Unfortunately, it didn't take long for Jim to start looking for ways to deserve his salvation. He was far more comfortable with earning his keep than relying on someone else's good graces. The more conscious he was of being good, the more aware he was of the fact that he wasn't. He was often reminded of how much God loved him, but the failures in his life made him seriously wonder if God *liked* him at all. He couldn't imagine Jesus smiling at him, any more than imagining his dad being pleased with him. Jim felt pretty convinced that if he had attended the last supper, he wouldn't have been reclining next to Jesus. At the far end of the table, more likely, or maybe the one serving food or bussing the table.

Another question presented itself in Jim's wandering mind: "What if God had been your dad?" The mere thought that God would consider being his dad flustered him. An image reluctantly pieced together of a father smiling proudly with a home movie camera, capturing his young son joyfully riding his bicycle with no hands, around and around the driveway. He imagined hearing the sweet words, "Honey, could you hold dinner for a few more minutes? Come and see how well Jimmy rides with no hands!"

Jim forgot he was holding a wrench, and it slipped from his hand to the concrete floor. He bent down and picked it up, grateful for the interruption. "I think this is a good place to end for the day," he said out loud, running his sleeve across his nose. He wasn't comfortable with his feelings, and was in no way prepared for the emotions that particular scene had just evoked. He gathered his tools, wiping each one down as he returned it to its places in his tool chest.

In the living room he found Gail curled up on the couch with a blanket and a book. "What's for dinner?" he asked.

"Popcorn. It's in the kitchen."

Sundays usually meant a late lunch, and often a large one, which meant Gail considered popcorn a perfectly suitable evening meal. Jim rummaged through the fridge for leftovers. Jackpot! Chicken pot pie. He scooped a pile onto a paper plate and heated it in the microwave.

As he waited, he thought about Caroline. He wondered how she could ever conceive of a Heavenly Father who loved her. It was hard enough for him, and his dad's greatest offense was his indifference. But Caroline? She had been a target of her dad's sick aggression. Indifference would have been a blessing for her.

Jim carried his meal into his office and sat down at the computer. After a couple bites, he set his fork down and began to type.

Dear Caroline,
Thanks for taking the time to stop by the other day. It was so good to see you. It stirred up a few things for me. Some really fond memories, as well as some painful ones, too. I remember how much I enjoyed looking out for you. I know you were older and probably didn't need me to, but thanks for letting me play that role. Remember when we were swimming and those boys came along and were teasing you, and I punched one of them in the face and he got a nose bleed and they took off? Or when you dropped the egg basket and I told your mom I was the one who broke the eggs? Remember when we were building our tree fort, and the branch you were on broke and you twisted your ankle when you landed? Then I carried you all the way home. Without any siblings of my own, you were as close to a sister as I would experience. I remember that time, too, in the barn, when I tried and failed miserably to protect you from your dad. I was so angry at myself for not being able to protect you. Then I was embarrassed that I thought I could. I can't pretend to imagine the damage you suffered at his hand. He broke something in me that day, too. I made myself not care. A couple years later when you met that boy, I knew what kind of boy he was. I had heard people talk about him. Everything in me wanted to tell him to get lost, with my fists if necessary. I wanted to tell you that you deserved so much better. But I stayed quiet. I'm sorry. I think I understand now why we both felt powerless to make better choices. By then, we already believed we were of little consequence.

—Jim

Realizing he didn't have her email or a physical address, he sent it to his phone and then on to Caroline as a text.

It seemed like Thursdays rolled around faster than ever. Sitting in Joel's office, Jim pulled his phone out and scrolled until he found the letter he had texted to Caroline.

"I think I might have made a vow," he said.

"Recently?" Joel asked.

"No, as a kid."

"Would you like to talk about it?"

"Remember you said I should be curious about my story, and vows I might have made? I think I made another one, besides not trusting my dad."

"What was it?"

"To not care about other people."

"Really."

"Well, it's not that I don't care about people. I really struggle to take responsibility for people."

"That sort of sounds like a good thing, doesn't it?"

"I don't think I'm saying it right. Can I just read you a letter I wrote?"

"Sure, please do."

Jim read the letter, and by the end, Joel was getting a clearer picture. "Jim, I think I see what you're saying. Would you mind trying one more time to describe your vow?"

Jim thought for a long time as Joel waited patiently. Then he said, "I wasn't ever gonna put myself out there, to protect someone else."

"Why?" Joel asked softly.

Jim's answer was even quieter. "Because I wouldn't be enough, and I never wanted to experience that feeling again."

"What feeling?"

By this time Jim's voice was barely a whisper. "Ashamed."

"Does the vow work?"

"No."

Jim's eyes were damp and Joel proceeded tenderly. "Why do you think you do it, if it doesn't work?"

"To hide the sign."

"And the sign…"

"Not enough!" Jim interrupted in full voice. "Other than in the shop, building furniture, I've never felt like I was enough!"

Joel tapped his chin with his pen. "So, not putting yourself out there for someone else's sake protects you from being found out as lacking?"

"Right."

"Any idea why you felt you had to make that vow?"

"I don't know."

"Could you take a guess?"

Jim was slow to answer. "Because I hated when I felt that way."

"What way?" Joel pressed.

"Little. Weak. Pathetic. Despicable."

"Those are harsh words, Jim. Is that how you see yourself as a young boy?"

"More or less. I was embarrassing when it mattered."

"So, the vow kept you from the pain of embarrassment?"

"I suppose so," Jim replied, looking at the floor.

Joel proceeded. "As children, we cope as best as we can with trauma. Someone who's drowning will grab a fishing line if it's available. An eight-pound test won't pull him out of the drink, but it might help keep him afloat. That's what a vow can do. At some point, though, he'll need to let go of the fishing line to grab onto a rope that can lift him out of the water. If not, the very thing that once protected us from the bad will protect us from the good as well. Are you curious if holding onto that vow has cost you anything?"

"I'm sure it has."

"What, do you suppose?"

"Well, for starters, just because I couldn't protect Caroline from her dad doesn't mean I couldn't at least warn her about that boy that got her pregnant."

"Anything else?"

"Maybe."

"How did you feel about searching for my son out in the woods last spring?"

"Honestly?"

"Sure, why not."

"Well, it kinda pissed me off that some stranger wanted me to take time out of my day to go hunting for their kid. I could've wandered around the woods for half a day, only to get a call that somebody else had found him."

"But somebody else didn't find him, Jim. You did. And you've been larger than life to J.R. ever since."

"I doubt that."

"Why do you say that?"

"After the way I treated him, he won't even come around."

"That's not because he thinks less of you. Oh, he has a healthy respect for you, and a measure of fear. But he also realizes that what he did was wrong. He blames himself for your actions."

"What!"

"Kind of like you blaming yourself for your dad's actions."

"Wait…I mean, I was surprised when I found him under my bike. But I was way out of line in the way I treated him. Way outa line. Surely you've told him that!"

"We've talked with him. Suppose that your aunt,

when she put your shoulder back in its socket, had told you that your dad shouldn't have treated you so harshly. How would that have felt?"

"I'd have appreciated her sympathy, I guess."

"Now, suppose your dad came to you, knelt down to look you in the eye, and said, 'Jimmy, I am so sorry I hurt you. You didn't obey your mom, but that was absolutely no reason for me to treat you the way I did. You should never be treated with such disrespect. I was wrong, and it will never happen again. Tomorrow let's buy a new front wheel for your bike, and I'm gonna talk to someone who can help me deal with my anger.'"

Jim didn't know whether to laugh or cry. He couldn't begin to imagine those words coming from his dad's lips. Yet, it stirred an extremely old desire that he had long abandoned.

"It would never happen."

"I'm sorry, Jim. Now that your dad's gone, I know it never will. But if it could, those words would be appropriate and true."

They both sat in the weight of the moment. Finally, Jim asked, "Is that what you want me to do for J.R.?"

Joel smiled. "If at some point you would like to do that, I believe it could be healing for your relationship. Especially since you are talking to someone who can help you with your anger. But, no. That's not what I'm suggesting. I'm wondering if it's possible that your vow has kept you distant from many more people than just my son."

Jim's head dropped. The movie reel that started to play in his mind confirmed Joel's inclination, and Kyle was at the top of the list. Jim didn't like feeling responsible without being able to control, so he errored regularly on the side of being overbearing or aloof. Overly involved or indifferent. Both sabotaged any opportunity to validate Kyle. He'd watch Gail and try to do what she did. But as long as he was committed to keeping his vow, it was no better than pretending.

"Yeah, I think you might be on to something, Doc." Jim grabbed a handful of tissues from the box and tidied his face. It was time to go. Rising reluctantly, he reached over and squeezed Joel's hand as firm as he dare. "Thanks. You've given me a lot to think about."

Joel looked him in the eye and replied, "You're worth the consideration. See you next week."

Chapter Seventeen

Do You Smell Something?

Friday morning found Jim busy in the office putting the finishing touches on a proposal. He had scheduled a 10:00 a.m. meeting with a potential client and was printing out some drawings when his phone rang. It was Gail.

"Hi, honey. Are you still home?" she asked.

"Yup, in the office."

"I forgot to get gas yesterday on the way home, and this morning I ran out. I'm on the side of the road just before the park where they have the farmers market. Could you come and get me?"

How could she be so doggone irresponsible? he wondered, but he composed his response. "I think I've got a full five gallon can in the garage. I'll be there in a bit."

Jim looked at this watch as he hung up the phone. "Man, I didn't need this today! I've still got to print this up, shower and shave, and now Gail's got me going fifteen minutes in the wrong direction."

He put the remaining three pages in the queue and hit print, then headed out to the garage. He loaded the gas can and funnel into the bed of the truck and drove off to find Gail.

When he pulled up behind her car, she was chatting on the phone. She had already released the gas door so Jim didn't bother to interrupt her conversation. He inserted the funnel and hoisted the gas can, doing his best to empty it without getting any on him.

Gail ended her call and got out of the car before Jim was done. She thanked him and apologized for interrupting his day. He said it was okay, but his tone didn't sound very convincing. He splashed the last of the gas from the can and retrieved the funnel, while Gail put the gas cap back on. As Jim climbed back into the truck, he realized he wasn't as successful as he thought. His pant cuff was wet and he reeked of gasoline.

His tires chirped as he did a u-turn and sped off for home. As he went, he dialed up the couple he was supposed to meet.

"Hi, Larry. How are you today?"

"Great, Jim. Looking forward to seeing what you've come up with for us."

"That's why I'm calling. I'm running a little behind this morning and wondered if we could bump our meeting to maybe 10:30 or so?"

"Oh, I'm sorry, Jim, but Nancy's got a doctor's appointment at 11:00 so we need to leave by 10:30. Is there any way you can still make it?"

"I will do my best."

Jim hung up his phone and watched the speedometer creep past sixty-five. He wasn't a fan of speeding, but he knew this couple was leaving for two weeks on Saturday. If he didn't make this meeting, there would be no chance of closing the deal yet this month.

Jim swung into his driveway with a swirl of dust behind him. Not wanting the laundry room to smell like gasoline, he kicked off his shoes and stripped from his jeans in the garage. As he passed through the kitchen, the time on the microwave said 9:52. Wearing only his socks, underwear, and sweatshirt, he checked the printer. Yes, they all printed. He slipped the drawings and the proposal into a folder and darted to the bedroom.

"Looks like no shower this morning," he grumbled

under his breath. "A little extra deodorant will have to do."

As he tied his shoes, he thought he could still smell gasoline. Not much he could do about it now. He ran a wet comb through his hair to try to tame his bed-head, and dragged a toothbrush over his teeth for a couple seconds. Good enough! It was 9:58 as he passed the microwave again, and it was a twenty-minute drive to the meeting.

Neither his schedule nor his wallet could afford a ticket, so he kept his speedometer to sixty-two, hoping to stay under the radar. The clock on the dash said 10:14 as he pulled up to their address. There was a car in the driveway, so he parked on the street in front of the house. With the folder in hand, he made his way across the lawn. SERIOUSLY? He didn't even make it to the sidewalk before stepping squarely into the very fresh evidence of a very large dog.

The rest of the way to the house he dragged his foot through the grass, desperately trying to rid the poo from his shoe. Reaching the porch, he rang the doorbell, and then knelt down to untie his shoes, thinking it best to leave them outside.

The door opened and a Larry's wife, Nancy, stood there looking through the screen door. "Oh, there you are." she finally exclaimed, "I didn't see you down there."

Jim stood up and she pushed the screen door open and let him in, where he was immediately greeted by a huge Saint Bernard. The dog's wet muzzle was all up close and personal, and he knocked the folder from Jim's hand, sending its contents all over the floor. Picking them up proved to be an irresistible invitation for the mammoth fur ball to shower Jim with all its slobbery affection.

Flustered, Jim apologized for being late, and he suggested they get down to the business at hand. Nancy offered coffee, which Jim politely refused; he was keenly aware that he had barely twelve minutes to sell this job. As they settled around the dining table, Larry spoke up.

"I smell something. Nancy, do you smell something?"

Jim quickly owned it. "I stepped in something your dog left in the front yard. That's why I left my shoes outside."

"Nope! It's gas. I smell gasoline. Do you smell it, Nancy?"

"Yes, yes I think I do."

Jim couldn't believe it. "Yes, that's me, too. I must've spilled some on me this morning. I'm so sorry. Now, here are the drawings laid out like we talked about."

Jim spread the drawings out on the table for them to look over. The request was to build cabinets for either side of their fireplace and build a new mantel to tie it together. They discussed how high the mantel needed to be above the firebox, and how it would be anchored it to the wall. Nancy wanted to know if Jim could match their existing stain, and if the hinges could be soft-close. At 10:26 they finally made it to the proposal. Larry looked it over. Nancy went straight to the price at the bottom of the page.

"Wow, I wasn't expecting it to cost that much. That's a lot more than we were thinking, isn't it Larry?"

Larry finished reading through the proposal. "Well, honey, it's custom work, and it's within the ballpark Jim gave us when he measured up a couple weeks ago."

"Well, I just wasn't expecting it to be so much."

Larry looked at Jim and shrugged his shoulders. "We better get going if we're gonna make the doctor's appointment. Thanks for stopping by, Jim. We'll let you know."

Just like that, Jim's opportunity was over. He thanked them both for their time, and graciously excused himself.

Back in the truck, he took a deep breath and slowly pulled away. He put way more time into that bid than he should have, and now he had nothing to show for it. If only he hadn't stepped in the dog crap, or poured gas on himself, or if Gail hadn't run out of gas. *Why couldn't she just pay attention to basic stuff like that? Who forgets to put gas in the car? It's not like the car just quits; there's a gauge and a light, for cryin' out loud! If I could've been there at ten like I planned this could have gone totally different. I could've been going to the bank with a down payment check right now. Instead, I'm going home empty handed.*

He didn't know if Gail was home yet, and he really didn't care to find out. Instead, he took the road back into town, and since he hadn't had time for breakfast, he justified an early lunch at the diner.

A bell announced his arrival as he pushed open the old wooden door. The sign inside said 'Seat Yourself', so he chose a table in the back. He was still licking his wounds when the waitress interrupted his thoughts.

"Coffee?"

"Yes, please."

"Well, I'll be darned. I don't remember the last time we saw you in here for lunch, Jim."

Jim looked up. "Well hello, Jenny. I don't get out of the shop much," he said with half a grin.

"It's nice to see you. Here's a menu. Clam chowder is the soup today, and our special is an avocado chicken salad wrap with fries and a pickle."

"Thanks," Jim muttered, but she was gone as quick as she came. He wasn't in the mood for salad anything. When she returned, he ordered a bowl of soup. "And maybe a mushroom burger. Could you make that a double with fries and a Coke? Wait, do you have Orange Crush by chance?"

"I'm sorry, we don't."

"Then Coke is fine."

"Absolutely," she replied with a smile, and again she was gone. Jim knew this was going to be way more food than he needed in the middle of the day but he really didn't care.

Still fuming, he nursed his cup of coffee. Most of his angst directed toward Gail. How could she be so oblivious?

It was like she had no concept of what her irresponsibility had cost him.

Again, his stewing was interrupted by Jenny. “Here’s your Coke and clam chowder. Your burger should be up in a minute.” Her smile was engaging, but Jim’s body language said he wasn’t in the mood for chit-chat. It had been so long since Jim had lunch at the diner that he had forgotten how good their clam chowder was. He drowned the little fish crackers and savored each spoonful.

His phone buzzed in his shirt pocket. Gail was texting that she was back home and would have lunch ready for him when he got there. He slid the phone back into his pocket without responding.

Jenny returned. She set a plate in front of him and pulled a bottle of catsup from her apron. Gathering up his empty soup bowl, she asked cheerfully, “Can I get you anything else?”

“Nope, this looks great, thanks.” And it did look great. Jim lifted the soft warm bun to his mouth and took a bite. Hot, juicy burger, mushrooms, Swiss-cheese, some kind of heavenly sauce. Jim closed his eyes and took it all in. There was nothing like comfort food to soothe whatever it was that had wound him up. In his own little corner of the diner, he relished every bite.

With the burger eaten, he mopped up every last drop of the sauce on his plate with the few remaining fries. That’s when the dessert menu at the back edge of the table caught his eye.

Jenny stopped by again to gather his dishes. “Anything else today?”

“How ‘bout a refill on the coffee and a slice of your lemon meringue pie?”

“Excellent choice. I’ll be right back with that.”

Jim wiped his mouth with his napkin and put it back in his lap. This was how he deserved to be treated.

He took his time eating the pie, and even longer with his coffee. He was in no hurry to see Gail. When the lunch crowd started to roll in, he decided it best to vacate his table. The burger was great, and Jenny had been very attentive, so he left a hefty tip on the table and paid his bill on the way out.

Walking to his truck, he tried to remember if there was anything else he needed while he was in town. Nothing came to mind, but he headed for the hardware store anyway. He was sure his memory would be jogged if he saw it in person. And sure enough, in the back of the store where the tools were displayed, he remembered the blade on his band-saw was getting dull. He studied the selection on the wall, finding the right size and type he preferred. He grabbed two. The cordless drills also caught his eye; he always liked to check out the latest models. They were progressively getting lighter and more powerful, and with longer battery life, but there was nothing new here. Heading down the automotive aisle on his way to checkout, he remembered that he was almost out of carb & choke cleaner. He picked up two cans, and since WD-40 was on sale, he grabbed one of those, too.

Placing everything on the checkout counter, he smiled politely when the cashier acknowledged him with a wink. In front of him was a candy display that included Clove chewing gum. Without thinking he reached for a pack, but then decided against it. Clove was Gail's favorite, and it was linked to some of her best childhood memories. It wasn't always easy to find, so whenever he did see it, he usually bought a couple packs and quietly left them where she would gleefully discover them. But he wasn't really interested in seeing her happy face right now. In fact, he wasn't keen about seeing her at all, but he'd run out of reasons not to go home.

Gail had finished her errands and was home by 11:30. *Jim's meeting must have gone well or he would have been home by now*, she reasoned. *He's probably finalizing details with the client, and then maybe going to the bank with a down payment. Otherwise, he would have responded to my text.* It was odd, though, when he still wasn't home at noon, and by 12:30 she started to replay the events of the morning.

He wasn't happy when I told him I had run out of gas. He barely spoke, actually, and was in a pretty big yank to leave as soon as the gas was in the car. I'd hoped he would start it for me to make sure it would run, but he was gone before I could ask him. He really would have been upset if I had to call him again.

She began to wonder if maybe the meeting hadn't gone so well, although she couldn't imagine why it wouldn't. Jim was always so good with his customers. *I suppose he may have been a little late. He hates being late. He wouldn't blame me for making him late, would he?* She went ahead and ate lunch without him, and was loading the dishwasher when she heard his truck pull in the garage.

"Hi, honey," she chirped up as he came in the door. "How was your meeting?"

"What meeting?" Jim replied gruffly.

"Your meeting this morning…the fireplace surround. Didn't you have your meeting this morning?

"It was a joke."

"A joke?"

"Thanks to you I was late!"

"What, like a few minutes?"

"Like fifteen minutes, and I only had a thirty-minute window to start with."

Gail felt blindsided. "Well, I'm sorry I ruined your day," she snapped incredulously.

"Yeah, you ruined my day all right. Because you're not responsible enough to put gas in your stupid car, I was late, I stunk like gas, and I stepped in dog crap on the way in! I never even had time to connect with them, much less sell the job. You screwed up that meeting before I ever got there. I never had a chance. It was a total waste of time, not to mention the two days lost on bidding."

"Oh, I'm irresponsible!" With that one word, Gail's hurt was swept away with a rush of anger, and she squared off directly in front of him. It didn't matter that he towered over her by nearly a foot; her face was as livid as her words. "Well, I'm sorry that you can't pour gas out of a can without dumping it all over yourself! And I'm not surprised you stepped in dog crap; you can't see the ground with your nose so high in the air!"

"If you hadn't made me fifteen minutes late, I could've walked over to use the sidewalk like a normal person."

"A 'normal' person would have put the five gallons of gas in my car last night, when I said I was low and wasn't sure I could make it to the station!"

"Oh, so your running out of gas is MY fault?"

"Just sayin' you could've dealt with this last night, and today would have looked a whole lot different!"

"NO WAY! This is not my fault. If you were Kyle, you'd be riding your bike for a week. Then you might appreciate that car that I paid for!"

Gail snatched her purse from the counter, pulled out her car keys, and slammed them against his chest. "YOU CAN HAVE YOUR DAMNED CAR! I'LL UBER!"

Without hesitation, Jim's massive right hand snapped up and grabbed her wrist like an iron cuff. It surprised them both. He had never laid a hand on Gail before. This was new territory. She looked him straight in the eye, her eyes narrow with fury. He released his grip. The keys fell to the floor, and she spun around and disappeared into the bedroom. Hearing the door lock behind her, Jim kicked the keys across the room. The fob shattered against the baseboard. It felt good to break something.

Knowing he wasn't in a good headspace to be working with sharp power tools, he retreated to his office rather than head down to the shop. He pulled his keyboard towards him and checked his e-mail. Nothing but junk. Then he started browsing the internet, hitting a few of his regular sites for parts for his Dream. After about ten minutes, a small green sedan rolled up the driveway. He figured Gail was expecting someone; and, sure enough, she went out and got in the car, and they drove away. *Maybe an Uber*, he chuckled to himself.

On his computer he came across a gal in Oregon who was selling vintage motorcycle parts. His inquiry led to an online chat with her. They started talking about restoring motorcycles, riding motorcycles, and raising families that got in the way of riding motorcycles. Eventually they found themselves talking about life in general. Nothing deep or specific, just life. Her husband was a long-haul truck driver who kept his eye out for vintage parts, and she would peddle them on the internet and at swap meets. Jim shared about finding the Dream that his dad had owned. It was fun to share about restoring it, especially with someone who was into old motorcycles, and this gal and her husband had restored many. They both rode older bikes now. His was a 1958 Harley, Duo-Glide that he brought home in boxes. She rode a 1968 Honda CB450 that they restored together. They mainly enjoyed day trips to the ocean or up to the mountains. It sounded like fun.

Jim couldn't believe he was getting hungry already, and was shocked when he looked at the time. Nearly six o'clock. They wrapped up their conversation, and he pushed his keyboard away. Gail wasn't home yet, so he foraged around and found a frozen pizza. He browned some Italian sausage and gathered ham and onions from the fridge to doll it up a little.

With the pizza in the oven, he sat down in the living room and turned on the TV to catch the local six o'clock news. A reporter was on the scene of an accident in town. It looked like a dump truck had plowed through a stop light and took out three vehicles in the process. As the camera panned the wreckage, Jim's heart sank. Crumpled beyond recognition was a small green car.

He dialed Gail's number immediately. It rang, and then again, and again.

"What do you want?" she answered. Clearly Gail was still miffed, but at least she answered.

"I saw on the news that a green car was in an accident in town. I, uh…just wanted to make sure you were ok. Are you ok?"

"I wasn't in an accident, if that's what you're asking."

"Oh…okay, good."

"I won't be home tonight."

"Wait, what?"

The line went dead.

Jim's hand was shaking as he set the phone down. The petty indifference he felt toward her prior to the newscast had been replaced. Fear, loss, relief, and confusion wildly chased each other around inside his head. His anger would be of no use here. The only thing left to control was…dinner.

He turned off the TV and waited for the oven timer to sound. *Wow, this was not how I saw this day going when I got up this morning.* Gail had left before, years ago, early in their marriage. She'd run home to her mom for a day or two until she calmed down. This time felt different, though.

He went to the fridge in the garage and grabbed a beer. When he came back to the kitchen, the timer was buzzing. He pulled the pizza from the oven, cut a couple slices, and sat down to eat, alone.

Chapter Eighteen

Make It Stop

Jim didn't sleep worth a tinker's darn. He replayed yesterday's events over and over. He hated everything about it – being late, losing the sale, and blaming Gail. He watched the clock until 6:00 a.m. and finally got up and made himself some coffee. Dissecting the scenes for the hundredth time, he was sure he'd never seen such rage on her face. It actually frightened him. Not that they hadn't had their fair share of fights over the years, but in light of her childhood, he knew better than to ever lay a hand on her — until yesterday.

He hated when they fought. Though he was still sore about yesterday, he didn't blame Gail anymore. He wanted to talk with her; he even imagined what that conversation might sound like. He hoped she might see things differently today, but her abruptness on the phone last night was not encouraging. He thought better of calling again.

The sun rose over the tree line, and the day looked promising, though Jim couldn't even think about tackling a Saturday project. *It's Saturday*, he thought, *and Gail loves the farmers market. I wonder if she'll be there this morning.*

He got dressed in a hurry and jumped in the truck. Imagining her looking over some produce or flowers brought a bit of a grin to his face. Maybe she'd turn and see him before he made it to her and break into a smile. He loved her smile; it meant all was well. They might embrace and share a few tender words. Then he'd buy her some cut flowers and take her to the diner for breakfast.

He wheeled into the parking lot and hopped out of the truck. She liked to arrive at the market early, so he felt good about his timing. One by one, he glanced down each short row of cars until he realized that hers was still in the garage. He'd have to wander through the crowd of neighbors and strangers.

He ran the gamut of tables and tents and tailgates, and then started around a second time. There was no sign of her anywhere.

"This is silly," he mumbled shoving his hands into his pockets and making his way back to the parking lot.

Before he reached his truck, Jim heard the unmistakable rumble of a Harley pulling into the market. He turned to see the only root beer-colored Harley in the county roll up into the empty spot next to his. Not wanting to be rude by getting in his truck and driving off, he waited until Joel removed his helmet to offer an obligatory, "Morning, Joel." Joel dropped the kickstand and stepped off the bike.

"Good morning, Jim. How are you on this fine day?"

Jim meant to respond with his standard "Fine," but when he opened his mouth, the words "I've had better" came out.

"I'm sorry," Joel said. He nodded in the direction of the market. "Couldn't find what you were looking for?"

Jim dreaded where this was going. If only he had left two minutes ago. He could have kicked himself.

"Naw, I screwed up with Gail yesterday." He could hardly believe he said it, but there it was, out in the open. Jim kicked at the ground bracing himself for Joel's reproach.

"Not able to patch it up yet?"

"Nope. She left for the night, I guess. Not really sure when she's coming back." Hearing the words out loud caused him to choke up a bit.

Joel could see his pain and embarrassment. By any

standard, Jim was not a man you'd want to mess with: tall and lean, with a quick eye. His sleeves were usually rolled up, and his forearms were thick. His leathery hands were massive. Yet, he stood there leaning against his truck bed like he barely had the strength to remain upright.

"I'm heading over to the office this morning to catch up on some billing," Joel offered. "Would you like an appointment?"

Jim eyed the ground. "Sure, why not?" he replied with no enthusiasm.

"Jim, if you'd rather wait until Thursday, that's fine."

"No, no; today would be good. Thanks."

"Alright, why don't you stop by around 9:30 or so."

Jim raised his head and met Joel's eyes. There was empathy that he didn't deserve. He quickly looked down again and opened the truck door. "I'll be there."

He thought about going over to the diner to grab some breakfast, but told himself he wasn't really hungry. That wasn't exactly true; he just wasn't in the mood for talking to anybody. Instead, he drove around town for a while before catching some breakfast at a drive-thru. He took it to a little park where the river crossed under the highway and shut off the engine. The sun had chased off the morning chill and he rolled down his window. The rippling water and the croaking frogs tried to lure him into fond memories of summers past, but he staunchly refused. There was no place for comfort today.

The coffee was okay and he ate the breakfast sandwich without really tasting it. Every few minutes he checked his watch. Finally, at 9:15, he started the truck and headed for Joel's.

Joel's Harley was parked in the back, and the back door was propped open with a stone. Jim opted to use it rather than be seen going in the front door. As he came in the exit door, Joel looked up from his laptop.

"Glad you found your way in. I really didn't want to unlock the front door on a Saturday. Have a seat. I'm almost finished."

Jim sat, grateful for the silence. He was ready to own what he had done, but wasn't ready for the reprimand that was sure to follow. Was Joel going to be required to report a domestic abuse case? Would there be legal ramifications? This wouldn't go over very well at church. Jim's brain began scrambling for an excuse to leave just as Joel closed his computer and looked at him.

"You seem pretty shaken up over what happened. Wanna talk about it?"

Like a dam breached, Jim spilled every detail from the previous twenty-four hours. After twenty minutes, Jim was a puddle of shame. Joel knew better than try to appeal to what he was feeling. Instead, he opted for a teaching moment.

"I can see that you're really hurting, Jim. Can we talk about the source of that pain?"

"Sure."

"I hear and see a lot of shame here. There two types of shame: legitimate and illegitimate. Legitimate shame is what you're feeling for how you treated Gail. Your behavior was bad. You controlled her, scared her, and made it about yourself at her expense. You created such a hostile environment that she felt it prudent to vacate her own home. It's appropriate and healthy for you to feel bad about that."

Joel adjusted himself in his chair. "But there is also illegitimate shame," he continued. "Illegitimate shame says your behavior was bad, thus you are bad. Illegitimate shame is less specific, too. Rather than telling you that you're bad in this way or that way, it just attacks your whole being as bad, very bad. It takes a gargantuan leap from 'you made a mistake' to 'you are a mistake'. From 'you screwed up' to 'you are a screw-up'. I think you may be struggling with both types of shame right now. What do you think?"

"I definitely feel like a screw-up."

"Ok, let's look at the process for a minute. Shame, whether legitimate or illegitimate, is one of the most desperate feelings on the emotional scale. It initially presents as embarrassment and all the uncomfortable bodily responses that we experience, such as flushing face and ears, etc. We feel exposed, and not in a good way. Like a spotlight is on our flaws. That is shame. Our response to shame is almost always contempt. And like shame, there are two types of contempt: self-centered and others-centered. If I'm feeling like the spotlight of attention is on my flaws, self-centered contempt would play out with me remaining in the spotlight while making self-deprecating jokes about my flaws. Maybe even retelling another embarrassing story that would solidify the audience's new and lower perception of me. Responding with others-centered contempt would have me in a flurry to draw attention away from my flaws and onto someone else's. Does that make sense?"

"Yeah, I think so."

"Going back to Friday morning, did you feel any shame?"

"When Gail called and I realized that I might end up cutting it close, I think I was bracing myself for the embarrassment of being late, which was exactly what happened. Then the dog poo, and the gas on my pant leg — they must've thought I was a real yahoo."

"Ok, a real yahoo. What does that sound like?"

"I'm not sure what you mean."

"Are you a real yahoo?"

"Well, I don't think so."

"Does that sound like a self-deprecating label?"

"Yeah."

"So there's a clue to what you were feeling. Shame, then self-contempt."

"Well, it would've been pretty unprofessional to tell them to pick up after their behemoth dog leaves a pile of manure in the lawn."

"It would have felt better, though, wouldn't it?"

"I'm tellin' ya."

"But then you got home and didn't need to be professional anymore, and you unleashed on Gail."

"Yeah, I really did. So was that the somebody-else contempt?"

"Yes, others-centered contempt. You took much of the shame you were feeling and threw it at her. And not surprisingly, some of it stuck."

"What do you mean?"

"I don't know Gail's story, but her response to your accusations suggests she might believe some of them to be true."

Joel saw Jim's face drop. "What is it Jim?"

"Her dad," he whispered, unable to look up.

"What about her dad?" Joel asked.

"He called her 'ditzy'." Jim took a deep breath before finally lifted his head. "He was physical with her; knocked her around some. But more hurtful was when he called her 'ditzy'. For her, that label epitomized irresponsibility. Gail is intelligent, witty, fun, kind…she's a big picture kind of gal. But details just aren't her thing. She has tried harder than anyone to change that, and I would never call her irresponsible…except I did. Yeah, that stuck."

"Jim, I'd like to go back and look at Friday morning again."

"Okay."

"I imagine Gail has disappointed you before, without such gross results."

"Yeah, usually we talk about it and move on."

"This time was different though. There wasn't room for talking. You went right to accusations and then it became physical. There was a lot more energy in this episode."

"That's for sure."

"I'm curious where that extra energy came from."

Jim looked puzzled.

"There's a phrase among counselors. 'If the response is out of proportion to the offense, the problem is not the problem.' Looking back, does your response to Gail running out of gas, seem out of balance?"

"Yeah, pretty much. So, what was the problem then?"

Joel leaned back in his chair and tapped his pen on his chin. "Do you remember when you were sitting in Larry and Nancy's dining room?"

"Yeah."

"You were late, you smelled of gasoline and dog poo, and they really didn't have time for you. On top of all that, your price was disappointingly high. How old did you feel?"

"Huh?" Jim recalled Gail asking him that question before. He thought for a moment. "Little."

"How little?"

"Nine, I think? I guess I felt about nine years old."

Joel discreetly thumbed back through his notes until he found this entry: '9 yrs – tried to protect cousin from uncle's sexual abuse – believes he failed.' He continued to press. "Nine, was that the first time you felt that way?"

"It wasn't the first time I felt embarrassed, but it was the first time I felt so inadequate. So lacking. Putting myself out there, only to have my efforts belittled."

Joel leaned forward a little. "What happened when you were nine Jim?"

"Caroline," he whispered. "Caroline…her dad…in the barn."

Joel gave Jim a moment before he gently responded. "You were trying to care for – rescue, if you will – someone who needed help, and there was no one else. It was up to you. And sadly, your best effort left you 'measured, and found lacking'."

There was a long pause before Joel went on. "I wonder if the energy in your response to rescuing Gail may have been fueled by the unaddressed pain of your 'failed' attempt to rescue Caroline all those years ago."

"That's a stretch, don'tcha think?"

"Did they feel the same?"

"Well, yeah, exactly the same."

"Jim, as a boy in that situation, you relied on your physical strength to stop it. Unfortunately, your strength wasn't enough. You weren't enough. But now, it's a different story. You could rip your uncle limb from limb. Your strength can easily put an end to a situation. It was the case with J.R. and again with Gail."

"What else was I supposed to do? She hit me in the chest with her keys!" Jim was sitting straight up in his chair.

Joel responded calmly. "Did it hurt?"

"No, not really," he admitted. "I just needed it to stop."

"Why did you need it to stop Jim?"

"I don't know. I just needed it to."

Jim's phone buzzed. Without hesitation, he snagged it from his chest pocket. It was a text from Gail. Jim looked at Joel. "Do you mind?"

"Go ahead, take it."

Jim read the screen silently

"R u home?"

Jim responded.

"No"

"Good. I need to stop by and get a few things. I'd rather you not be there until I'm gone."

Jim's shoulders slumped forward as he keyed his reply. "I'll wait until 11:00."

"You ok?" Joel asked.

"Yeah, I'm fine," Jim lied, hoping his face wouldn't

betray him.

Joel scribbled a few lines on a fresh page of his notes, tore it out, folded it, and handed it to Jim.

"What's this?"

Joel smiled. "Homework."

Jim stowed it in his pocket with his phone. "Thanks for seeing me this morning, Doc, but I think I'm ready to go."

"You seem exhausted, Jim, but I'm glad you came in. I'll see you Thursday."

Jim got up and made his exit. As Joel finish up his notes from their session, Jim poked his head back in the door.

"Am I…I mean…is this…well…normal?"

Joel gave him an understanding smile. "Healthy? Not in a million years," he said. "But in light of your story? Yes, I'm afraid it's more normal than you know."

Jim nodded and left.

Chapter Nineteen

A Skilled Friend

Donna kept the car running while Gail gathered up some clothes with more intention than she had yesterday. She did a once-through-the-bathroom to gather her conditioner and blow dryer before she zipped the suitcase shut. Then she stopped in the kitchen to give the flowers a drink. Lord knows, Jim won't remember. She found her water bottle in the dishwasher and filled it before returning to the car.

"How was that for you?" Diana inquired.

"Fine, I suppose. Frozen pizza box on the stove and a beer bottle on the counter. Didn't take him long to revert to his bachelor days," Gail said.

Gail and Donna had met in church years ago. About twelve years ago, Donna went through counseling, and a couple years later Gail met with the same counselor. Donna liked Gail, but kept her distance until Gail had made substantial gains in addressing her own pain. Donna had no desire to be a mother figure, or the "cheese" to go with Gail's "whine." But Gail had done a lot of hard work with her counselor, and in the last couple years Gail and Donna had become fast and skilled friends.

Donna's husband, Bud, was out of town when Gail called yesterday, and Donna opened her home, spending the evening hearing Gail's side of the story. Now, Gail was just stewing.

"Sweetie," Donna said as they made their way back

to her house, "I'm really sorry you're going through this. Like I said last night, you did nothing to deserve this."

"Thanks. And thanks for running me around this morning."

"Don't mention it. Are you interested in talking about what really went on yesterday?"

Gail looked confused. "What do you mean? We spent all last night talking about what went on."

"Honey, I think you know what I mean. We spent last night talking about what happened on the outside, but we haven't talked about what was happening on the inside."

Gail looked out the side window. She could feel her neck turning red. In one motion, she pulled up her sleeve and stuck her bare forearm in front of Donna's face. It was still red where Jim had grabbed her. Donna got the message: Gail wasn't ready to go there, and Donna was willing to honor that for now.

Jim swung into the gas station and filled his tank, and also the five gallon can that was still in the back of his truck. After retrieving his receipt from the pump, he took the long way home, pulling into the driveway at 11:03. He was proud and disappointed at the same time. Proud that he honored his word, but disappointed that he hadn't at least caught a glimpse of Gail. Talking with Joel had helped, and though he still struggled with Joel's questions, he was feeling truly sorry for how he treated her the day before.

He decided to spend the rest of the day working on the Dream. By 3:30 he had done all that he could do. The seat was installed, and the left mirror that was missing and the right mirror that J.R. broke were replaced. It was, for the most part, complete. Though he was able to get the engine to fire a few times, it still wasn't running, so he planned on taking it to a mechanic that was rumored to be well-versed in vintage motorcycles.

He had backed the truck up to a small bank by the shop and laid a ramp between the lawn and the truck's tail-gate, when he noticed a slight figure slowly walking up the driveway. He stood there, straining to see if it was Gail. Everything in him wanted to run down to meet her, but his feet wouldn't move. Slowly he could make out the person's features. Familiar, yes. Gail, no.

"Hi, Mister. Jim." J.R.'s voice carried across the yard. "Is Miss Gail home?"

It surprised Jim that he wasn't more disappointed that it was J.R. "I'm sorry, J.R., she's not here. Somethin' I can do for ya?"

J.R.'s eyes dropped, trying to hide his disappoint-ment.

Jim pressed. "Whatcha got there J.R.?"

"Candy bars," he answered hesitantly.

"Are ya sellin' them?"

"Yes sir."

"Raisin' money for something'?"

"Yes."

Something inside Jim needed to prove that he was good. "I like chocolate. What kind are ya sellin?"

J.R. was a bit bewildered. Mister Jim didn't seem nearly as scary as the last time he was there. He opened his box and began digging through the chocolate bars.

"Milk chocolate with almonds, medium dark with caramel, medium with peppermint, and dark with sea salt," he said. "They're two dollars apiece, or a box of three of each for twenty dollars."

Jim had no idea what he would do with it, but choc-olate suddenly sounded like a good idea. He took some cash out of his wallet. "Put me down for two boxes."

J.R. pulled a wrinkled piece of paper from his pocket

and wrote down Mister Jim's order. Then he looked up with a smile.

"Thank you, Mister Jim. Thank you very much!"

Jim sensed the shift in the boy's demeanor and hoped to capitalize on it. "Say, do you think I could talk you into doing me a favor?" J.R.'s smile disappeared, but Jim quickly continued. "I'm getting ready to put that old motorcycle in my truck and I'm wondering if you could sit on it and steer while I push it down here from the garage. If you'd rather not, that's okay."

"You want me to sit on your motorcycle?" J.R.'s eyes got huge. "Sure!" Dropping his box of candy bars, he stuffed the order form and cash into his pocket and followed Mister Jim up to the garage.

At the garage door, J.R. hesitated a moment before going in. His memory of the last time he was in this garage shook him a little. But after taking a brave breath, he walked in and right up to the motorcycle.

"I'll hold the bike if you're ready to climb on," Jim said.

J.R. had to step onto the foot peg to be able to get his other leg over the seat. Jim reached forward with his foot and released the kickstand, then started pushing the bike toward the door.

"What if it starts going too fast?" J.R. wanted to know. His voice was a mix of excitement and concern.

"You can squeeze the brake lever or push down on the foot brake on the right."

Jim started trotting as he pushed. "Do you want to go fast?"

"This is fast enough."

They came around the shop to where the truck was parked. "Gently press down on the foot brake and aim for the center of the ramp," Jim told him, and J.R. did exactly as instructed.

"Okay, J.R., squeeze the front brake lever once we're in the truck."

Again, J.R. followed his orders, bringing the bike to a stop right where Jim wanted it. Jim put the kickstand down and helped J.R. climb off.

"Well done young man. Well done!"

"Thanks! That was fun. I can't wait to tell my dad I drove a motorcycle!"

Jim chuckled to himself as he strapped the bike in, while J.R. retrieved his chocolate and disappeared down the driveway.

That evening Jim sat down at his computer with a slice of leftover pizza on a paper plate. The house was especially quiet without Gail there. He aimlessly checked his e-mail, the weather, and a news site before remembering he had homework. Reluctantly, he pulled Joel's paper from his shirt pocket. It had four questions scribbled on it:

1. What options (or resources) did you have when challenging your uncle?
2. What options (or resources) did you have when challenging Gail?
3. What label felt like it was showing at Larry and Nancy's?
4. Why did you need it to stop?

Jim pushed the list off to the side and took his pizza back to the living room to find a movie on TV. His phone buzzed; it was a text.

"Hi Jim. Missed you on the roof today. Hope everything's OK."

"OH, CRAP!"

He had totally forgotten about the roofing project. They needed his ladder, too. All day long Jim had felt like he was forgetting something, but he just attributed it to all the disruption going on. Pressing through the shame, he keyed just four words: “Sorry, something came up.”

Donna had a commitment that afternoon, so Gail opted for the chaise lounge next to Donna’s pool. She hadn’t thought to bring her suit, so she just rolled her shorts up into a cuff, and drew her shirt up to get a little sun on her tummy. Armed with a glass of iced tea, Donna’s sunglasses, and a good book, she was ready for a well-deserved break.

The sunglasses didn’t fit very well. Unfortunately, Gail’s were on the visor of her car. The sweat on her face didn’t help either, as they kept working their way down her nose. Her face wasn’t the only part of her that was perspiring, and the pool looked inviting. Even though no one else was around, she resisted the idea of borrowing one of Donna’s suits and going for a swim.

The sun crested high overhead. She tried to plow through another chapter. A stalwart bee refused to leave her tea alone. The more she swatted at him, the more determined he was. Hot and miserable, and having read the same paragraph three times, she got up, emptied her pockets, kicked off her sandals, and dove in.

The silent weightlessness consumed her as she curled her knees to her chest and exhaled just enough to settle on the bottom of the pool. She lingered there until her lungs started to feel like a vacuum. Pushing off the bottom, she broke the surface, took a breath and returned to the bottom again.

I wonder if this is what a preborn infant feels, she thought. *Suspended in warm liquid, muffled sounds, blurry vision, safely hidden from all the outside chaos.*

She pushed to the surface again, and this time rolled onto her back. Her eyes cleared; it looked as though a bag of cotton balls were spilled across the sky. Small and puffy, they lazily shifted as they dawdled eastward.

Now you can't float on your back unless you're relaxed, and Gail was made keenly aware of how much tension she was still holding onto. Mentally, she isolated each part of her body, forcing her neck, shoulders, arms, torso, and all the way to her feet, to slacken. She was surprised how uptight she still was.

Floating with no resistance, her world quieted enough that she allowed herself to hear Donna's earlier observation: "We haven't talked about what was happening on the inside."

She knew Donna was right. Yes, Jim's behavior was way out of line, but her response was also out of proportion with his accusations. What was her part, she wondered? And try as she might, she was striking out at seeing the bigger picture.

That evening as the two women sat down to dinner, Gail started. "I'm sorry for how I responded to you in the car this morning. I was still really mad."

"You don't say," Donna replied with a grin.

"I know if I want any kind of resolution, I need to get to the root of my part in this," Gail continued. "I'm just struggling to see my part."

"I know, it's really hard sometimes, especially if we're still angry."

"Yeah. In the pool this afternoon — I used your pool by the way — I realized how angry I still was. More than angry, actually. It's like my body was still afraid."

"Were you afraid of Jim yesterday?"

"No, not really. I knew he wouldn't hurt me. He just wanted it stop."

"Beneath the anger lies the fear, right?"

"That's what we were taught."

"So, what were you afraid of?"

"I'm not sure. Before he grabbed my arm, I was

already triggered."

They both sat silently while Gail replayed the scene in her mind. Her hand went limp and her fork settled onto her plate. "It's like my world went from color to white hot."

"When?"

"When he said I was ditzy."

"He called you 'ditzy'?"

Gail paused a moment. "No, he called me irresponsible." Her eyes started to puddle.

"What's wrong, honey?"

Gail remembered feeling the disappointment sink deep into little heart when her Daddy called her ditzy. He'd chuckle whenever he did it, but it deflated any hope of garnering his approval. Now the tears fell from her cheek onto the plate.

"Gail, honey, what are your tears for?"

Gail looked across the table at her friend. "Daddy would call me ditzy. He thought it was playful, but it always hurt. I would forget stuff, like leaving my homework at school, or my gym clothes at home. One time I went to bed without putting my horse in the barn for the night. He made me go out in my nightie to round her up from the pasture and put her in the stall. My feet were so cold. I remember him chiding me as I went back up the stairs. 'You are such a ditz. How will you ever care for a husband, or a family, if you can't even care for a horse?' It haunts me. Every time I miss something or forget to do something, his words haunt me. What if I am too irresponsible to be a good wife? Or mom? Jim was right. I should have gotten gas before letting the tank get so low."

Donna paused for a moment before responding. "Sweetie," she said, "I'm so sorry your daddy planted that seed of doubt in your tender little soul. I'll bet you were full of wonder and imagination as a girl. And as a woman, you're more responsible than most." Donna paused again. "You don't talk much about your dad. Were you close?"

"I wanted to be. Oh, how I wanted to be his little girl! But, no. I was always on guard, always feeling judged, sometimes by his words, sometimes with his hands."

By now Donna was leaning in so close that her shirt was in her plate. "Oh, darling, no little girl should ever know the anxiety of not trusting her daddy. I'm so, so sorry that's part of your story."

It was clear they were done eating, though neither had hardly taken a bite. "Why don't you go out on the deck, honey?" Donna suggested. "I'll clear the table and join you in a minute."

Gail gladly obliged. It was cooler now, and Donna's deck was lovely with a variety of comfy places to relax among the potted flowers and hanging bird feeders. Donna reappeared a few minutes later. They sat in silence, watching hummingbirds come and go from the feeder. The sun was hinting that the evening was drawing to a close when Donna pressed once again.

"What were you afraid of, Gail?"

Gail let the question sink deep, and the crickets sang a verse and a half before she replied. "That my daddy was right," she said with a distant lilt, followed by another lingering pause. "That I really don't deserve a husband, or a family. That I'm not enough."

Donna reached over and took her hand. Without another word they watched the sun bid farewell before they got up and went inside.

Chapter Twenty

Where Do I Belong?

Jim hung his leg over the edge of the bed — except it wasn't the bed. Apparently, he had fallen asleep on the couch. The paper plate and half-eaten pizza were on the floor next to the remote. At least he had turned the TV off.

It took a minute to realize it was Sunday. Church was a given on Sundays. For a moment he processed his new situation. How would he explain showing up to church without Gail. That was a can of worms he had no intention of opening. But what if Gail went? He played that scenario out in his head, too. If she was at all open to an apology, maybe he could talk to her. But what if she was still angry? He didn't have the courage or desire to risk being ridiculed in front of his peers.

He poured a cup of coffee and stepped out onto the deck to clear his mind. Sitting down at the table, he let his head tilt back as he scanned the morning sky. It was clear, with dark blue in the west, succumbing to a robin egg blue in the east. A few stars still had the nerve to compete with the rising sun, and a sliver of moon hung just above the horizon. The blue jays were complaining at the bird feeder, and Jim could hear a pair of loons back on the lake, calling out to each other with their familiar forlorn cry. He could relate. It was a perfect morning in every way — except Gail wasn't here. If he could have, he would have joined the loons in their lonely lament.

His thoughts were interrupted with the sound of someone coming up the driveway. The lights were off inside, so maybe if he stayed really quiet, they would leave. Sure enough, he soon heard the crunch of tires on the gravel fade into the distance. It was safe now, so he got up and went inside to get another cup of coffee. He decided to skip church; it seemed prudent and easily justified, especially in light of missing yesterday's work bee. He filled his cup and turned.

There stood Gail.

He quickly set his mug down on the counter. He was more than thrilled to see her, yet, wasn't sure of the intention of her visit. He wanted to hug her so badly, but didn't dare. He awkwardly plunged his hands deep into his pockets and just stood there.

Gail finally broke the silence. "Jim, we need to talk."

Jim exhaled; this felt hopeful. *Maybe talking means staying,* he thought. "Yes, talk, talking is good, we should talk. May I go first?"

"Ok. If you'd like"

Jim tried to read her face, her posture, anything for a clue as how to proceed. At a complete loss, he simply blurted out, "Oh, Gail. I am so sorry I grabbed you and yelled at you, and that I didn't fill your car the night before like you asked, and blamed you for my bad day. I'm sorry I caused you to not feel safe here." He paused to breathe. He wanted to take her hand or touch her arm so badly, but refrained and continued his apology. "I'm so sorry I said you were irresponsible. That is not true. You are one of the most responsible people I know when it comes to stuff that really matters."

Gail's brow furrowed as she looked him in the eye. "What do you mean, 'stuff that really matters'?"

"Stuff, about people. You are so attentive to detail when it comes to caring for people, especially Kyle and me."

Jim knew she wasn't about to be sweet-talked, but sensed that she was appreciating his words, as she allowed herself to smile slightly. But then her serious face returned.

"Jim, it really hurt me when you said I was irresponsible. What I heard you say was that I was ditzy. Jim, I know you're not my dad, yet the anger I unleashed on you was fueled with the hurt and longings that I felt toward him. I'm ashamed and sorry for the way I responded to you." Her eyes probed his for a response. "Did that make any sense to you?"

"I think so. I'm so sorry too. I'm not as clear as you are yet about why I was so upset. I talked to Joel about it, but this is still pretty new to me. I am sorry. Can I get you a cup of coffee?"

"No, thank you. Donna and I had breakfast on the way over. I'm not going to church this morning. I'm gonna change and take a walk."

"I wasn't planning on going to church either. Would you like me to come with you?"

"Jim, I love you and I forgive you, but I'm still pretty raw and not quite ready to trust you. I'm gonna take my journal down to my spot by the pond, alone."

"Okay. You think maybe we could get lunch when you get back?"

He was hoping to hear that she would only be gone a couple hours, but all she said was, "I don't know."

Gail realized her response bordered on withholding, but that wasn't her intent. She knew she loved Jim; but at the moment she just didn't like him very much. She also knew that "not liking him" was more about her than him.

She slipped on a pair of sweat pants and pulled a hoodie over her t-shirt. Sitting on the edge of the bed to put on her old running shoes, she let her hand sink deep into the down comforter. It was white with lilacs embroidered into it. She had fallen in love with it when it caught her eye at the fair. The comforter they had was just fine, but she really loved this one. And even though Jim wasn't a fan of frilly flowers, he was happy to oblige.

She found her journal and favorite pen in the living room, along with her Bible. "See ya, Jim. I'll be back in a while."

Everything in him wanted to follow her, but he had returned to his chair on the deck with his coffee, and there he stayed.

Gail skirted the edge of the pond until she came to an old fallen beech tree. Its large trunk lay parallel to the shore a couple feet from the water. Deer had a worn path between it and the pond. A portion of the trunk had a smooth, flat spot on top, and it was Gail's favorite place to sit and think. She set her journal down and opened her Bible to Jeremiah 29:11. The dog-eared pages nearly fell open to that passage on their own. Gail loved this verse as much as she loved this place. Her eyes fell to the words highlighted in yellow:

11 "For I know the plans I have for you," says the LORD. "They are plans for good and not for disaster, to give you a future and a hope."

"God," she prayed out loud, "I remember how many times I felt like I had no future. Wondering if I had what it would take to trust a man…to have a family. I look back over the years and I can see the success that You had in store for me. I've experienced Your goodness. Why do I forget so easily and just assume my life is going down the crapper every time I get triggered?" Gail's eyes followed the page to the verses that followed:

12 "In those days when you pray, I will listen. 13 "If you look for me wholeheartedly, you will find me. I will be found by you," says the LORD.

"Thank You, Lord, for hearing me…for seeing me… for being safe for me no matter what. Thank You for not hiding or withholding from me." She continued to read:

14 "I will end your captivity and restore your fortunes. I will gather you out of the nations where I sent you, and will bring you home again to your own land."

"Lord," she prayed, "so often I feel held captive by what Daddy did. It warps everything. I know you can set me free. I know I'm freer now than I was ten years ago. But I hate when my story still trips me up. Please restore me. Help me to feel like I belong in my own home."

Her own words surprised her. Did she believe it was her home, her car? Why was she so quick to leave them? It was Jim she was mad at, right? She sat quietly and let the questions ruminate. Did the house and car represent the same security she longed for with her dad, only to train herself not to embrace them for the pain that would surely follow? Did she still keep Jim slightly at bay under the same reasoning? "Jesus, help me to trust more and protect myself less."

A memory emerged. Gail was just sixteen and it was 11:08 p.m. She had borrowed her mom's car and driven her friends to the football game, and then to the dance. The new-found freedom her driver's license afforded was exhilarating. It had been a perfect evening, and after dropping off the last of the gang, she headed home. She parked in the driveway and shut off the headlights. The moon was so bright that she hardly noticed the porch light wasn't on. Gail hated to see the evening end, and she hesitated before pulling the screen door open. Grabbing the knob on the front door, she reluctantly gave it a twist. Nothing. She twisted it again, and again, still nothing. Then she noticed a note in her dad's handwriting, taped to the door. Curfew was 11:00. Her eyes blurred, and her mind was reeling. An internal pendulum was swinging hard, from responsible young adult allowed to take the car, to irresponsible child who couldn't keep track of time. She slowly backed away from the door, slumped back into the car, and pulled her collar snug around her neck. Gail couldn't remember a longer or more lonely night. It would be the last time she sat behind the wheel for a month, because her driving privileges were promptly suspended the next morning. There was a pulling away that night. Gail felt herself choose distance from her dad. It was a distance she both hated and needed at the same time. She did not want to repeat the posture with Jim.

Gail set her Bible down and picked up her journal. While thumbing through it to find the first blank page, she stopped abruptly at an entry from the prior week. Her eyes grazed the page and settled on some verses she had meditated on and written out. It was Colossians 3:10-15.

10 Put on your new nature, and be renewed as you learn to know your Creator and become like him. 11 In this new life, it doesn't matter if you are a Jew or a Gentile, circumcised or uncircumcised, barbaric, uncivilized, slave, or free. Christ is all that matters, and he lives in all of us. 12 Since God chose you to be the holy people he loves, you must clothe yourselves with tenderhearted mercy, kindness, humility, gentleness, and patience. 13 Make allowance for each other's faults, and forgive anyone who offends you. Remember, the Lord forgave you, so you must forgive others. 14 Above all, clothe yourselves with love, which binds us all together in perfect harmony. 15 And let the peace that comes from Christ rule in your hearts. For as members of one body you are called to live in peace. And always be thankful.

Gail's eyes became blurry. She had written this verse down to share with another friend who was struggling. Little did she know how much she needed these words to call her from her own perspective and see the bigger picture. She smiled as she looked upward. "It's not about my earning or deserving, or holding on tight, is it?" She felt the tension in her chest dissipate as she picked up her pen, and on the following pages she continued to flesh out what forgiveness might look like while maintaining healthy boundaries.

Gail's return that morning had lit a fire under Jim. Hoping to gather a little more insight on why he behaved so poorly, he found the homework Joel had torn from his notebook, and returned to the deck. He read the first question, and then read it again:

1. What options (or resources) did you have when challenging your uncle?

It wasn't easy going back into that scene, much less taking an objective inventory of the resources at his disposal at the time. It seemed like attacking his uncle was more of a reflex than a thought-out response. He finally wrote down, "My strength." It was all he could come up with. He moved on to the next question:

2. What options (or resources) did you have when challenging Gail?

Jim thought. His voice? No, that didn't really seem to be working with Gail. So once again he wrote, "My strength" and moved on to question three:

3. What label felt like it was showing at Larry and Nancy's?

Jim remembered the discussion he and Joel had about labels. The image of the pieces of wood hanging around his neck, with a word carved into each one, was forefront in his mind. He replayed the fiasco at Larry and Nancy's house, and was able to connect quickly with the feeling, but struggled to put a word to it. At first he wrote 'Little.' Then erased it and wrote 'Irresponsible.' That felt a little closer, but he erased that, too. 'Inconsequential.' That was it. On that miserable Friday morning, he had felt like he didn't matter — that his plans, time, and work didn't matter. He felt of little consequence and easily overlooked. Feeling good about his progress, Jim proceeded to question four:

4. Why did you need it to stop?

Jim let his mind wander back. As the events of Friday morning replayed, he noticed his body becoming tense all over again, especially picturing Gail reaching into her purse for the keys. He squirmed in his chair and sipped his coffee. Distracting himself with watching a pair of hummingbirds drink from the feeder, the image of Gail's face, twisted in rage, began to fade. Jim got up abruptly. *I should probably fill this feeder*, he thought as he reached up and released it from the hook. Now the image had successfully disappeared, and as he mixed the warm water and sugar, he felt much better about himself.

Rehanging the feeder, refreshing his coffee, and checking his phone kept him feeling better for the next few minutes; in fact, they kept him from feeling at all.

Back on the deck, his eyes glanced at the question again. Why did you need it to stop? This time he thwarted the imagery before it began. But without it, his mind was blank. "I needed to maintain order, for Gail's sake," he told himself. But no. As honorable as he tried to make it sound, he knew that wouldn't fly. Was he afraid? That rang hollow, too. He finally settled on writing 'I don't know.'

"There, that's done," he said out loud as he folded the paper and put it back into his shirt pocket.

Gail eventually returned, and the two of them spent the rest of the day maintaining an awkward distance, trying to disguise it as necessary busyness.

Chapter Twenty-One

What Else Was I Supposed To Do?

Jim rose early the next morning. When Gail shuffled sleepy-eyed into the kitchen in her PJs and slippers, Jim met her with two plates, eggs over-easy, toast with strawberry jam, and a half orange each, peeled and separated. Two cups of coffee already waited at the table along with silverware and cloth napkins.

"What's all this?" she asked, a bit guarded.

"Breakfast, dear." Jim searched her face for a hint of approval, but it was hard to read.

"Thank you, Jim. This looks nice," she said matter-of-factly. She sat at the table as Jim brought over the salt and pepper shakers and joined her. Reaching out, he took her hand. It was a habit formed many years ago; holding each other's hand when they prayed at the table. Habit outranked emotion as Gail rested her hand in Jim's. It felt right, good. It also exposed the disparity between what she thought she felt toward him and what she was actually feeling. She didn't hear a word he was praying until he said "amen." She gently squeezed his hand, and when he looked up, she whispered, "Thank you."

They enjoyed breakfast, and afterward Jim cleared the table, rinsed the dishes, and put them in the dishwasher. Then he washed and dried the frying pan and put it away, and wiped down the stove. As he said good-bye before heading out to the shop, he hoped their routine may have returned.

but rather than poking her head around the corner for a quick kiss, Gail simply responded with, "Have a good day." Jim was neither surprised nor discouraged. Breakfast went well, he thought.

The week passed quickly. Jim had to work a couple long days to catch up from taking the previous Friday off. Their exchanges were cordial, even pleasant. Gail was still cool, and Jim wasn't sure if she was still hurting or punishing him. But either way, he didn't blame her; he was happy just to have her home.

Thursday afternoon found Jim sitting in Joel's office again.

"How is your week going?" Joel started out.

"Better since we talked on Saturday. Gail came home." Jim filled him in on the details.

"That's great," Joel said. "Did you get a chance to look at your homework?"

"I did," Jim announced with a bit of pride, reaching into his pocket and pulling out the paper Joel had scribbled the four questions on. Jim laid it on the desk and tried to smooth the wrinkles out.

"Let's take a look," said Joel. He seemed pleased to see that Jim had put some time into it. "What was the first question?"

Jim cleared his throat and read aloud. "Question one: What options (or resources) did you have when challenging your uncle?"

"How did you answer?"

"I put down 'My strength."

"That's good, Jim. Any other resources?'

Jim shook his head. He couldn't think of any.

"Okay, what's next?"

"Question two: What options (or resources) did you have when challenging Gail?"

"And what did you write down for that?"

"All I could come up with was my strength again."

"Let's think about it some more. Were there any other options for you, other than grabbing her arm?"

Jim felt put on the spot. Joel wouldn't be asking if he didn't think there was. He drew a blank as he replayed the scene in his mind. Not one single alternative was obvious. "Sorry, Joel. I got nothin'."

"It's okay, Jim. It's okay." Joel flipped back a couple pages in his notes. "When you were nine years old, the resources you had available to you were very limited. Due to your age, even your strength was limited. When you talked to your dad about what you saw, it didn't help at all, and maybe even made it worse, right?"

"Yeah. I never did see Sammy after that."

"If I were a betting man, I'd bet no one ever talked to you about conflict resolution. You were on your own, and eventually your strength was enough, so that became your 'go to' remedy when life wasn't working for you."

"But this was the first time I ever grabbed Gail like that."

"Yes, but you've grabbed others, right?"

"Yeah."

"Would you consider your strength only physical?"

"It kinda seems that way."

"What about your words, your tone, your look, your posture, your intolerance? Aren't they all a part of it? Does it seem like you resolve conflict with power?"

"Well, I'm the man. What else am I supposed to do?"

Leaning forward slightly, Joel smiled. "That is a most splendid question."

Jim was confused, but maybe a little relieved. At least they were on the same page.

"Your answer will be next week's homework," Joel said.

"Oh come on, Doc; I already told you I have no idea

what else I could have done."

"I know, but you will. Let's go to the next question."

Jim was ready to move on. He took a breath. "Three: What label felt like it was showing at Larry and Nancy's? Inconsequential. That's how I felt, like my time and energy weren't worth a darn to anybody."

"That sounds painful, Jim. And it's a very descriptive word."

"It felt just like when Daddy told me to prune the orchard, but didn't tell me how. I wasted all that time doing it wrong." Jim was feeling pretty good that he was able to make that connection all on his own, and apparently, Joel was impressed too.

"Good job! Now, are you inconsequential?"

"No! And I have a list of happy clients who would agree with me!"

Joel smiled at Jim's enthusiasm. "That's right, and I'm sure the list is much longer than just your clients." Joel made a note and then continued. "How about number four?"

"Four: Why did you need it to stop?" Jim looked up at Joel. "I don't know."

"Is that what you wrote?"

Jim held the wrinkled paper out to him.

"This might seem unfair, but I have always felt that 'I don't know' often means 'I don't want to think about it that hard.' Let's try again. Why did you need it to stop?"

"I thought about it a lot. I was just so uncomfortable inside."

"How so?"

"Like anxious, I guess."

"So, you needed the anxiousness to stop."

"Yeah."

"Did you feel in the spotlight?"

"Yes."

"Did you feel accused?"

"Yes, especially when Gail said running out of gas was my fault."

"Did you feel accused before then?"

Jim thought for a moment. "Yeah, when Nancy thought my price was too high."

"How about before that?"

A puzzled look came over Jim's face.

"Let's go back to when you received the call from Gail that she was out of gas. What was the very first feeling you had in response to that?"

Joel gave Jim plenty of time to search. "I felt bad for Gail," Jim finally said.

"Excellent. Then what?"

"I remembered what she had said the night before, about being low on gas. Normally I take care of stuff like that if she mentions it, but I didn't."

"What did you feel?"

"Like I let her down."

"Can you name the emotion?"

"Shame." Jim wore it as he said it, his eyes lowering along with his voice.

"What did you do with that shame?"

"You mean like follow it up with contempt?"

"Is that what you did?"

"Yeah, at myself for a bit. But then I was mad at her, so 'somebody-other-than-me' contempt?"

Joel couldn't help but smile a little. "Sounds like it. Then what happened?"

"She took a little of it, then she threw it back on me."

"What did that feel like?"

"Like shame all over again. Like the spotlight you talked about. It was on me, and I couldn't get it off. She wouldn't take it, and I had to get it off me. I had to make it stop!"

Joel let the weight of his statement sink in, then

posed the question again. "So, if you had to venture your best guess, why did it have to stop?"

Jim hesitated before proceeding cautiously:

"It *had* to stop, because, the shame I felt for disappointing her was *just too painful.*"

Joel concurred with an empathetic nod.

"So I'm the one who pulled out and polished up the 'inconsequential sign' for everyone to see?" Jim asked.

Joel didn't respond; he didn't have too. The light bulbs were starting to come on for Jim.

"Why would I do that to myself?" Jim asked.

"Because you still believe some of those old signs are true?"

"Aw, crap." Jim shook his head. "What do I do?"

Joel smiled again. "That brings us to next week's homework. Remember the phrase you used, 'I'm the man, what else was I supposed to do'?"

"Yeah."

"I'd like you imagine you're nine or ten years old, and your dad is treating you much like the way you treated to Gail."

"That'll be easy." Jim muttered.

"I'd like you to imagine him stopping and asking you, 'What else am I supposed to do?' What would your nine- or ten-year-old self want to say to him?"

"That's my homework?"

"That's your homework." Joel ended the session with a glance at the wall clock. "I'll see you next week."

"See ya, Doc."

For several days, Jim and Gail's conversations had been limited to the logistics of living together. At dinner, he thought about sharing some of what he and Joel had discussed, but there wasn't a natural opportunity, so he let it pass.

Later in the evening, though, Gail was on the couch with a book. He sat down in his chair and decided to just put it out there. "Joel wants me to imagine myself as a boy, with my dad treating me like I treated you the other day. He wonders what I might say to my dad if he stopped and asked me, 'I'm a man, what else am I supposed to do?'"

"Is that what you said to Joel? 'I'm a man, what else am I supposed to do?'!"

Crap. That didn't go at all like I was hoping. Jim wanted to defend himself, but was afraid that whatever he came up with would only make it worse. So, he sat there silent. Gail got up abruptly and went into the kitchen. Jim didn't know what to do. "Dear Jesus, please help me. Help us." Prayer seemed like the only thing he could do that wasn't detrimental.

Gail stood gripping the edge of the kitchen sink. She couldn't believe what she just heard. She muttered the words under her breath with growing disdain. "What else was I supposed to do? What else was I supposed to do? I'll tell you what else you were supposed to do, you bloomin' nincompoop!" Her blood pressure was rising.

Pulling a glass from the cabinet, she drew a cold drink of water, giving her nerves a chance to settle. Why would Joel even suggest such an asinine question? She had enough respect for him to think twice about it, and wondered if maybe it got lost in translation. Jim had been known to do that on occasion. "Lord, what's up here?" she prayed. "I need your perspective on this, and I really don't want to fight."

She set her glass down and leaned on the counter, running the question through her head one more time. *"He wonders what I might say to my dad if he stopped and asked me..."* She closed her eyes and smiled, realizing Joel was trying to get Jim to connect with what little Jimmy was feeling way back then. She remembered the first time her counselor had proposed a similar question to her. "What did nine-year-old Gail feel?" Alone, invisible, never enough, ditzy...the labels had filled her soul. But years later, her counselor offered an honest perspective that challenged the conclusions she had drawn as a little girl. Lies about her value were exposed, and the truth was offered in it place.

This must be Joel's intention. For Jim's sake, she wanted to capitalize on the moment before the opportunity got away. But how?

She returned to the living room with two cups of coffee. Handing one to Jim, she settled back onto the couch, and proceeded. "So, if your daddy was ridiculing you, or being physical with you to make a point, and then he stopped and asked what else he was supposed to do, what would you say to him?"

Jim wasn't sure if this was a set-up or if she was being helpful. She had brought him a cup of coffee; hardly a spiteful move. Shifting in his chair didn't relieve the uneasiness he felt.

"It's hard to imagine. I don't know what I would say. What would you say?"

Gail didn't fall for his attempt to pass it off. She asked again, "What might you want to say to him?"

Jim thought her voice seemed softer, and she tilted her head just a tinge as she asked. *This feels a little more like the old Gail,* he thought.

She gently continued to probe. "What if you were assured your daddy wouldn't be offended? What if you knew he would listen to you, like he wanted your input? What would you want to say then?" She was looking directly into Jim's eyes as she spoke, searching.

Everything about this conversation felt risky to Jim, but he had started it. He drew in a long breath and answered slowly. "I'd ask him why he was so angry. Could he just sit down and talk to me? Explain if I'd done something wrong, and show me how to do it better? Could he put his hand on my shoulder like he was proud of me instead of angry at me?"

The images prompted emotions that Jim wasn't prepared for, but he pressed on. "What if you said I was good for something instead of always pointing out where I wasn't enough? What if you said you liked me? What if you treated me like you liked me?" Jim's eyes were spilling over, but he couldn't stop. "Why did you sell the Dream? Why didn't you adore mom like I adored her? Why didn't you beat the crap out of your brother when I told you what he was doing to Caroline? Why didn't you hold me after knocking me off my bike instead of walking away? Why did you have to knock me down in the first place? What if you thought of someone besides yourself, you selfish son-of-a …?"

A dam had broken inside. Jim was finally putting words, loud words, to feelings that he had stuffed since childhood, and Gail was writing frantically. "What if you figured out a way to make me me feel like you approved of me? Why couldn't you ever say you loved me?"

Jim felt very big and, strangely, very small at the same time. His body shook a bit as he sank deep into the chair. He was done.

Gail put down her pen and reached over, placing her hand on his forearm. "I'm really proud of you Jim," she said softly. "Really proud."

He pushed through the shame that was trying to crowd in and looked at her. Her cheeks were wet too.

"Thank you," he whispered.

Chapter Twenty-Two

I Already Have

Not much was said for the rest of the evening, and the next morning started as if that past week had never happened. Jim received a call from the mechanic who was working on the Dream. The parts had come in, and it would likely be ready by midweek. Jim was almost giddy with the news, something he hadn't felt in a long, long time. He put in a few more long days so he could cut out early on Friday to pick up the bike.

On Wednesday afternoon a car pulled up the driveway and stopped at the house. Jim wasn't interested in being bothered and continued working until he heard the shop door open.

"Can I help you?" he hollered without looking up.

"Naw, just wondering if mom is home yet?"

"The word 'mom' grabbed his attention, and he spun around to see Kyle standing there.

"How are ya, Dad?"

"I'm great. I didn't know you were coming home."

"It was a last-minute thing. I got a couple days off and thought I'd bring home some stuff from the apartment to lighten your load later."

"So mom doesn't know you're here?"

"No, I just found out about the schedule change last night. I thought I might surprise her."

"Go get your car and park it behind the shop," Jim

said. "She'll be home around 4:30. You should be waiting for her in the kitchen when she comes in."

Kyle smiled and followed the plan. He never quite knew what mood he might find his dad in. Playful was a pleasant surprise.

An hour later, Gail pressed the button and waited for the garage door to fully ascend before pulling in. She worked later than she planned and hadn't taken anything out of the freezer for dinner. Chinese sounded so good, but if felt too indulgent for a week night. They couldn't just go out every time she came home tired. She gathered her purse and a few groceries from the passenger seat and trudged inside.

"Hi Mom!"

She nearly dropped the groceries. "OH MY GOSH!" She threw her arms around Kyle's neck and babbled something, but he had no way of possibly understanding it among her blubbering. She finally let go of his neck, put down her purse, and returned to the mannerly mother she was. "When did you get here? I didn't see your car. Does your dad know you're here? How long can you stay? Is everything alright?" Kyle helped her put groceries away as he patiently answered each inquiry.

Eventually, Jim came in to silently enjoy the show. "Look who's here, babe! He can stay for a few days. Isn't that wonderful?"

"It's wonderful, hon."

Jim smiled. "How 'bout we order Chinese for dinner?"

Gail looked like she was going to cry. "Yes please!"

After dinner, they headed to the living room to continue their visit. Jim had kicked off his work boots at the door, and it felt good to sit for a spell. He was tempted to close his eyes, but thought better of it. The conversation about how he wished his own dad had shown up for him was still fresh in his mind. He wondered if Kyle had ever felt the same way. Jim hoped it wasn't too late to try.

"So Kyle, how are the plans coming together for your trip to Mexico?" Jim asked.

"Uh, good." Kyle was a little taken back by his dad's interest. "Really good, in fact. Housing is arranged. We've raised about eighty percent of our goal for funding the projects at the school, and about fifty percent of our travel and living expenses."

Jim nodded. "Do you have fund raisers coming up to cover the balance?"

Gail raised her eyebrows slightly and held her tongue. She had so many questions stirring, but she was happy to let Jim continue the dialogue.

"The youth group will finish up a three-month can drive next week," Kyle went on. "They have a semi-trailer of returnable cans and bottles almost full. We're pretty confident that will cover the school's needs."

"That's exciting," Jim said.

"And the church staff is going to host a really nice dinner and silent auction for the community, so that should get us fairly close. Then it's just our personal spending money on top of that."

Jim made a point to maintain eye contact, and he really wanted to ask another question, but he couldn't think of one. Gail saw the opening and stepped in.

"How's your Spanish coming along?"

Jim remained engaged but was grateful for Gail's assistance.

Later that evening, Gail was rinsing the glasses. She stepped aside so Kyle could toss the paper plates in the waste basket under the sink. "What's up with Dad?" he whispered.

"Wanna be a little more specific?"

"Well, he asked about my trip, and then he listened like he wanted to know. I just wasn't expecting that, I guess."

"Gail smiled. "Don't underestimate your old man. He's full of surprises."

Thursday afternoon found Jim in Joel's office, clutching the notes Gail had scribbled down for him. He felt ambivalent as he laid them on Joel's desk. He wasn't sure why, but there was a sense of pride and accomplishment for addressing his dad in light of his childhood memories. But he was also a little embarrassed displaying tenderness toward the little boy in his story. It was all just so unfamiliar.

Joel reached over and picked up the list. Jim silently watched Joel's eyes moisten as he read line after line. Then he looked up and waited for Jim's eyes before responding intently.

"Jim," he began, "no little boy deserves to live under the anxiety of an angry father. I'm sorry he wouldn't talk to you…with you…listen to you. I'm sorry that his touch made you wince, instead of relax. I hate that he led you to believe that you were never enough. Jim, every child deserves the security of seeing their dad adore their mom…you included."

Jim's unblinking eyes remained riveted on Joel's as he listened.

"When you share about seeing Caroline with your uncle…you were braver than your daddy could ever hope to be. It's such a loss that you never got to experience the down-in-your-gut warmth of receiving your daddy's approval, and that you didn't get to learn what it looked like to pass it on. Jim, even though you had a tender heart to receive and hold your dad's love, I hate that he left it empty."

Jim drank in every word. Each one was foreign, and a bit awkward to hear, but welcome just the same. "Thank you," was all he could say as they each pulled a tissue from the box.

Jim was in the shop by six the next morning. He

wanted to get the all the mantel pieces stained so they could dry over the weekend. He also wanted to be done by noon so he could pick up the Dream. Each piece rested on a rack, waiting for the stain to be applied and wiped off. Nowhere was Jim more patient and thorough than in the paint room. Years had taught him that all of the craftsmanship he exercised in the shop could be diminished to waste with a poor finish.

It took about thirty minutes to get the color just right. After each piece had a once-over with a tack cloth, the staining began. He would often choose lumber with specific grain patterns for certain pieces of a project, and though he had an idea how they might look, it was still quite gratifying to see the woodgrain come to life as it was wetted and wiped beneath his rag.

He remembered Gail coming alive that way. She was always so fun and smart and caring. He loved being around her. After she saw her counselor for a while, Jim started to notice a depth to her that wasn't there before. She was more mature in the way she interacted with people. More secure, more stable. He hoped he might be changing in a similar fashion.

Maybe the Lord can put a shine on me yet, he told himself with a chuckle.

By 11:45 each piece was stained and wiped down on both sides and systematically perched back on the rack. He cleaned his hands with a splash of lacquer thinner and headed up to the house.

"Good timing," Gail piped up as Jim came into the kitchen. She was just pulling a batch of cookies from the oven. The warm aroma of melted butter and chocolate chips permeated the room. Jim inhaled slowly through his nose and smiled.

"Kyle and I were just talking," Gail said. "I've got errands to run this afternoon, but he's available if you'd like him to come with you to pick up the motorcycle?"

"Sure, that sounds great," Jim replied as he searched the fridge for some leftovers. "I could use the help."

"There's stew out in the garage fridge from last night. It's in the big pot."

Jim made a sandwich while the stew warmed on the stove. "Where is Kyle anyway?" he asked.

"He was here checking out my cookie dough until a few minutes ago. I think he wanted to put away some of the stuff he brought home."

Jim was about to holler for him, but he thought better of it. Instead, he finished his sandwich and went to Kyle's bedroom to find him. "Mom says you might want to go with me this afternoon?"

"Yeah, if you'd like."

"Sure, I'd appreciate the help…and the company," he awkwardly added. "I thought we'd try to leave by one. That work for you?"

"Yeah, I just have a couple more things to put away and I'll grab some lunch."

Jim returned to the kitchen and the stew was bubbling. He stuck his finger in it and then stuck it in his mouth. "Mmm, just gets better each time ya heat it up." He scooped two bowls and buttered a piece of bread for Kyle and brought them to the table. He waited on Kyle like one hog waits on another, and was almost finished by the time Kyle came out of his room. Rinsing his bowl in the sink, he looked toward the dining room.

"I'm gonna gather up the ramp and a few ratchet straps. See ya in the truck in a few?"

"Sure, Dad," Kyle replied, looking at the clock. It was 12:40. He glanced at his mom. Gail smiled an apology.

"I think your dad's a little excited," she said.

Kyle scarfed down his stew, grabbed a few cookies for the road, and was out the door.

It was about a forty-five-minute drive each way. Jim was tempted to turn on the radio to avoid the uncomfortable silence, but pressed through and started a conversation instead.

"Were ya able to get your stuff put away?"

"Yeah, some of it had to go under the bed, but most of it fit in the closet."

"Good. How much more still needs to come home?"

"Between this trip and what I can bring home at Thanksgiving, I think we can probably fit the rest in your truck when you come down. That way you won't have to bring the trailer."

"That'll be good."

"I know you're not keen on dragging that trailer around in the city."

"Yeah."

After driving a few miles in silence, Kyle initiated the next round. "So, what's with this motorcycle?"

"The Dream?"

"Yeah."

"Oh, nothin' really."

"Really? You seem pretty excited over nothin." Kyle grinned at his dad, "Mom said you had one as a kid?"

Jim bit. "Oh, not just any one, but this one. This very same one." He started to wax nostalgic as he recounted the anticipation of restoring it with his daddy, and dreaming about riding around town on the back. He even risked mentioning the hope of putting his arms around his daddy and holding on tight as he imagined them racing through the gears. Kyle listened intently.

"Then," Jim explained, "one day I came home from school and it was gone. Disappeared before we even started on it. Dad sold it." Jim paused. "I saw it a couple years later. A kid at school was riding it."

"Wow, Dad; that sounds really hurtful."

"Somethin' changed in me the day he sold it." Jim paused again, keeping his eyes straight ahead. "I swore I'd never trust him again."

"I know," Kyle whispered.

"What?"

Kyle took a deep breath before repeating, "I know."

"What do you mean, you know?"

"Today, when I was in the closet moving things around…I found my yellow remote-control car. The one Nana and Pop's gave me for my birthday."

"You still have that?"

Now Kyle kept his eyes straight ahead, as the images of that painful day came into focus. "After you drove over it with your truck, I collected all the broken pieces and put them in a box."

Jim could feel his neck turning red. Inside he was thinking, *How dare you accuse me? Running over your toy was nothin' compared to how my dad would've treated me!"* But what he actually said was, "If I remember right, you left it in the driveway. I don't know how many times you were told to pick up your toys. I figured if it cost ya something, ya might learn."

Kyle sat silently as his dad's words echoed in the cab of the truck. After justifying his position, Jim expected to feel vindicated, but instead he just felt alone. The silence grew thicker as the miles continued, but there was anxious posturing going on in Jim's mind. Kyle had been put in his place. *Who does he think he is to not even respond? Did he think I was wrong? After all, I was the man; Kyle was only a little boy. What else was I supposed to do?*

The familiarity of the question caught Jim off guard. He remembered his homework. He had just processed those very words with Gail, and then with Joel. Suddenly, he saw history repeating itself. He had done to Kyle just like his daddy had done to him. He bit his lip. He wanted to clear the air, but what could he say? *'What would you have wanted to hear from your daddy?'*

The question haunted him. The only response that came to his mind was, 'I'm sorry.'

Apologize? Are you kidding? To Kyle? Ten years after the fact?

A few more miles couldn't dissuade Jim from the obvious. He knew he needed to — *wanted* to — apologize. The words were so foreign to Jim that he would have to force them out. But he couldn't not say them. If Kyle longed to hear them half as much as he had longed to hear them from his dad, he would speak them if it took his last breath. He turned to Kyle.

"I'm sorry."

It caught Kyle off guard. He had never heard his dad apologize before. Oh, maybe a few time to mom, but never to him. Kyle knew the power of a true apology, as well as the weakness of lip service.

"May I ask what you're apologizing for?" he asked.

Jim wasn't prepared for a conversation about it. "Ah...um..." He exhaled silently and let his resistance fall. "I'm sorry for defending myself."

For a split second, the image of the truck tire rolling over the toy flashed across Jim's mind from Kyle's perspective. A distant sense of hurt welled up.

"I'm sorry I ran over your toy car…on purpose. I'm… so sorry."

Kyle smiled at his dad. "Thank you."

"I know I was kinda cruel at times," Jim went on. "I wouldn't expect ya to forgive me."

"I already have," Kyle responded softly. "A few years ago, after I left home, I asked mom why you were like you were. She told me about your dad, and his dad. It all made sense. I decided to forgive you then. I didn't trust you, but I didn't hate you anymore."

Jim bit his lip again. Kyle's words revealed the cost of Jim's offenses as clearly as any invoice, and he knew they were true. Fair enough. He knew forgiveness was a gift, and he would take it. Trust…he was willing to earn that.

They loaded the motorcycle and headed back home without much more said. It was puzzling to be caught and exposed, to be held accountable and forgiven. By his son, no less. Now, he felt it was a strange honor to be sitting with him. Kyle was a man to be reckoned with, and that made Jim just proud enough to break a smile.

Chapter Twenty-Three

Hero or Zero?

Saturday morning found Jim in the garage dusting off his old helmet. Throwing his leg over the seat of the Dream, he was twelve again, just for a moment. He remembered barely being able to touch the floor when he sat on it back then. He imagined the *thump, thump, thump* of those twin cylinders, and hanging on tight to his daddy.

Jim reached down and gave it some choke, turned the key, and touched the starter button. It fired right up, and the smile of a twelve-year-old spread across his face. He twisted the throttle. Now he was no longer imagining the *thump, thump!* He could hear it, feel it, and smell it. Rolling forward from one foot to the other, he waddled toward the door before shifting it into gear. With a gentle roll of the throttle and a smooth release of the clutch, down the driveway he went.

Once his tires left the gravel and encountered the smooth asphalt, he accelerated. The morning sun had burned the dew off the road. He anxiously rummaged through his memory. *One down, three up, I think*. He was pretty sure that was the shifting pattern. *Squeeze the clutch, lift the shifter with the left toe, ease out on the clutch again, and give it more throttle.* Jim hadn't ridden a motorcycle for years, but the logistics were slowly coming back to him.

The rush, however, was instant. It may have only been a 305, but being on a motorcycle is distinct from any other sensation. It's like a bicycle, but no pedaling; like a horse, but no asking it to go or stop. He let up on the throttle just enough to upshift again, and then rolled the gas back on.

Approaching a sweeping curve, he pulled ever so slightly on the opposite handlebar and the bike gently leaned into the corner. Only a few cars used this road on Saturday mornings and Jim was grateful. He assumed he had a less than distinguished smile on his face. Who was he kidding? He had a sloppy grin from ear to ear, but it felt so good.

As the road descended near the creek, Jim felt the air chill on his face. The earthy smell of the creek couldn't have been more present if he were standing in it. The cedars that flanked the riverbed shared their spice, followed by a hint of sweetness as the road passed through a stand of basswood. The aroma of cows and freshly cut hay was also on tap, marking his transition into the farming community. It was like a nature hike with a shot of adrenalin. He couldn't believe how much he was enjoying himself.

In time, he turned west and followed the county road until he found his favorite gravel two-track, which led him under a canopy of oaks and maples and to a grassy clearing high above the rest of the county. He rolled to a stop, turned off the bike, and removed his helmet. Beautiful farmland stretched out for miles below, and he felt like a kid on top of the world, without a care. It was a fine place to bask in the feeling. His dream had come true. Or had it?

Jim lowered the kickstand and climbed off. Removing his denim jacket, he rolled it and placed it under his head as he stretched out on his back in the grass. Puffy clouds chased each other like turtles across the sky. The sun warmed his face, and he could hear squirrels chatting like neighbors at a fence. A robin hopped around, hunting for a snack, while a pair of goldfinches perched curiously on a nearby sapling. "Who is this happy, old fellow lying on our lawn?" they seemed to ask each other.

Jim propped himself up on his elbows. "Man, what

I wouldn't give for an Orange Crush right now." Humored that he had said it out loud, he closed his eyes. He could have been nine again, resting on the bank of the creek with a pole in the water, while Caroline unpacked the cooler. It had been a long time since Jim had felt this untethered.

Eventually the ground got hard. Jim got up and brushed himself off. Donning his jacket, he mounted the bike, fired it up, and took one last, long look around before heading back out to the county road. Shifting through the gears and coming up to speed, he lowered himself over the gas tank and twisted the throttle. Going down the hill seemed like a perfectly good place to see what she'd do. The speedometer atop the headlight climbed: 62…65…68...70. The wind pulled at his jacket and buffeted his helmet. His eyes started to tear up behind his sunglasses. He knew it was capable of more, but that was fast enough.

Letting it settle back to 55 mph, he shifted himself to a more dignified, upright position and enjoyed the scenic route home. The miles left him settled inside, like hanging out with old friends or thumbing through photos of a favorite vacation. There's a pleasant satisfaction with the experience, and then a tug when it's time move on.

Jim rolled into the garage and parked it back in the corner. It had been an amazing morning, better than he imagined. But as he stepped away from the bike, a strange thought came to mind. He wondered if he'd ever ride it again. To be honest, it was a little small for him, and underpowered for some of the hills around there. It wasn't even that comfortable, especially if Gail wanted to go along. He set his helmet on the bench and went inside.

Gail and Kyle had planned to go to the farmers market and then get some breakfast. They weren't back yet. Passing through the kitchen, Jim saw there was a message on the machine.

"Hi, Jim. Larry here. Say, Nancy and I finally had

some time to talk about your proposal for our fireplace cabinets. I really appreciated the way you handled some of the details that had us concerned. Anyway, I just wanted to let you know we'd like you to put us on your schedule. We'll drop a check in the mail on Monday for the down payment. Thanks. Bye."

Jim always liked getting those calls, and this one in particular. *I sure didn't plan on hearing from Larry again. Nice.*

He made a cup of coffee and went out to the deck. Sitting silently, he let his mind wander. The images, sounds, and smells of the morning were still fresh. The view of the clouds. The smell of the dirt as he lay in the grass. Remembering happy-go-lucky summers with Caroline. Then the sudden disconnect with the motorcycle when he parked it. What was that about?

The Dream had been a source of joy and hope, of disappointment and mistrust, and finally of worth and redemption. Then why didn't he feel more redeemed? After all, his dad may have felt like he didn't deserve it, but Jim knew better. He deserved to be riding that bike as much as that other kid in high school. And now he had the means to make it happen. So why didn't it feel better?

Gail pulled into the garage, where she loaded Jim up with more produce than they would ever eat. She had also picked up a couple wraps from the deli. After putting stuff away, they returned to the deck to eat lunch.

"Did you lose Kyle along the way?"

"He ran into a high school friend and they decided to hang out for a while. How was your morning? Did the bike run well for you?"

"Yeah, it ran great."

"Was it fun?"

"It was amazing." Jim paused, basking in the morning again. "I rode for...well, I left around nine and didn't get back 'til eleven, eleven fifteen. Yeah, it was fun." Jim's voice trailed off.

"Do I hear a 'but' coming?"

"No. Well, no. Maybe. When the initial excitement of finding it, and fixing it, and finally riding it wore off, I thought I'd still feel some kind of redemption. Like I was finally showing my dad that I deserved a motorcycle, *that* motorcycle, and this time he couldn't take it away from me."

"But?"

"But it's...well, now I've got it, and nothing's really changed."

"Like changed with your dad?"

"I don't know. I mean, he's not even alive anymore. How could it change? I'm not sure what I was expecting. I just thought I'd feel more...I don't know...vindicated by it, maybe?"

Gail smiled. "Maybe it wasn't about the motorcycle after all?"

They finished their lunch. As much as he tried to push her last statement aside, it wouldn't go away. Jim gathered their plates and left Gail enjoying the sun on the deck.

The bike sat in the garage until Thursday afternoon. Once again, he uncovered it, rolled it to the garage entrance, and started it up. It would be his first trip into town with it, and he was a little nervous about riding it in traffic. But he arrived at Joel's without a hitch, and even got a few nods and waves along the way. He parked behind the office in his usual spot, next to Joel's Harley.

Once Jim got settled, Joel dove right in. "Jim, we've talked about you responding to situations out of your strength, both when you were a boy and then as a man. I'd like to revisit that if you're willing."

"Sure, I remember. You wondered what options I had, and I couldn't think of any."

"In the incident with Caroline, your display of

strength was more likely a reflex than a planned show of might. You were trying to influence a bad situation with your physical force."

"It wasn't very influential though." The memory was still embarrassing.

"Later, you used your words with your dad."

"That didn't get me anywhere, either; except I never saw Sammy again."

"I imagine as you got older, your size increased and your strength increased, to the point where you could rely on it to subdue a situation."

"I'll never forget the last time my dad tried to lay a hand on me." Joel nodded for him to go on. "I was in the barn helping him work on the tractor. He asked for a wrench, so I handed him the one he had used earlier. It wasn't the one he wanted and he turned around cussing and took a swing at me. I deflected it and grabbed his arm." Jim paused, reliving the memory. "I twisted him hard to floor before he knew what hit him. I held him there just long enough to tell him he can get his own damn wrench, and then I walked away. He never asked me to help him again."

"How did that feel?"

Jim's shoulders were slumped. "I'm not proud of it. There were times I wanted to help him, but it never happened."

"So what I hear you saying is, your strength is your only option, and it's either not enough, or it's too much."

Jim looked up. "Sounds about right."

"Let's go back to your uncle and Caroline. What did you want to communicate to him in the barn that day?"

Jim thought for a minute. "That what he was doing was wrong, and it needed to stop."

"Did you succeed?"

"No."

"Are you sure?"

"What do you mean? He didn't stop."

"Maybe not Jim, but your actions, and later your words, made it clear that it was wrong and needed to stop. He just didn't listen."

Jim skewed his face. "I'm confused. Are you saying I was successful?"

"Yes, I am. We can't control people, but we can show up and take a stand. You've said Caroline didn't acknowledge you at the time, but if she could have, what do you think she might have said?"

"I don't know. 'Thanks for nothin,' maybe?"

"How about, 'Thanks for trying; it means a lot that you'd stick up for me'?"

Now Jim was totally bewildered. "Are you sayin' she might have seen my lame attempt as a good thing?"

"I would've."

Jim was clearly struggling with this perspective, and after a pause, Joel continued. "Every time you speak of that event, I see shame in your face and body. I hear shame in your voice. Jim, you were a hero in that situation. You couldn't control the outcome, but you entered it on behalf of your friend, without thought of what it could cost you. That is a hero in my book."

Jim was following, but made no reply.

"Do you care for J.R.?" Joel asked.

"Of course I do," Jim shot back.

"I know you do," Joel said with a smile. "Just for the sake of example, I wonder what your strength said to him that day you pulled him from the river? Hero or zero?"

Jim shrugged. "Hero, I suppose?"

"Yeah, the way he went on about you for the next week, you were right up there with Superman."

Jim's brow furrowed in disbelief.

"Hey, I'm not kidding," Joel insisted. "He wouldn't stop talking about that kind, big man that saved him from freezing to death in the icy river, and then carried him all the way home."

Jim looked back at the floor. "I'll bet he doesn't think that now."

"Why do you say that?"

"Cause of how I treated him in the garage."

"What resource did you rely on in the garage?"

Jim was cautious to answer, "My strength."

Joel tilted back in his chair and tapped his chin with his pen, while Jim braced himself. "I wonder if there was another option," Joel asked.

"Like what?"

"Jim, you're a pretty resourceful man. I'm curious if there might have been another way to enter that situation?

"Man, I don't know."

"How did Gail show up that evening?"

"Are you comparing me to Gail?"

"No, I'm just curious."

"She didn't manhandle him, if that's what you're asking."

"Did she do anything?"

"Yeah, she got out of the truck and talked to him."

"Was that helpful?"

"I suppose so."

"So, can you think of anything you could've done differently that may have facilitated a better outcome that evening?"

Jim stared at the floor for a long time before answering. "My voice."

"Tell me what you mean?"

"Instead of using my strength, I could've used my voice. Gail used her voice. She talked to him. I guess I could have used my voice."

"That's good Jim."

"I also could've turned on the light to see what was

going on before charging in…with my gun drawn."

"Okay, how might that have played out?"

"Well, I probably would've seen it was J.R. and not somebody breaking in. I would've seen his relief that we were there. And I probably would've been a little gentler in helping him up."

"Sounds like you could've been a hero again." Joel smiled empathetically. "You have resources now that you didn't have as a young man. It might be beneficial for you to discover and tap into them." Then he flipped to a fresh page on his pad and started to write.

"Each of us has pages in our story where we were a victim..."

When he finished writing, he tore it out and handed it to Jim. "Why don't you take a look at this, and maybe ask Gail for her perspective? We can talk about it next week."

Jim took the piece of paper, folded it, and put it in his shirt pocket.

Chapter Twenty-Four

Unexpected Satisfaction

Joel followed Jim outside. "Wow, Jim, nice bike! How long have you had it running?"

Jim smiled as he pulled on his jacket. "I picked it up from the mechanic a couple weeks ago."

"It's got great lines. Mid-sixties?"

"Sixty-five."

"Sweet. Was it hard finding parts for it?"

"It was pretty complete. I found some parts from a guy downstate, and the mechanic had a couple donor bikes he pulled some stuff from."

"You like riding it?"

"It's a fun little scoot."

"This is the one you hoped to enjoy with your dad?"

"The very one."

"That's pretty cool that you found it again."

Just then, J.R. poked his head around the corner of the building. "Hi, Dad! Oh... hello, Mister Jim."

"Your mom dropped you off?" Joel asked.

"Yeah," J.R. said. "And I had a good check-up. No cavities! She still has to get groceries, so I asked if she'd drop me off here so I could go home with you."

"Sounds like a good plan to me. I hope you don't mind waiting, though. It'll be another forty-five minutes before I'm ready to go."

J.R.'s chin dropped a little. He looked at Jim's bike.

"How's it ride, Mister Jim?"

Jim's eyes met Joel's with a grin. "Oh, she rides fine J.R. I'm heading home now. If you'd like, and if it's okay with your daddy, I could drop you off."

J.R.'s eyes lit up. "Could I, Dad?"

"I think that would be fine," said Joel. "Let me get your helmet from my tour-pack."

Jim strapped on his own helmet and steadied the bike so J.R. could climb on behind him. It started flawlessly, for which Jim was grateful since he had an audience. Joel patted him on the shoulder with a very pleased look on his face, and then stepped back. Jim let out the clutch, and they were off.

J.R. gripped the folds in Jim's denim jacket as they idled through the parking lot. Jim braked smoothly at the exit, but J.R.'s helmet bumped Jim in the back.

"Sorry, Mister Jim."

"No worries, buddy," Jim said pleasantly.

He gently navigated a few blocks of city driving before turning onto a winding county road and heading west. It was a splendid day to be on a motorcycle. The trees were getting ready to show their colors soon, and the air was dry and warm. The sun filtered through the leaves and danced on the asphalt. When Jim got up to speed and had navigated a few sweeping corners, J.R. shouted, "Thank you, Mister Jim! This is so much fun!"

Jim turned his head slightly. "It's my pleasure!"

What he felt next surprised him. J.R. loosened his grip from Jim's jacket and wrapped his arms around Jim's middle instead.

Jim remembered sitting on this bike in the shed all those summers ago, envisioning hugging his daddy from behind while exploring back roads. Dreaming about all the fun they would have. Imagining the smells and sounds and sights they would share. An unexpected satisfaction settled over him. It was the odd contentment that comes when a dream is realized in a way never imagined. Jim relaxed the throttle a little just to savor the moment.

Soon enough, they rolled into J.R.'s driveway. J.R. slipped off the seat and dropped his helmet to the ground. "That was so much fun, Mister Jim! That's way different from my daddy's motorcycle. Thank you so much!" And with another quick squeeze around Jim's waist, J.R. picked up his helmet and darted toward the house.

A broad grin swept across Jim's face as he waited to make sure J.R. got inside. He turned the bike around and made his way back onto the road. He was just into third gear when he started to downshift for his own driveway. As he approached the garage, the door suddenly started up on its own. He looked in his mirror. Gail had pulled in behind him and used her remote opener. He rolled the bike into its corner and climbed off as Gail followed him in.

"Good timing!" she chirped as she grabbed a bag from the back seat.

"Need a hand?"

"Naw, just got a couple things from the store. How was your afternoon?"

"Good. Really good."

"I'd like to hear about it. Can you get the door?"

Jim opened the door and followed Gail inside. "I gave J.R. a ride home from Joel's office," he told her.

Gail set the bag on the counter and slipped her purse from her shoulder. "How did that go?"

"Great." Jim beamed as he said it.

"How did that come about?" Gail kicked off her shoes and pulled up a dining chair, poised to hear all about it.

"Well, after my meeting with Joel, J.R. showed up wanting to get a ride home with his dad. Joel wasn't gonna be ready to leave for a while, so I asked if he wanted to ride home with me. And he did."

"Did he like it?"

"I think so. He said he did…and he hugged me."

"Wow, Jim, that's pretty cool!"

"Yeah, I thought so, too."

Gail's smile grew. "So, he hugged you, huh?"

"Yup. What's for dinner?" Jim said, in a hurry to change the subject before she got too analytical. She was fine with that.

"I picked up a couple steaks at the market. Would you mind starting the grill?"

"Yes ma'am."

It was a perfect evening to eat on the deck. After dinner, Jim cleared their plates and returned with a glass of wine for each of them. Gail slouched in her chair, and reaching for the adjacent chair with her toe, she pulled it close enough to use it as a foot stool. The sun was setting earlier this time of year, and warm nights were not to be taken for granted. They both sat in silence for a while; Gail, drinking in the delight of a pair of hummingbirds at the feeder, while Jim casually scanned the orchard. The apples were coming along nicely and the deer hadn't done much damage yet.

Gail interrupted the quiet. "What's in your pocket?"

Jim looked down at the folded paper sticking out from his shirt pocket. "More homework."

"Anything interesting?"

"Don't know; haven't really looked at it. Joel thought maybe we could work on it together. Ya know...get your perspective."

Gail sat up. Ever since becoming familiar with her own story, she had prayed for the opportunity to help Jim enter his. Containing her delight, she casually proceeded.

"We have a few minutes now. Wanna take a look?"

Jim pulled out the folded page and handed it to Gail. She unfolded it and read it to herself. "Wow, Jim," she said, "this is really good. You haven't read it yet?"

"No. What's the assignment?"

"Hmm...I'd say it's more of an observation. Here, you read it."

Jim had already rested his head back comfortably on his chair and closed his eyes. "Do you mind reading it out loud?" he asked.

"Sure." Gail swiveled in her chair toward him and started to read:

"Each of us has pages in our story where we were a victim. If we respond to life out of that pain, there is a likelihood for harm. If we address those wounds, it frees us to respond from the truth of who we really are, in spite of that pain. Then, there is a likelihood for heroism.

Jim still had his eyes closed when she finished. "Hmm, interesting," he said.

Gail wasn't about to let him off that easy. "How so?"

Jim didn't answer right away. He wasn't stalling, just trying to get his head around what she had just read.

"When Joel and I talk about my story, he says I've been a victim. To me it just feels like the bumps in life. I learn from them and move on."

"What do you learn from them?"

Jim paused once more. "What to do, or not do, next time."

Gail slouched in her chair again and put her feet up, then took a sip of wine. "Any examples come to mind?"

"Not right now."

"How about when your dad sold the Dream?"

"I learned not to trust him. Not sure how that makes me a victim."

Jim's resistance to her line of questioning was rising. Gail paced herself. "Didn't he lead you to believe that you would get it running together?"

"Yeah."

"Then he sold it without telling you?"

"Yeah."

"Well...it sounds to me like you were lied to." Gail paused to take another sip. "Did it hurt?"

"It made me really mad. So, yeah, I suppose it hurt."

"Then wouldn't it be fair to say that, on that page of your story, you might have been a victim of your dad's dishonesty?"

"I suppose."

"And then what did you do?"

"I carved NTD on my headboard."

"NTD?"

"Never Trust Dad. Joel says it was like I made an agreement with myself."

"Like a vow?"

"Yeah, that's what he called it, a vow."

Gail slowly spun the stem of her glass between her finger and thumb, and then stopped when she saw the setting sun through the remaining wine. It playfully distorted the evening sky and made her face glow. It also reminded her to consider the bigger picture. "Honey," she said, "I wonder if you were a victim every time you chose not to trust because of that vow."

Jim pondered that. "You mean, not trust my dad?"

"Oh, sure, it probably started there. But whenever we take a position, like, to never trust someone, it seems like it would make it easier for that posture to bleed over into other relationships."

"You lost me."

Gail continued to look west, through her wine glass. "Oh, I don't know. Did you find yourself more suspicious of people after that?"

"Probably, it was probably a good life lesson."

"What was the lesson?"

"Not to trust people."

"All people?"

"Well, yeah. I mean, yeah, until they prove themselves trustworthy."

Jim was already sensing that his case was frail, and Gail's next question caused it to crumble completely.

"So, who has ever proved themselves trustworthy?"

Jim had no answer.

"Honey, I think that's what Joel meant by responding to life out of the pain of being victimized. Unfortunately, your father taught you out of the pain of his own story, and you are sadly aware of the likelihood for harm." She let her words hang in the evening air.

Jim's hands rested in his lap; he looked past them a hundred miles into the ground beneath the deck. "Do you remember that dream I wrote down a few months ago?" he asked. "About a boy and a girl near a well, and some people came and took the girl and tied up the boy?"

Gail nodded that she did.

"When I shared it with Joel, he said I referred to myself as the boy."

"Okay, that makes sense."

"And he said I was a victim in that dream."

"That's interesting."

"He said I was subdued, berated, and abandoned."

"Sounds abusive to me," Gail said. "It also sounds a lot like the situation with Caroline and her daddy in the barn."

"That's what Joel said."

"Except, in both of those situations, you chose to show up as the hero."

"Yeah, Joel mentioned that, too," Jim said, minimizing her perspective. Gail's relaxed posture in her chair didn't change but her tone became very sober.

"Jim, I love you, and I pray you can hear this. When you show up like the man you are — when you use what God has put in you — being a hero is as easy as falling off a log. It's second nature for you. But when you respond to your world through the eyes of that precious, but insecure, scared little boy you once were...well, that's when you hurt people. Often, the people you love."

Neither of them said a word for a long time until Jim broke the silence. "So, this is story work?" he asked softly.

Gail didn't have to answer. The dots were starting to connect for Jim. She could tell by the questions he was asking.

Did you have to look at your crap like this when you were in counseling?"

Gail flashed a wry smile. "Oh, honey, you have no idea!"

The day gave way to moonlight and stars, and their conversation drifted into small talk about autumn plans. Harvesting apples and raking leaves would take up a couple weekends. Jim wanted to do some maintenance on the snow blower before mounting it to the tractor for the winter. As they verbally ping-ponged through their mental checklists, Gail asked out of the blue, "What do you think about supporting Kyle financially for his Mexico trip?"

"I guess I assumed we would."

"Any idea what that might look like?"

"I dunno," Jim said. "What were you thinking?"

"I figured we'd help with logistics and moving his belongings. But I hoped we might support him financially, too."

"Yeah, maybe when he makes his presentation at church."

"Any idea how much we'd want to give?"

"I'm not sure yet. I've put a little away since he

mentioned he might be going."

Gail was pleased to hear Jim was already invested. "I've been saving some, too."

They sat in the dark for a few more minutes, washed in a warm southern breeze and serenaded by tree frogs and crickets. Suddenly, Jim's deeper thoughts spilled out.

"I think I'm gonna sell the Dream."

He was surprised that he said it out loud. It surprised Gail, too.

"Are you serious?"

"I don't know. It's just a thought. Whatever I get for it could go to help Kyle's trip."

"Wow, hon. You and that motorcycle go back a long way, and now you've got it running so good."

"Yeah, we'll see. It's just a thought."

Gail got up and walked around the table to where Jim was sitting. She leaned over and kissed his forehead. "You are full of surprises, James Robert. I'll see you inside."

Chapter Twenty-Five

FOR SALE

Traffic on their county road had picked up over the last couple weeks. It usually did this time of year. Autumn meant color tour for the folks from the city. A stream of cars, campers, buses, and motorcycles would trek north from downstate, searching out the rolling hills and winding tunnels of trees that graced the rural lanes. It was Friday afternoon and Jim was wandering the aisles of the hardware store.

"Hi, Jim."

He spun around to see who had interrupted his search.

"Hi, Joel. What brings you here?"

"Bobbi called from home. The bathroom faucet is leaking. It's old, so I figured I'd replace it rather than try to find the parts to fix it."

Jim nodded. "Plumbing's in aisle four, I think."

"Thanks. You seem to be on a mission, too."

"Yeah, I'm looking for a 'FOR SALE' sign."

"Oh, what are you selling?"

"I'm thinking about selling the motorcycle."

"The Dream? The one you just got running, after all these years?"

"Yeah, seems kinds funny, doesn't it? I wanted it so bad for so long. Now that I've got it…" Jim looked down. "I guess what I really wanted was just to connect with my dad."

"Jim," Joel said, "he missed out on knowing a very amazing man."

Jim looked up with a smile. “Thanks, Doc. A lot of water’s gone under that bridge, but I sure hope I can start connecting with my boy a little better.”

“I hope so, too, Jim. That would be nice for both of you.” With that Joel proceeded to the plumbing section.

Jim found the sign, paid for it, and made his way out to the truck. As he climbed in, the unmistakable sound of Joel’s Harley firing up put a grin on his face. He must have found a faucet.

Back home, Jim backed Gail’s car out of the garage and uncovered the Dream. He rolled it to the middle of the garage and put down the kickstand. Looking through a cabinet, he found a bottle of car wax, then snuck a towel from the kitchen. Pulling his rolling stool out from under the workbench, he wheeled it over to the bike and took a seat.

After ripping the towel in two, he proceeded to apply the wax with one piece and remove it with the other. The bike was clean, but its shine had long since faded, and a wax job wasn’t going to help much. Jim wasn’t sure why he was doing it, but once he started, the memories of hours spent after school in the shed, going through these exact motions, came flooding back. He fought it at first, but then gave in. It felt kind of good; then his eyes went misty, though he wasn’t sure why. It almost felt like he – a fullgrown man – was sharing this experience with a little boy who was overjoyed to be invited in.

He polished every inch of the motorcycle, imagining himself showing little Jimmy how to check the tire pressure and read the oil dipstick. Jim worked on the bike all evening. Somehow, it seemed honoring to a little boy from long ago. His plan was to roll the Dream out to the road the next morning, where he would put the FOR SALE sign on it. It was more of a declaration, actually. He already knew of an interested party. When he and Kyle picked up the motorcycle, his mechanic had told him that a guy stopped in while he was working on it and wondered if it was for sale. The mechanic took his phone number and passed it along to Jim in case he ever wanted to sell it. Jim had intended to give him a call, but there was something deliberate about putting it out by the road and leaving it there, like some kind of declaration that he was ready to sell it. He wouldn't let it slip away unnoticed again.

The next morning, he did just that. Then he and Gail took her car to the farmer's market, followed by breakfast at the diner and a 'five-minute stop' at Donna's to borrow her crock pot (which, of course, turned into twenty minutes). Jim waited patiently in the car. He knew if he'd gone in with her, it would have been an hour.

That afternoon, Jim's phone rang. He saw that it was Joel, so he shut off the mower and answered.

"Hello, Joel. Need a hand changing out your faucet?"

Joel chuckled. "No, but thanks for the offer."

"What can I do for you?"

"Bobbi and I were out for a ride this morning, and we went past your place."

"Yeah?"

"You're serious about selling the Dream, aren't you?"

Jim smiled. "I think, as for my journey, that bike has taken me as far as it can."

"Hmm, well said my friend. Then you're sure about this?"

"Yeah, Joel, I'm sure. I want to use the money to help Kyle with his mission trip this winter. Why, do you want it?"

"Ah, well, yes, I'm interested."

"Seriously? You look pretty comfy on that Harley."

"Well, it's not for me."

"Does Bobbi want her own ride?"

"Oh, she might ride it a little. Actually, since you gave J.R. a ride home on it the other day, he hasn't stopped talking about it. Quite honestly, it's driving us a little nuts over here. Anyway, I saw you had the price listed on the sign. Bobbi and I talked it over, and I'd like to buy it from you. I know he'll have to grow into it. Until then, he can learn to ride it around the farm."

Jim's response was instant. "I would love that! But there's only one condition. Don't you dare sell it without J.R.'s approval." Jim caught himself. "I'm sorry, I know you wouldn't do that; I just couldn't help myself."

Joel laughed. "Not a problem Jim. Would it be okay if I stop over to pick it up Monday after work and we can settle up then?"

"Sounds like a plan to me. Thanks, Joel. Thank you."

"J.R.'s gonna be beside himself. Thank you. I'll see you Monday."

Jim slid the phone back in his pocket and finished mowing the lawn. After putting the mower away, he walked to the end of the driveway, pulled the key from his pocket and started the Dream one last time. He swung his leg over the seat and rode straight back to the garage. The thought of taking it for just one more short jaunt never crossed his mind. He was more excited with the idea of J.R. finding it in his own barn in a few days.

That evening, Gail rinsed while Jim loaded the dish-washer. At one point he stopped. "Gail, I know I apologized for when I got angry with you and grabbed your arm. You remember?"

Gail shut off the faucet and looked at him. "Oh yeah, I remember."

"Well, I remember apologizing for how I treated you, but I didn't apologize for why I behaved so badly."

"And why did you behave so badly?" She tried to stifle a grin.

"I'm serious, Gail."

"Sorry."

"Joel thinks it was my 'precious, but insecure, scared

little boy' – as you called him – who showed up that afternoon. I allowed him to lash out at you."

"And what do you think?"

"I think he's probably right."

"Then thank you, Jim. I accept your apology."

Jim returned to placing the plates in a row on the bottom rack. "How long do you think it will take until I can stop him from influencing my behavior?"

"Him, meaning what you experienced and felt in your story, your little boy?"

"Yeah. Like, when will I be over this?"

"Gail didn't even try to stifle her amusement. "Oh Jim, the stuff you experienced throughout your childhood will influence your perspective until...well, until you die."

"So, I won't get over it?"

"Sorry, babe, you won't get over it. But you don't have to repeat it."

"So I'll still hurt you, and Kyle, and J.R.?"

"Sometimes, yup. But the beauty is, if you continue to expose the lies that were planted in you all those years ago, and replace them, one at a time, with the truth of who God created you to be, it will improve. Jim, we are both broken people, and we will both continue to hurt each other; but less often and with less damage as we continue to grow in the truth of who we really are."

"You mean, like taking off the signs that other people hung around our necks?"

"I have no idea what you're talking about."

"Joel said it's like Daddy made a sign that said 'lazy', and another that said 'irresponsible', and hung them around my neck."

"Oh, like labels."

"Yeah, like labels."

"Yes, identifying and stepping out from under the curse of those false labels, rather than letting them suffocate us in shame, produces a ton of freedom."

Jim groaned. "How long will I need to keep seeing Joel?"

Gail handed Jim the last dripping plate. "As long as you like. I eventually stopped seeing my counselor when I was able to identify for myself the fears and longings of my little Gail. Once I learned to address them before they became demands that leaked out onto those around me, I was done. And some days I still succumb to that little girl's perspective. You've seen it. But now I have the tools to honor her while taking back control."

"Man, that sounds like a lot of work!"

Gail smiled and tossed the dishtowel at him. "Oh, it is. But it's good work, Jim. And you're worth it!"

Chapter Questions

You may want to jot your numbered answers in a journal or note pad.

Chapter 1

Jim appears to have a pretty low tolerance for interruptions. Constants are good, variables are bad. Control seems to be important to him.

1.1 What areas in your life make you frustrated if you're not in control?

1.2 What is your initial response to an interruption?

Jim had the opportunity to be a hero in chapter one.

1.3 Have you ever been celebrated for your actions?

1.4 How did you feel about it?

Chapter 2

Jim minimized the sting of their son Kyle choosing to text Gail instead of him.

2.1 Where do you minimize similar hurts?

The "sting" represented Jim's lack of relationship with Kyle.

2.2 Can you identify a loss connected with your hurt?

Jim had been trained to believe that his worth was based on his performance (i.e. what he did and what he could produce).

2.3 What were you taught about where your worth came from (either directly, implied, or modeled)?

2.4 What activity do you engage in when you want to feel good about yourself?

Jim envied Kyle's freedom to dream and make plans, but couldn't embrace that kind of freedom for himself.

2.5 In what areas of your life do you wish you could experience more freedom?

Chapter 3

Gail seems to make people a priority.
3.1 Do you know someone like that?
3.2 How does it feel to be around them?

Jim, on the other hand, seems to value his things over people.
3.3 Do you know someone like that?
3.4 How does it feel to be around them?
3.5 Are you more likely to identify with Martha (busy serving) or Mary (more relational)?

Jim seemed hypervigilant in his concern about the "Honda Dream."
3.6 What things do you find yourself protecting with hypervigilance?

It's helpful to understand why the Dream meant so much to Jim.
3.7 What losses did you experience as a child that cause you to guard something now?

As a boy, Jim experienced feeling invisible, silenced, and without consequence when his dad sold the motorcycle without a word.
3.8 When in your childhood did you feel deeply insignificant?
3.9 What conclusion(s) did you draw from that (those) experience(s)?

Chapter 4

When Jim finally had the opportunity to restore the motorcycle, it included an "I'll show him," attitude.
4.1 Can you relate?
4.2 If yes, how so?

Jim's shop was his domain of competence. When Kyle and his buddies decimated it with their paintball guns, Jim took control by destroying Kyle's gun to ensure it would never happen again.

4.3 Would you consider that an overreaction?

4.4 Who has responded to you in a similar fashion?

4.5 When have you responded to someone else in similar fashion?

If the response is out of proportion with the offense, we can assume that the problem isn't the problem.

4.6 What do you think the deeper problem might have been in the previous two questions?

Chapter 5

If Gail and the police officer had not entered the situation, Jim might have felt totally justified in his treatment of J.R.

5.1 Why do you think he saw his behavior as appropriate, while the others didn't?

5.2 Watching his granddad and father respond to life with outbursts of anger, how do you suppose Jim felt when he was reprimanded for it?

5.3 What do you think allowed Gail to push through her own fear with a desire to control the situation, entering Jim's world with empathy?

Chapter 6

6.1 What were some of the methods used to teach you a lesson as a child?

6.2 Which of these methods did you continue to use as a parent?

6.3 Which ones did you refuse to use as a parent?

6.4 Why?

6.5 Has anyone ever suggested you might want to "talk with someone?"
6.6 If so, how did you respond?

Chapter 7

When Gail found J.R.'s science project in the garage, she wanted to return it, but refrained, feeling like she needed to let Jim and J.R. sort it out.
7.1 Do you agree with her approach?
7.2 Have you ever tried to fix someone else?
7.3 What did the thought, "Consider the lilies of the field," mean to Gail?

It took Jim weeks two fill out his intake form.
7.4 Why do you suppose he was so reluctant to talk to a counselor?
7.5 Can you identify with his reluctance?

Chapter 8

8.1 Why do you think Jim struggled to connect with Kyle?
8.2 Have you ever desired to feel like you belonged?
8.3 Have you ever desired to quiet down on the inside, and pretend a little less on the outside?

Jim's go-to antidote for "feeling too much" was work. Call it soothing, if you will. Many of us soothe with work, TV, food, alcohol, drugs, sex, pornography, shopping, internet surfing, etc.
8.4 How do you soothe?

Chapter 9

Joel gave Jim an assignment: "A chair is rarely damaged when it is being cared for properly, so, I'd like you to pay special attention to events [in Jim's story] that may have left you feeling bruised or injured." Listing these things can feel a bit like we're taking inventory, but it can also help us accurately count the cost of what has happened to us in the past.

9.1 Have you ever made a list like Joel asked of Jim?

9.2 Have you ever viewed childhood photos of yourself from this perspective?

9.3 What is the pain hidden in some of those pictures?

Chapter 10

10.1 Why was Jim so put off with being compared to a "simple-minded" sheep?

10.2 What were the nicknames, characteristics, or labels assigned to you as a child?

10.3 Who gave them to you?

10.4 Do you still hear them?

10.5 Even if you know that they're not true, do you still respond to them as if they are? (A clue might be how hard you try to distance yourself from them.)

Chapter 11

When Jim shared how his dad responded to his pruning the orchard, Joel offered a different perspective on how Jim should have been treated. Joel's words stirred longings in Jim.

11.1 What do you suppose the longings were?

11.2 What did you long for from your parents?

Jim compared the scene of his motorcycle lying on the garage floor to the Harley lying on the pavement in Joel's parking lot. He recalled that "when his dad came down hard, it seemed easier to not care, to distance himself from the offense and the offended." Now the tables are turned.

11.3 In the case of the Harley, how did Jim distance himself from the offense?

11.4 In the case of J.R. and the Dream, how did Jim distance himself from the offender?
11.5 How are you tempted to distance yourself from an offense, and the offended or offender?
11.6 How did your parents respond to offenses when you were growing up?

Everything in Jim's life — his farm, his family, his business, his skillset — had been acquired to shake the 'disappointment' label. But one stupid little mistake could made him feel so small again. Sometimes he felt like 'insignificant' could be his middle name.
11.7 What does it take for you to feel insignificant?
11.8 How do you respond to feeling insignificant?

Chapter 12

Jim's uncle stole from both Caroline and Jim, decimating their boundaries for his own gratification.
12.1 Can you relate to either Jim or Caroline?
12.2 Who from your past has shown up and stirred old hurts?
12.3 Have you ever talked about it?

Chapter 13

Jim felt uncomfortable dealing in the currency of mercy and grace. He was more familiar with the currency of judgment.
13.1 Which currency are you more comfortable with?
13.2 If justice, how do you make "them" pay?
13.3 What does it cost you?
13.4 If mercy and grace, how do others respond?
13.5 Have you received mercy when you were bracing to be charged more than you could pay?
13.6 How did that impact your life?

Chapter 14

14.1 When you were a child, who was delighted to see you?
14.2 Who had your back?
14.3 Who did you depend on to look out for you, and they failed?
14.4 When that happened, what internal shift took place in your belief system?
14.5 What vows did you make as a result?

Chapter 15

Jim overheard Joel defend him to J.R. at the campfire.
15.1 Have you ever prepared to defend yourself only to have someone else step in and defend you instead?
15.2 How did that feel?
15.3 Have you ever done it for someone else?

Jim's uncle used the lamb to leverage loyalty from Jim.
15.4 What has been used to leverage relationship with you?

Jim struggled to imagine Gail's father helping him restore the motorcycle.
15.5 Can you think of a time when you have you been helped by someone who had nothing to gain, but simply wanted to help you?

Chapter 16

16.1 Do you suppose the disciple John may have simply acquiesced to being loved by Jesus, to the point that it actually became his identity?
16.2 Have you ever wondered if God likes you?
16.3 How might your childhood have looked differently if Jesus had been your dad?

Jim made a vow to not extend himself for someone else's benefit, so that if he failed, he could avoid the embarrassment.
16.4 What did you commit to as a child to avoid embarrassment?
16.5 Did you ever make a vow to avoid certain people or situations that could cause emotional pain?
16.6 To reiterate Joel's question, "Are you curious if holding onto that vow has cost you anything?"
16.7 If so, what does/has it cost you?

Chapter 17

Gail's "lack of planning" caused Jim to violate his childhood vow to not be in a position where he was expected to come through for someone else. Rather than disappointing someone else, he was the one disappointed that morning. The dog poo, smelling like gasoline, and being late caused Jim a level of embarrassment. When feeling ashamed or undone, we often turn to certain behaviors, or activities, to calm us, or soothe.
17.1 Can you name three things Jim did to soothe?
17.2 Did this make Jim's situation better or worse?
17.3 How?
17.4 Can you recognize a recurring incident or feeling (trigger) that causes you to soothe?

Chapter 18

There are two types of shame: legitimate shame (you did something bad) and illegitimate shame (you did something bad, thus, you are bad).
18.1 Can you identify the difference between legitimate shame and illegitimate shame in yourself?

Contempt (either self-contempt or contempt toward others) follows shame.
18.2 Following Jim's failed sales meeting, did he engage in

self-contempt or others-centered-contempt?
18.3 What did it look like for him?
18.4 When you feel shame, do you usually blame yourself or someone else?
18.5 How might that play out?
18.6 How did Gail respond to Jim's contemptuous behavior?
18.7 How do the people in your life react to your contemptuous behavior?

Chapter 19

Jim purchased 24 chocolate bars from J.R. to stave off the feeling that he was bad.
19.1 What do you do to quiet those same feelings in your own life?

Beneath anger often lies fear. Gail was afraid that Jim was right; that she really was irresponsible.
19.2 When you get angry, have you ever considered what fear might be lying beneath your anger?
19.3 Have you ever asked yourself, what am I afraid of?
19.4 What fears may cause you to respond with anger?

Chapter 20

Gail chose to distance herself from her dad, a distance she both hated and needed at the same time. In looking back, Gail could see areas where she never trusted Jim because she learned to not trust her dad.
20.1 Are there areas of mistrust from your childhood that you're transferring to your spouse or loved ones?
20.2 What does that look like for you? (Avoiding accountability, secrets, withholding, unrealistic expectations, etc.)
20.3 Have you ever felt like you don't belong in your own home? If so, where else have you felt that way?

Chapter 21

Jim learned early on to use his strength to make his life work.
21.1 What did you use as a child to make your life work? (Intimidation, kindness, helpfulness, moral justification, humor, etc.)

As an adult, Jim was still prone to relying on his strength to control his life, especially when he was feeling shame.
21.2 How do you respond when you feel shame?
21.3 Do you still use the same tactics you used as a child?

Sometimes, offering grace is easier when we choose to see the bigger picture. Gail was able to overlook an offense for the sake of helping Jim move ahead.
21.4 How easy does this come for you?

Chapter 22

Jim found it puzzling to be caught, exposed, held accountable, and forgiven by Kyle, in the account of driving over his remote-control car.
22.1 Have you ever been confronted with one of your past offenses and been given unexpected grace?
22.2 How did it feel?
22.3 How did you respond?
22.4 Did it make you want to offer forgiveness to someone else?

Chapter 23

After buying, restoring, and finally riding the Dream, Jim wondered why he didn't feel vindicated.
23.1 Why do you think he still felt lacking?
23.2 Have you ever pursued an object to bolster your sense of value?

23.3 How did that turn out?
23.4 Can you identify where Jim was powerless as a child?
23.5 What resources did he have to rely on at the time?
23.6 What resources did he come to rely on when he was older?
23.7 Were there other resources available to him as an adult?
23.8 Can you identify where you were powerless as a child?
23.9 What resources did you have to rely on as a child?
23.10 What resources do you have now that you didn't have then?
23.11 Do you see where you've been a hero?
23.12 Do you see where you've caused harm?

Chapter 24

Joel wrote: "There are pages or chapters in each of our lives where we were a victim. If we respond to life out of that pain, there is a likelihood for harm. If, instead, we respond from the truth of who we really are in spite of that pain, there is a likelihood for heroism. It's good to eventually come face to face with it all." J.R. for instance, had experienced Jim as a hero, but had also experienced harm at the hand of his neighbor. When we make it about others, there are hints of heroism. When we make it about ourselves, we often offend.
24.1 What fear in you lies behind the need to make it about yourself?
24.2 Where did that fear come from?
24.3 What confidence in you lies behind your ability to make it about others?
24.4 Where did that confidence come from?
24.5 Can you identify the heroism and the harm modeled for you by your parents/family?

Chapter 25

Jim could start to see where his "precious, but insecure, afraid, little boy" could cause chaos in his relationships if allowed to dictate how he showed up as a man.

25.1 Are you aware of what causes your precious, but insecure, afraid, little boy or girl to show up?

25.2 What does it look like when they show up?

Others may often recognize when our little boy or girl is vying for control before we see it.

25.3 Is there someone you trust enough to speak into your life when your little boy or girl is taking charge? (A good counselor, life coach, or mentor is a good place to start.)

Some of us may have spent a lot of energy trying to distance ourselves from our youth and the vulnerabilities we may have experienced. It can feel counter-intuitive to venture back into our memories with compassion, protection, and advocacy for that child. Listening to that child's fears rather than minimizing them, hearing their concerns rather than dismissing them, and helping them find answers to questions they may never have been able to articulate can settle years of insecurity. It helps us compare the "truth" we knew as a child with the real truth of God's Word. A loving, sacrificing, perspective from the only perfect Father can heal the deepest places in our souls. It's hard work, but good work, and you're worth it!

Bibliography

Allender, Dan. ***The Wounded Heart.*** NavPress, 1995. Colorado Springs, CO

Allender, Dan and Tremper Longman. ***Bold Love.*** NavPress, 1992. Colorado Springs, CO

Bonham, Mark. ***The Heart and Soul of Loving Well.*** Bridge To Life Ministry, 2014. Spring Lake, MI

All Bible references are from the ***New Living Translation.*** Wheaton, Ill: Tyndale House Publishers, 2004.

Strong, James. ***The New Strong's Exhaustive Concordance of the Bible*** (2nd ed.). Thomas Nelson, 1997. Nashville, TN

The Journey Begins. Open Hearts Ministry, 2011. Kalamazoo, MI

About the Author

Pete Norris and his wife Vicki reside in northern Michigan, where they raised their four (now adult) children. Along with owning and operating a small custom cabinet shop, he is also a life coach with an emphasis on marriage and relationships. Pete and Vicki have worked with couples and individuals for over 20 years. Story work is at the core of their efforts, helping adults recognize how the pain from their past is often the culprit that is raising havoc in their current relationships.

In 2001 Pete began his journey by attending a week-long intensive conference hosted by Open Hearts Ministry in Muskegon, Michigan. When introduced to the director, he quietly confided, "I'm really just here to support my wife. I don't have a story." Her response was endearing and terrifying at the same time. "Oh," she said with a warm smile, "we all have a story." And she was right.

Made in the USA
Middletown, DE
05 November 2023